Night Mare

Books by Franci McMahon:

Staying The Distance
Night Mare

Night Mare

Franci McMahon

Odd Girls Press, Anaheim, CA

Original artwork and cover design commissioned from
ArtByLucy, reachable via Internet at <artbylucy@hotmail.com>
or <ArtByLucy@aol.com> Cover art Copyright © 2001
ArtByLucy.

First edition, 2001
10 9 8 7 6 5 4 3 2 1

Library of Congress
Cataloging-in-Publication Data   2001087927 CIP

McMahon, Franci
Night Mare : a mystery / Franci McMahon
p. 256 cm.
ISBN (trade paper): 1-887237-14-3

Women detectives – Fiction.
Horses – Fiction.
Lesbians – Fiction.
Investigative reporting – Fiction.
Women ranchers – Fiction.
Quakers – Fiction.
Ranch life – Fiction.
Montana – Fiction.
Vermont – Fiction.

This book is dedicated to my No. 1 fan

Micah Brown

A novel takes shape with the help of many voices. I would like to thank Katherine V. Forrest, whose trained eye for the unneeded word helped hone this book and who asked all the right questions, kindly. And Margaret Gillon who made the book possible. The woman behind the author, Jenifer Wise, whose dry comments point to the flaw, and who sustains and puts up with me. Readers Peggy Marquis, Barbara Du Bois, Nancy Owens, Randi Levin, Martha Ayers, Melissa Kwasny and Karen Davidson, all were very helpful.

Prologue

I heard nothing but the drone of tires on pavement. Every rough pimple on the highway ran through my body like a telegraph message: getaway getaway get away get a way.

Yellow flyspecks covered the gray ceiling. Slowly, fighting despair, I looked around my prison. There must be a way out. Sunlight shone in through four small windows set high in one side of the van. A large sliding door for unloading the horses was on the right. I lay facing the horses with my head to the driver's end, tight up against the wall with windows. Three trunks sat snapped to the back wall.

I recognized the horse looming immediately in front of me. The black mare, the nasty one into whose stall I'd jumped that day looking for clues. She had been stolen along with the others, handpicked for new identities. I wondered if her owners would miss her, or they would say, good riddance.

A longing to be missed and searched for filled me. As well as regret for ending the relationship with Rhonda. Had the relationship really been all that bad?

1

Newly out of their buds, maple leaves dancing above the driveway mottled the morning sun when I returned from Putney Quaker Meeting. I found Rhonda cross and sullen. I was over our fight, why couldn't she move on? I couldn't understand why she had to be jealous of Victoria. Vic was straight, for God's sake, and she'd been my best friend since we crawled around in diapers and took naps together in nursery school.

Well, okay, some women get jealous. I don't quite understand it, but, perhaps I needed to court her now. Walking up behind Rhonda, I put my arms around her, nuzzled my lips into the fuzz at the back of her neck and said, "Let's go out for breakfast. We could go to Santa's Land Pancake House. Don't you love it in the Igloo? You could have the Elves' special."

I snuggled my body into her back and whispered, "Or would you like to make love first?"

"Jane, get off. Santa's Land is for kids," Rhonda said, shaking me away like something disgusting. "I'd like to go someplace elegant for a change. Let's drive to Brattleboro. Why not the Back Side Cafe? Or T. J. Buckley's?"

I didn't say anything, torn between speechless and pissed.

She finished moussing her short, dyed red hair. "Muffy was there last weekend. She said almost everyone was there."

I seriously doubted this. T. J.'s, a small classy diner, only had five tables. It was probably Vermont's smallest restaurant. Therefore, it must be a very select "everyone." Curious as to Rhonda's definition, I asked, "Who?"

"That new dentist in town and her lover, and Babs — she was Muffy's date. You know, they all play tennis together. I'd like to meet some sophisticated women. All you and Victoria ever talk about is horses." Rhonda gave a little laugh meant to soften her words a bit.

"We love horses. Besides, we talk about other things, too." I struggled to stay connected to Rhonda and the conversation, and not slide away, into my thoughts or out the window. This sense of detachment had been growing lately.

"Horses, though! Really, Jane, it feels like I'm living with a teenager." Rhonda tossed her head.

I heard my voice become cold as I said, "This smacks of the Arrested Development school of thinking when it comes to women and horses. I've gotten this all my life. We're supposed to outgrow horses when puberty hits. We supposedly don't leave childhood behind until we get laid by a guy. Hey, we grew up to be revolutionaries. We're queer. We can love whomever we want. And I love horses!"

Rhonda groaned with theatrical boredom as she carefully applied lipstick, stretching her mouth into a silent scream.

"My dear, I'm simply saying I'd like to go to town for breakfast."

"But, Rhonda, I don't really enjoy being around those people. There's a brittle — "

"What do you mean, darling? You don't even know them." Rhonda returned to her grooming.

Stomping around the bedroom, I picked up things and put them down somewhere else. It looked like tidying, but wasn't. I sat down on the bed to watch Rhonda through the bathroom door. I knew we would do what she wanted and I hated myself for it.

Rhonda had taken to using eyeliner lately and I watched as she put it on now with studied detachment. I was willing to bet that was why women used makeup, as a distancing tool. Probably fights were engineered to happen right before the makeup was due to go on. So that afterward she could come out of the bathroom a new woman, wearing a mask. I tried to suppress a laugh but wasn't successful.

"What are you laughing about in there?" The querulous voice echoed from the tiled bathroom.

"Oh, the feminine mystique." I entered the makeup chamber to watch in the mirror as Rhonda drew a fine black line around the edge of her eye. Fascinating. Her eyes were a pale icy blue with a darker rim, the kind of eyes that could stop you in your tracks. She was slender and went to a great deal of trouble to look thin and successful; the two were synonymous in Rhonda's mind. She dieted constantly, worked out at a gym, and did aerobic dancing. One year Rhonda tried to claim the cost of staying thin on her income tax as a business expense — she was an agent for Vermont artists and crafts-people, traveling around the country to place their work.

Her attitude had shocked me to the core. The amount she'd tried to claim was exactly the same as my yearly donation to the local food kitchens, which I'd previously considered generous. I decided to double it.

I never gave my size or weight a second thought, unless it related somehow to horses. The right weight to ride a young horse, too short to braid the mane of a sixteen-hand horse without a stool, and so on. My exercise came from tossing hay bales or mucking out the barn, walking behind the lawn mower and riding for miles over the rolling green hills, getting off now and then in the winter to run beside my horse to stay warm.

Rhonda came out of the bathroom into the bedroom and started putting on upscale clothes. I followed her a short way, brought along in the wake of the smells and the intensity that goes with grooming oneself. It was captivating to watch, and I felt a small awkwardness as I realized arousal was part of it. That drained away as Rhonda turned her cloaked face toward me. "Aren't you going to get ready?"

With a sigh, I said, "All right." Rhonda would never have a clue why I sighed.

There had been a time in our relationship when Rhonda thought it a lark to go to the Igloo at Santa's Land. Maybe if we'd run into some of the community's Lesbian Lionesses we would still be going there.

The tight, select, social-climbing circle of Muffy and her friends would instantly accept me, and as my partner, Rhonda would be "in" on a superficial level. What she didn't know was that her foot-in-the-door access would slam shut if our relationship ended.

Rhonda wanted to climb. This climbing rope is feeling a little frayed, I admitted to myself.

Rhonda craved status, the right connections with "professional" women, and being on the inside group's party list. Rhonda was good at meeting people, making witty conversation, and she always livened up any group. When I'd first met her she charmed the socks off me. I honestly admired the ease Rhonda had with everyone, but the clever social scene always wore thin with me very quickly.

Splashing cold water on my face, I drew a brush through my short hair, watching it bounce back after the brush. I went downstairs to my own bedroom to change. Stepping into and zipping up my favorite old honey brown corduroys, wonderfully baggy and soft, I reflected over the increasing conflict in our relationship. Whenever Rhonda was home for the weekend she seemed to want control over my life. Even reading a book resulted in a frustrating struggle. It became easier to use a bookmark when Rhonda walked into the room. And easier still to read only during the week when Rhonda was out of town. The more I tried to stand up to Rhonda the more willing I had to be to face an ugly scene.

I was acquiescing way too much. Why did I need to be so agreeable? Looking in the mirror over my dresser I was shocked to see the underlying sadness in my face.

"Dearest, what are you doing down there? I'm starving."

"I'll be up in a minute."

I pulled on a green turtleneck and over it a dark blue Guernsey sweater knitted from yarn so fine and close that it shook its fist at wear and weather.

On some level I knew I had a handsome butch air about myself, with my short curly brownish-red hair and the easy athletic way I moved. I turned in front of the full length mirror by the door, pleased. I could be a North Sea sailor, just off the fishing boat.

The thought of the North sea and Scotland saddened me. The memory would have this power all my life. My parents died in a plane crash over Scotland.

Traveling as a passenger into Brattleboro, I looked out the side window of Rhonda's British-racing-green Saab. A passing hay field was dotted with newly arrived robins.

"Look! There must be hundreds of robins in that field. Each one has its own territory maybe five square feet. Isn't that neat?" Pleased as a child, I turned to see boredom on Rhonda's face.

Feeling squashed, I said, "Okay. What's the matter? Are you going to tell me or am I going to get the deep freeze all morning?"

Rhonda's eyebrows shot up. "Oh, have I been giving you the impression that I'm upset?"

"Rhonda, don't give me that crap. Of course I can see that you are. Let's air it."

Slipping off my clogs, I folded my feet under myself and leaned against the car door. It would take a few minutes for Rhonda to gather herself to talk about her feelings. Idly I plucked a stem of hay from my corduroys, then, feeling warm, pulled the sweater off. I suspected I looked a little rumpled now. Always within a short time of dressing to go 'out,' I seemed to achieve my look.

Rhonda, on the other hand, always looked groomed. She had a Thoroughbred show horse aura, mane and tail braided, brushed checkerboard on the rump, while I was in the Mustang or Exmoor pony class, usually with a burdock or wind twist in my mane.

"It's Victoria — that's the problem."

Here we go again, I thought, but my outrage came out in a sputter. Rhonda raised her hand imperiously and continued. "Now, Jane, I've thought this over. You *must* make a choice about where you spend your time, and if I am not as important to you as she is . . . " She let the consequences dangle.

Here I got the words together to coherently object. "Rhonda, of course you are an important part of my life, but I will not compare you to Victoria. She's been my friend forever. You must admit, it's awkward that you're only home two days out of seven. It's as if you're a perpetual guest who I'm supposed to drop everything for."

"You mean Victoria is more real to you?" Rhonda asked, checking her teeth in the rear view mirror at a stop sign.

"Come on, Rhonda. Victoria works all week, has a family, and often the weekend's the only time we can get together. Can't you see it's hard for me, too?" As I spoke I could see little reaction on Rhonda's face.

In a voice loaded with manipulation, Rhonda said, "I know you don't care about me anymore. You ignore me when I'm here and you're probably relieved when I leave every Monday morning."

Oh, my God . . . here we go again. What she said was true; I couldn't wait for her to leave each time. Another damned breakup was on its way. I didn't know what to say and sat silently as this sank in, watching the big old houses pass by as we drove down the long hill of Western Avenue.

Then words seemed to spill out of me, as if it weren't me talking. "Maybe it would be a good idea if you got a room or apartment in town. I feel this question of time is putting a real strain on our relationship."

She tried to interrupt, but I kept talking. "It might help to take the pressure off."

"How can you say that? You know I love you."

"I don't think this issue is about whether we love each other or not. It's gotten all murky around how we spend our weekends. Living together can't be done on the usual model. Living apart doesn't mean we need to end the relationship." Oh, yeah. Liar.

"It all seems easy to me," Rhonda responded. "Just save your weekends for me." She pulled into a parking place at Harmony lot, killed the Saab's engine, then turned and looked straight into my eyes her eyebrows, arched above cold eyes.

I shivered, then said, "I won't do that, Rhonda."

2

"Jane! How would you like to go look at a horse? There's one for sale, a chestnut mare."

My best friend's voice cheered me. "Just a minute, Victoria. Rhonda left in a snit last night and I'm not really awake yet."

I placed the receiver on the rumpled bed. After pulling on a velour polo shirt, I ran into the kitchen, pushed the coffee maker button, then made for the living room.

Settled on the couch, I said into the extension, "Okay. I'm ready. Tell me about this horse."

"It's hard not knowing if I'm going to call at an awkward time. Is she away on one of her buying trips or . . ." Victoria paused significantly, "away."

I laughed, hearing a touch of bitterness in its sound. "The shackles have been slipped from my ankles. Temporarily. She returns Friday. What's up?"

The excitement in Victoria's voice came across clearly. "Listen to this: Chestnut Arabian mare, seven years old, 14.3

hands, gentle. Twelve hundred dollars. I called her owner. It's just over the Connecticut River into New Hampshire. So, do you want to look at her with me?"

"Now?"

"Yes, now." Victoria's voice tapered off. "Or do you have other plans?"

"Nothing that's any competition for going to look at a horse. But Vic, do you want to waste your time looking at a twelve-hundred-dollar Arabian? It can't have ever won any ribbons. That's only a little more than dog food price."

"That's my price range."

"Well, I can't understand why you don't buy a horse you can do something on. I'd be more than happy to give you the money."

"No," Victoria snapped.

People usually didn't rebuff my offers of money. But then, Vic was different. "Look — I'll meet you at the Putney General Store in, how about half an hour?"

"Great. Michael can deal with the kids this morning."

While drinking my first cup of strong black coffee, I felt my house around me, familiar as an old shoe. Whenever a lover moved in, it seemed to get corns or bunions as if trying to accommodate this other person. I had a rush of anxiety. I was definitely feeling pinched and cramped.

There once had been something comfortable about the relationship with Rhonda. Now, for the life of me, I couldn't think what it was.

Abruptly I stood. I'd be late if I didn't boogie.

I ate my breakfast standard of a cutup banana, corn flakes and some yogurt, while Bugs, the orange marmalade male cat, in his youth a foundling, rubbed his warm body against my legs.

"You have the world's loudest purr, Mr. Bugs," I said as I spooned a large dollop of yogurt into his bowl. Instantly his purring grew in volume, then stopped altogether as he began to eat. Bugs had a way of holding his whiskers close to his cheeks to keep them tidy when he ate.

I returned to the bedroom, replaced the phone in its cradle, retrieved last night's shed corduroys from the floor, and a somewhat clean shirt from a pile of "briefly worns."

A pesky surge of loneliness caught me. It wasn't about Rhonda. It was a memory, so vivid the voices almost echoed in the room. My father's voice, always soft and calm, explaining, "Mary, I've only worn this shirt once. There's no need for it to go into the hamper."

"I don't care, Spenser. We don't want anyone to think I would let you go around filthy."

"I'm not going to the village. Just some gardening."

Mother's sharp voice: "No matter."

I had no doubt there was love in their marriage. But how could they have been so very different from each other? Opposites attract. That must be it. Was that my story, too?

One sock dangling from my hand, I caught myself looking in the mirror as if a stranger had sat down in my bedroom. Her brown eyes showed gold flecks, reflecting the morning sunlight. A lean angular woman of thirty. Not a bad-looking woman. Her slightly bushy eyebrows lowered into a frown. Softly I said, "Damn," while watching my lips move.

With certainty I knew the relationship with Rhonda could be counted in days. I felt hollow. Hastily, I turned away from my image, like a bird dog leaving the water, shaking droplets of distress into the air.

Border Scout, a female Norwich terrier I'd adopted from the Humane Society, followed me to the barn. The horses, waiting for me to get a move on since dawn, greeted me with their big morning whinnies. The blind mare, Moonglow, and her son, Star Dust, both grey Thoroughbreds, neighed with different voices.

"Singing again! What a duet. Here's your grain." I dumped their respective rations into the buckets, then filled the hayrack. "That ought to keep you busy for a while."

For a moment I paused to admire the smooth silk of their new spring coats, pushing out the last of the winter hair. "You two need a good brushing." I kept Dusty blanketed most of the time so his coat would look good for shows. Free to come or go from their stalls, they chose most often to hang out on the downwind side of something, seeming to meditate on nature.

The green Toyota 4-Runner, parked by the barn, started as if relieved that the subzero weather was past. I sure was. The winter had seemed unusually long. Driving by the farmhouse, built in the early 1700's, I noticed it could use a fresh coat of white paint. Brittle, dead weeds framed the entrance to Black Locust Lane. The place looked totally neglected. Where had my head been lately?

Putney Village, the General Store at the hub, was a mere two miles away. I passed the *Thickly Settled* sign going down Kimble Hill. I had always loved this sign, purely New England, indicating many houses, most of them painted white, like white-haired dowagers, primly lining either side. They seemed to guard towns from interlopers, and from those who might entertain the unthinkable idea of tossing a candy wrapper onto the ground.

Victoria Marsh was there ahead of me, pumping hazelnut coffee from the thermos on the lunch counter, her fine blond hair brushing the tops of her shoulders. Her lips were wide and soft for such an angled face. Her intense face concentrated on what she was doing, as usual. Her sharp nose swooped hawklike, between sky-blue eyes. I'd seen those eyes change from the sky of a mild summer day to the gritty underside of a glacier.

She was the dearest person in the world to me. If I ever lost Victoria it would be unbearable.

Vic smiled her most relaxed smile. She swept her hair back and took a swig of coffee.

"Morning," we both said at the same time, hooking little fingers the way we had done since grade school.

On the way down Route 5 to the bridge over the Connecticut River, Victoria told me what she had learned in her telephone conversation with Velma Smith, the mare's owner. She had asked all the standard questions: Any vices? Recent injuries? Was she sound? Suitable for active trail riding? Velma had assured her the mare had no problems.

"Velma said she's shown horses for years. Do you know her?"

I tried to put a face to the name, but couldn't recall this woman. Wasn't one of the regulars. "No."

"She told me she bought this mare for her husband, but he doesn't ride much. She wants to sell her to free up a stall."

"Why so cheap? She's a registered Arabian, isn't she?"

"Yes, Velma said she had the papers." Victoria checked her sketched map of the directions. "Turn right up ahead. I don't know why the price is so low." Victoria gave a little shrug, shot her eyebrows up and pursed her lips.

"I wish you'd let me give or loan you the money for a better horse." Quickly I added, "I know we've been through this before, but . . ."

"No. Thanks, Jane." Victoria smiled and reached out to squeeze my hand.

Mentally I kicked myself. This was one of those times when the money didn't make life easier. Would I ever learn the power of it? At times I wanted to give it all away. Victoria and I had been around the block a few times on this subject, and right when I thought I'd maybe learned something, I'd stick my entire foot in my mouth again. Patience was Vic's middle name. Actually it was. Perhaps she tried to live up to it.

I wished my name were Jane Tact Scott. I sure needed it. With Michael, Vic's husband, out of a job and the whole family to support she didn't need me throwing my inherited money in her face.

After college I'd tried living in denial by closing up the farm and renting a small apartment in Boston. I worked the graveyard shift at a newspaper, writing blurbs and doing layout. For one year I lived within the income I earned, working forty hours a week. All I really missed were the horses. I learned what a luxury they were when I could barely support myself, let alone a horse, too. In the Spring I went to a riding academy, splurging a near fortune for an hour on a rental hack. By the end of the hour, I'd decided to stop living in renunciation and return home to Putney.

Victoria broke in on my thoughts. "I'm free this afternoon, you want to go riding?"

"I'd like to, Vic, but I have to work on an article for the *Chronicle*. Deadline's coming up."

Victoria glanced at her written directions then checked a passing road sign. "What's it about?"

"Remember the disappearance of the Brach candy heiress?" Victoria looked up, then nodded. "Vaguely."

"Well, it seems she got caught in bad company. They say Helen Brach took in every stray dog dropped off at her door. She pampered nearly a dozen dogs, but had no friends. She answered a personal ad that a con man put in the Chicago paper. She must have been so lonely to answer one of those ads."

Up ahead the road looked rough so I slowed the 4-Runner to a creeping ten miles an hour. "Once he'd gotten her confidence he sold her a bunch of worthless race horses. My research suggests she may have learned too much about the sting operation."

"Usually that kind of con artist has acted before. There must have been other women he bilked. Any rumors?"

"Lots of them. It's been close to eighteen years since Helen Brach disappeared and people are finally talking. Some say there's a horse hit man called the Sandman, who'll put your horse to sleep for a mere five thousand dollars. This is, of course, a deal if your horse is insured for fifty or a hundred thousand."

"Killing horses to collect on insurance? Who would do that?" Victoria asked in disbelief.

"The very rich. People who want to win beyond reason at shows. I admit I've had surges of desire for trophies, which left me blushing. At the shows, I've heard rumors this Sandman does exist."

She stared at me. "I'm having trouble taking it in. My experience is that wealthy people retire their old show horses to pasture."

"Those were the days when showing was for fun. Everything's changed now. Too much money is involved. Horses are worked too hard at their specialty until they're sour. You've seen it. Nobody who's paid over thirty thousand dollars for their show horse wants to give dobbin a vacation or go for a relaxing ride through the woods. They're kept in small paddocks or stalls and never turned out in a big pasture to risk getting kicked by other horses. The horses get bored and stale."

"I can certainly understand that. I hate riding in the ring, and expect the horse does, too." Victoria pointed to a right turn ahead.

"I've heard people talk about their car with more warmth than some of the top riders refer to their show horses." I slowed for the turn.

"Commodities. Or status symbols, not living beings."

"It's so cold-blooded. It reminds me of that wreck on the interstate two years ago. Remember?" I knew she did, this was an event we talked over periodically in an effort to defuse the memories and put it to rest.

Victoria nodded. "Wish I could forget it."

"Ugly. I'm a realist and know that horses get eaten, but what happens to them up to the point of slaughter must be as humane as possible."

An envelope of silence held the dark horror of that night.

Those horses should never have been loaded into that double-decked stock trailer. Driver speeding. The weight must have shifted going over the bridge. I can't even remember now who called me to bring my horse trailer. Only half of them survived . . . if you could call it that. There were maybe ten of us with horse trailers lined up along the shoulder of the interstate . . .

Vic broke into my thoughts.

"That mare and foal you took home. I see them now and then when I drive to Bennington. The girl you gave them to leads that young horse everywhere."

I couldn't let the men from the packing plant have them. I'd paid the meat price.

Victoria rubbed her hand over her eyes. "I can still hear the sound of the veterinarian's gun, the screams of those horses. I see the spinning blue lights — they flash through my brain."

I had written the story for the *Reformer*. It had seemed like solid news to me; a driver's speeding the cause of twenty-nine deaths. I couldn't believe when they didn't consider it news. Nothing. Not even a blurb in the local section. I said, bitterly, "If that had been a bus full of people and twenty-nine had died, it would have hit the AP wire."

"You walked around with tears in your eyes for a week."

With a lopsided smile, I said, "So did you."

A solid mile of uphill, passing old dairy farms and large new houses, brought us to the far side of Chesterfield, along the border of Pisgah State Forest.

"Turn left, third farm. Go one half mile. Farm on right." Victoria read off. "New barn."

Arriving at farm on right, new barn we both groaned. Crammed among trees, road, and hillside, was an unkempt house trailer, not far from a tilting, chipboard barn, the roof, as yet, unfinished. A blue plastic tarp covered some of the hay in the loft. Trees and bare ground were fenced in with draping barbed wire stapled to leaning posts and once-living trees. Stripped of bark as high as the horses could reach, the trees were dead and ready to shed brittle, lethal branches on the horses.

We could see a few thin horses standing listlessly, tails to the wind. Not one strand of leftover breakfast hay wafted across the dirt.

While the engine idled we stared at each other. "Oh, dear," I said, putting the 4-Runner into reverse. "Still want to look?"

"Of course. She obviously needs to sell a horse or two." Victoria opened the door and started toward the house trailer. Resignedly, I cut the engine. Before I could join her, the trailer door opened and Velma Smith stepped out. The barrel-like body was top-heavy over her thin bandy legs. Her head was large with small watchful eyes. A smile with no warmth was pinned on her face. Her hair was that kind of brown that had no color, hung long and lanky, and was held back by a barrette in a style that might have looked tolerable on a twelve-year-old.

I watched as the women shook hands, the one, my dearest friend, the other, a woman I instantly distrusted. I walked toward them.

"Hello," I said, reaching out to shake Velma's hand as Vic introduced us. I realized we were both sizing each other up.

"This way," Velma said, leading us to the unmistakable barn where the chestnut mare stood, tied.

The sound of gulped air, like a belch in reverse, could easily be heard as we walked toward the horse. Ye gods, a cribber, I thought. The mare pressed her top front teeth against a board then tensed her neck muscles to draw a gulp of air into her stomach. Cribbing was positively a vice in anyone's book. Other horses learned it by observation; a nervous habit, like nail biting. It was self-destructive and indicated too much confinement and boredom.

The mare looked thin. The chestnut coat still had large patches of unshed winter hair, a sign of worm infestation. Wordlessly, Victoria ran her fingers down the mare's washboard ribs, then rested her fist in the hollow where ribs met hips. The feet had been neglected, but appeared fundamentally sound.

Of course I wondered how much of the horse's easygoing disposition was depression from starvation. The honey-colored mare turned her head and stared full into my eyes, as if to say, "Get me out of here." A depth of kindness shone out of her eyes that would last through being fat and frisky.

"What's her name?" I asked.

"One of those Arabian names you can't spell or pronounce. Bent Jamball or something. I'll get her papers."

Velma headed for the house trailer, but was cut off by a huge red pickup truck carrying every accessory which could be chrome-plated. It was pulling a gaudy, matching two-horse trailer, complete with dressing room and tack compartment. Not a scratch on it. Brand new.

Velma turned with pride, announcing, "My better half."

Frankly I couldn't tell what the pride had to do with, or which was the better half — the husband or what he was hauling. But as he climbed out, it became clear to me it had to be the trailer, hands down.

"Hi. I'm Chuck." He had a smile like a car salesman, showing every tooth in his head.

Victoria and I murmured polite greetings as Chuck came over to take charge. He tripped as he neared the mare, reaching out toward her in an effort to save himself. Both he and the horse were equally startled by his sudden embrace. Pushing himself away from the mare, he brushed with disgust at some mud on his jacket.

"Nice to meet'cha," he said as he stepped backwards. "Looks like you girls have it under control." He about-faced and headed for home.

I rolled my eyes and tried to suppress a giggle, which if it got away would turn into raucous laughter. I felt Vic's hand on my arm. "Don't!" she said firmly.

We turned to look again at the mare. Victoria laid her hand, fingers spread out, over the mare's shoulder blade in a reassuring gesture. She hummed a tuneless thing. I never knew if Victoria's humming was an attempt at music or a meditation hum.

Sliding her hand down over the rough brown coat, sharp bones and flabby muscle, Victoria kept humming and shaking her head. Across the mare's back were scabs of rain rot, a fungus afflicting horses that had no shelter. Caked mud held the long winter guard hairs together in chunks under her belly. Watching Victoria's gentle hand, listening to her soothing song, a deep sadness washed over me for all the world's neglected animals.

"I'm trying to imagine her in better condition. She's not exactly pretty, is she?" I said.

"She would be." Victoria said adamantly. "This is a good mare, fallen on hard times, you might say." She plucked at one of the chunks of dirt hanging from the mare's belly.

I halfheartedly nodded agreement. "Needs a good scrubbing. Not to mention a dose of worm medicine. I don't think Velma will be freeing up a stall by selling this horse." I pressed my lips together, shaking my head. It upset me when people had more horses than they could adequately care for. This was Victoria's show, however, so I needed to restrain myself from delivering one of my scathing lectures.

"Here they are," Velma called, waving papers as she walked toward us. She paused, sorting her way through the registration papers.

Curious, I stepped up to read over Velma's shoulder. "Her name's Bint Jameel." Then, with surprise, "She's freeze-branded."

Walking around to the mare's right side, I lifted the mane. There, sure enough, were the symbols representing her registration number, the white hair growing out of the freeze-branded hide.

"Oh! So that's what those marks are. I thought it was some kind of weird scar."

I looked at Velma, startled to realize the woman did not know what the brand meant. It was a quick and easy job to verify this was the same mare as the one shown on the papers. Turning the registration papers over I noticed they had not been signed over to a new owner. The registry frowned on that.

"I would think you would have transferred her papers into your name?"

Velma's startled eyes slid around a minute before she answered. "I didn't know if she would work out for my husband or not. It's no problem, though. You can transfer her." She pointed to a form on the back, then folded, and crammed the papers into her jacket pocket.

"Have you had her long?" Victoria asked.

Picking up a brush resting nearby in the mud, Velma responded, "Bought her January, at a sale."

"So, why didn't you transfer ownership?" I persisted, knowing I pushed the question too hard.

Velma hadn't taken her eyes off me as she made a few swipes with the brush over the mare's back. Her eyes narrowed. Like a lizard slipping off a rock, her gaze turned to Victoria. "If you don't want her, no sweat. I'll sell her easy enough. The grass will be up in a couple of weeks and she'll shed out and probably sell for a couple of hundred more."

Velma chucked the brush back to the mud, then turned to walk toward the house trailer.

Victoria spoke up and I had enough sense to stay quiet. "Oh, but I am interested. I see that you care where your horses go."

A soft snort made a feckless exit, which earned me a scathing look from Victoria.

"I'd like to try her out," Victoria said.

Velma stopped and turned halfway. "Fine," she said, though she cast a dark glance in my direction before heading toward the barn.

I edged closer, but Velma said, "I'll get her gear."

"Please let me help," I offered in an appeasing way.

Velma actually held out her hand to stop me and said, "Wait here."

I obliged, though dying of curiosity. I took another step closer, trying to see through the door.

Velma snapped, "The barn's off-limits. Insurance." Ducking inside, she closed the door behind her.

Oh, well. I figured the stalls were probably filthy and Velma had the decency to feel some embarrassment about that. But why was she so secretive?

Soon Velma returned carrying a black and pink western saddle.

Vic and I looked at each other. Recognizing one of our silent signals, I headed to the 4-Runner for Victoria's tack.

Returning with saddle and bridle over my arms, I also carried a pair of scissors. I set the saddle on the mare's back, but before securing the girth, I snipped the long hairs which held cakes of mud and manure.

Velma demanded belligerently, "Hey, what do you think you're doing?"

"Cutting off the chunks of dirt that will cause the mare pain if I tighten the girth over them," I explained, trying to keep the anger in my voice under control.

"You're going to make the hair all chopped and uneven. If you used my string girth you wouldn't have to do that," she complained.

Of course, I ignored her. Victoria could deal with her, and I was absolutely not going to let anyone tighten a girth up over this crusty mud. I bent down behind the mare and continued snipping.

I heard Vic say, "Velma, I'm afraid your cinch won't fit my saddle. Now, tell me about your horses. Appaloosas, aren't they? It's not a breed I'm familiar with." That age-old, irresistible invitation to talk about your own horses worked on Velma. Their voices faded while I furiously snipped. Good old Vic.

Finished, I tightened the girth, then stood back. I admired Victoria's way of charming the socks off Velma Smith, who now helped Victoria mount the mare.

Watching my friend ride the mare up the road I was glad we had come. Even though the mare obviously had some flaws, she was too nice a horse to be living like this. When Vic turned to ride back, her grin told me everything I needed to know. Victoria's heart had been won. Her old gelding, Nutmeg, could be retired.

When Victoria jumped off, I said, "Come on. We have to talk. Reality check time."

We carried the gear to the Toyota, then swung the back door wide for a place to sit. Legs dangling from the end, I said, "I know you are smitten with this beast, but let's look at her drawbacks."

I methodically listed my concerns. "The mare cribs. There's swelling in her tendons, which may never go down. You have no idea how she is around other horses, she may be nasty."

Victoria turned and looked at me like a woman in love, eyes dreamy, distracted. "Isn't she wonderful?"

Inside I smiled, but I asked, trying to narrow it down, "She's a good ride?"

"Oh, she moves like a dream. Just the lightest squeeze with my calves and she responds."

"You may not be able to get her registered."

Victoria looked at me as if I'd just made the most crass suggestion. "So?"

I slipped off the tailgate. "I'd rather see you on a Thoroughbred. Those Arabians can be such dingbats. And if you're going to show hunter, they're never pinned. Arabians simply don't fit the hunter frame."

"You know I don't show, Jane." Victoria departed to make arrangements to buy the mare.

I'll stay clear of this, I decided, moving in behind the steering wheel. Absorbed in events of the day, hoping this would be a good horse for Vic, I stared blankly out the window.

Surprised, I saw my blacksmith pull his truck into Velma's driveway. Opening my door, I waved over the hood at him. "Hi, Buster."

He half-raised his hand. After looking at me, then at Velma talking to Victoria, he put his truck in reverse.

I called again, "Hey! Buster?" But he was gone.

3

The next day Victoria dropped me off at the end of my driveway. We had spent the morning watching a Sally Swift horsemanship clinic in Massachusetts. "I still haven't heard anything from Velma. I'll call her tonight."

"Call me when the mare arrives." I waved good-bye to my friend, then looked around the entry to the drive with a critical eye. Slowly walking up the driveway, planning my weed attack for that afternoon, I veered around the Saab before it registered on my distracted brain. I was amazed to feel a tiny rush of pleasure that Rhonda had returned early.

It wasn't hard to locate her. Rhonda took up the entire bedroom, her energy filling the room, the suitcases and their contents spilled all over the bed. "Hi, when did you get in?" I asked. "I didn't expect you until tomorrow."

"That's obvious. I must remember I need an appointment to see you." As Rhonda closed the empty suitcase her silver bangle bracelets rang like wind chimes. "On the way here I stopped at Foxmeadow stables to sign up for a series of riding lessons. Seems to me it's the only way I'll be able to spend any time with you." Rhonda smiled.

Nonplussed, I didn't know what to say. Rhonda had never shown the least interest in my horsy doings before. My first response was to wonder what she was up to. The second was to mentally kick myself for being so suspicious. Mustering my best smile I said, "Great, Rhonda."

"And I think I should take more of an interest in the maintenance of the farm, as well as the care of the horses."

This time the smile felt wooden. "Oh. Yes. I could use some help." I wondered why I was lying. Rhonda knew nothing about lawn mowers, weeds versus garden plants; in other words the entire world of outdoors. "Actually, I was on my way out to groom the horses and rake the paddock. Then, I really have to do something about the state of the flower gardens. Want to join me?"

"Sure, I'll be right out." Rhonda smiled agreeably.

Dressed in L. L. Bean country-at-home fashion, Rhonda arrived at the barn in the middle of a grooming session with Moonglow. I attempted to suppress my intense irritation with her for persisting to buy from L. L. Bean, in spite of one of the owners' anti-gay stance. My lips pressed tight and my rubber curry comb got very active. Hair flew, airborne white clouds of it; gigantic puffs scampered across the ground in the light spring wind. I was covered with white fuzz. Rhonda halted about ten feet away, aghast.

"Is there always so much hair?" she asked in distaste.

In spite of my annoyance I laughed. I couldn't take her very seriously, though I should've known better. "Last month it came out in handfuls."

Hesitating only a moment, Rhonda spun on her heel. She shot back over her shoulder, "Forget it. I'm not going to trash my clothes."

So much for togetherness.

I spent more time with the horses than I'd planned. The peepers emerging from the mud in the small pond at the bottom of the lower pasture were in full chorus by the time

I shook off my sweater on the back stoop.

Passing through tantalizing aromas in the kitchen, I was told by Rhonda, "Dinner in twenty minutes. Why don't you shower first, dear?" She pushed up the sleeves of her African burnoose, preparing to rinse the salad greens.

"Hmmm," was the best I could do. Walking down the hall to my bedroom I wondered if I was in for a little dinnertime seduction. After showering, I stepped softly into my regular flannel PJs, topped by my beloved, slightly ratty, white terry cloth robe.

The dining room table had undergone a metamorphosis. Junk mail, riding clothes catalogs, odd bits of horse-related leather, and, to the best of my memory, a pair of dirty socks, had all been cleared away. Now residing on the freshly polished cherry surface were two hand-woven table mats. Upon the white-on-white texture of the mats rested hand-built porcelain plates of the most delicate lavender and white, with tiny snails and fish built along one section of rim. Hell to clean, they were nevertheless stunningly beautiful. Hand-forged eating utensils pressed their worthy weight against the mats. Blown glass goblets stood high, their round bellies shining.

My lover swept into the room carrying a hot dish. The burnoose made it appear that she was footless and moving about on well-oiled rollers. "You can open the wine," she said.

Wine, burnoose, sumptuous dinner, and next would be song.

"Darling, why don't you pick out some nice music?" came from the vicinity of the kitchen. I knew my snort of laughter was audible at fifty paces. Rhonda was so predictable.

Bach is my favorite dinnertime music. Harpsichord, or a not too busy trio. Thumbing through the CDs I decided on Vivaldi for Rhonda's seduction. An observer corner of my brain wondered at my own detachment.

Taking a bunny nibble of salad, Rhonda said, "I can't figure out why you like that funeral music. Really, just too deadly."

I responded, "Find something you like better."

To the strains of elevator music Rhonda floated back to her chair. Settling in, she told amusing stories of her most recent trip. Rhonda was very clever with words, and often had an incisive insight into other people's behavior. She frequently padded out the real with total fantasy.

I relaxed in my chair and listened. She was funny and I laughed often. Maybe this night wouldn't be as miserable as I feared.

Then abruptly Rhonda said, "So, what do you see in Victoria? Does Michael know?"

Sitting up, frowning, I said, "I can't believe it, you think I'm having an affair with her, don't you?" I was filled with a mixture of disgust and amazement. Yet, a pang of sadness caught somewhere deep inside, to realize how insecure Rhonda must feel.

"Well, aren't you? Why else would you want to see her instead of me? Like the weekend before last?"

I rose to collect dirty dishes. I didn't want to hash this one over again. But I paused, knuckles resting on the place mat. "It is true that I love Victoria, but in love with her I'm not. You've got to get that straight — "

"I think she's homely," Rhonda interrupted, playing with one gold earring.

"We are not having an affair," I stated flatly, then left the room carrying the dishes.

Rhonda followed me. "You can't expect me to believe that!"

"Oh, but I do." I set the dishes down a little too hard. "Can you tell me, Rhonda, why you have difficulty accepting that intimacy can be in a relationship without sexuality?" Or sexuality without intimacy, I thought.

"I don't expect you not to see your friends," Rhonda said in a tone proclaiming her reasonableness. "I simply do not understand why you had to run off all day Saturday. I was so bored. There was nothing to do. We could have gone to see that new show at Windham Gallery."

Endless times we had gone over this same ground. "Don't you see Rhonda, if you had your *own* friends you could call them up to do things with you. Sometimes I feel like you expect me to fill all of your entertainment needs."

"You act like I'm a child who has to be amused." Rhonda placed some dishes on the counter and visibly calmed herself. "I simply don't understand why you refuse to buy a dishwasher."

"Whatever for? I'm perfectly able to wash them."

"You can easily afford one." Rhonda shook her head, puzzled.

"It's a simplicity thing. Why own more than you need? I can't think of one Quaker who has a dishwasher." I laughed, recognizing how silly this was and yet loving this desire for plain living, the commitment to simplicity.

"Would you like some coffee with dessert?" She used her best hostess smile.

"Yes. Decaf?" I was so sick of scenes. I turned the music so low it could barely be heard, and curled up in a comfortable chair.

Rhonda came into the room, rustling silkily, with one of my mother's silver trays in her hands. She placed the tray laden with silver pot, no less, on the coffee table. Sitting on the couch she patted the space beside her.

Like an obedient dog, I shifted from chair to sofa, checking out the dessert on the way. "Hamellman's fruit tarts! You know how I love them."

"Yes, darling. I've been thinking. Why don't we get married in your Quaker church?"

"It's not mine and it's not a church," was my stunned response, slightly muffled by a mouthful of peach tart.

"Wouldn't it be nice, though? Last year they married those two gay men. Why not?"

"Wait a minute, Rhonda. Just wait a minute." My brain scrambled to find words. I began again. "Being taken under the care of the meeting as a couple is a lengthy process. It is done in the utmost respect and agreement."

"Do I have to convert? Is that what you're saying? Well, I can do that, no problem."

I closed my eyes. What a nightmare. "You don't convert, you become a convinced Friend. Look, Rhonda, why do you want this?"

"It would give us stability in our relationship."

"That doesn't come externally. Commitment and centeredness come from within the couple." Why did I always sound so pompous when I was freaked?

Rhonda took a tiny bite of tart, her lips working over the tender crust. "This may sound avaricious but what will happen to your money when you . . . if you . . ."

I was struck dumb. So that's what she was after. A lot of money had come to me when my parents died, not only from the sizeable insurance settlement, but also from generations of carefully cultivated wealth. The Scott family had worn money like a favorite hand-knit sweater, many times darned. We felt no need to live beyond our simple needs just because we could. A long history of being socially responsible to our community and in our investments was something I honored. My father, Spenser, had taught me well. He'd also warned me about men like Rhonda.

"Die? Is that what you want to know?"

"Yes, dear. As your wife it would add support to any claims."

My smile was stiff. I tried to lick my lips in order to unstick my teeth from the inside of my upper lip. "These tarts are lovely."

Even though I knew it was coming, the seduction scene took me by surprise. Longingly eyeing my peach tart, only one bite removed from the perfect circle, I grew increasingly angry. It figured that Rhonda would test herself against my pleasure with this piece of food. And I was sick of fielding avaricious women.

The tie on my terry cloth robe proved small barrier to Rhonda. I could feel her reptilian hands, slow and cool, slither under the PJ top and across the skin of my back. Christ! I was just not into this. What if she tried kissing me next . . . of course she would. I couldn't fake that. The lights were on; she'd see my expression. Why couldn't I tell her I didn't want this?

I could feel Rhonda's warm breath on my neck as she undid the buttons on my PJs, then her wet tongue crept across my breasts.

It wouldn't be hard to shift the focus to Rhonda, and slip out of it myself. I firmly untangled her, saying, "Let's go to bed."

Proof of my easy success came with Rhonda's theatrical screams of orgasm. My sigh of relief was almost as loud.

Hollowness and a sense of having disconnected from myself in the process of this charade kept me awake watching the moonlight slowly fill the room. Shame at my behavior made me wonder how I could participate in this most intimate act with the detachment of a prostitute. Why on earth did I do that?

Or was it that now I knew where I stood with her? I thought back to Kate, both wanting to remember her yet shying away. We had a great couple of months together and when spring came and she told me she had to go back to her job as a smoke jumper again, it was the first time I'd realized that she wasn't like me, a trust fund baby. From the moment she told me this I began packing my feelings on ice. I could have loved that woman but instead I'd witnessed the pain in her eyes when I took up with Rhonda.

I never explained anything to Kate. Well, what could I say?

I groaned, disentangled myself from Rhonda, then rolled into a solitary ball.

∽

I never escaped into sleep. All night I worked things over in my mind. Morning came and in the end it all come apart with a huge fight. I told her that I was far from interested in a life commitment with her. I asked her to find another place to live, and further, if she hadn't moved by the end of next month, then I would find a place for her, move her belongings and leave the key to the new apartment with my lawyer.

The next few days ground by, leaving a constant sensation in my mouth of rough corn meal.

One morning as I pulled the bales of hay away from the base of the house I shook my head over the neglected gardens. It was sad to see all the twisted plants trapped beneath the bales. This would never have happened when my father was alive. Spenser had a deep awareness of nature in all of its cycles and rhythms. Shame filled me, because this was one of the things I'd learned from him. From the time I was big enough to hold the strings on the bales, we had done this job together. I wondered how I had let the right time slip past. Perhaps it was the distraction of Rhonda; the disintegration of our relationship.

Now I felt my father's nearness as I worked. Spencer's ability to work as a silent companion was something I'd cherished. Even though he had been dead for thirteen years the yawning space where he lived inside me waited; no one else had ever been given access to it. There had been one or two perceptive women who pushed at the door to my deepest rooms, but I kept the entry barred.

Most women, once the initial rush of passion was over, took up too much of my life. Too much energy. It would be a cold day in hell before I'd ask any lover to live with me again.

Finished moving bales, I saddled Dusty, hungry for some true intimacy. As I swung into the saddle, I realized how much I'd needed this ride.

Old farms — houses painted white, barns red — stood solid and comforting at regular intervals on our twelve mile loop, oriented not to the passing road but to the path of the sun. Stone walls neatly enclosed the fields which were dotted with black and white cows. We rode beside woodlots of sugar maples and beech trees, where a sudden flare of white birch trunks startled my eyes. Along the top of the ridge, views opened of orchards near the Putney School. The tame apple trees were in blossom. Planted in orderly long rows they stood protected by high deer fencing. The little wild apple trees flaunted their freedom in the woods, prancing in white party dresses.

Dusty's regular strides, hooves striking the ground to accent the rhythm, was as dear and familiar to me as the beat of my own heart. The motion of the horse brought me to a centered place where I could explore my emotional crevices.

I tried to look underneath the immediate relief of the ended relationship with Rhonda. One thing I knew for sure; I'd never been friends with Rhonda. Never, even once, had I felt as close to Rhonda as I was most of the time with Vic.

A chilly sensation rushed into me, like a cold drink of water; it spread with running fingers through my chest, on the edge of pain.

Maybe there was something lacking in me. A distance which filtered out closeness, as if intimacy were a poison. My mind skipped away from the honesty. Really, I was better off with just my friends. They truly sustained me. Lovers were always so much trouble.

Once Rhonda told me that I needed to stop looking like a church mouse. There was some truth in that. She'd even bought me clothes, using my charge cards, of course. Outfits hung in the closet, worn only when we went out. Rhonda had said, "I like it, Jane, when you look the part."

That had stunned me speechless, but I didn't have to wonder about *the part to what*? I knew. The part of a rich woman.

A snort of sardonic laughter erupted from me. Dusty flicked an ear back. Patting the gelding's neck, I said, "I'm afraid I'm turning into a bitter woman. It's the money again, Dusty." The rest of my thoughts rose up with surprising anger and I kept them from Dusty's ears. I could never trust a woman to be attracted to just me. The damn money was a lure, like the hot scent of the fox to the hounds. Blood money.

Perhaps I never loved Rhonda and that was why I was attracted to her.

"Did I want that?" I asked my confidant, Dusty.

Into my whole self swept the realization that this was my own flaw, not Rhonda's. Sex without intimacy. Relationships without friendship. Going through the motions of love without any substance. My thoughts had come full circle.

⟋◦⟍

Home again I rinsed the bit in the water bucket, then put the saddle and bridle in the tack room. Stepping into the mudroom, I removed my brown field boots using the cricket jack, and hung the wool tweed riding coat on a hook. Rhonda had always objected to the horsy smell that followed me like a friendly dog. Shedding the main gear in the mudroom helped limit the aroma of my favorite perfume, and it had become a habit.

In my bedroom I stripped off turtleneck and riding britches, dropping them on the closet floor. Ignoring the nagging voice in my head, I closed the door on the mess.

With a pang I recalled the dinner date I had that night with Rhonda to "discuss closure of the relationship." It was the last thing in the world I wanted to do.

The next morning I awoke with scenes of the previous night seeping into my mind in the same way the sunlight filtered into the room through the small panes of glass, splinter segments of discomfort, misunderstanding, and resentment.

Groaning, I rolled over in bed and looked at the clock. Six-thirty-one. Swinging my feet over the side of the bed, I moved to the windows. Even in the middle of the conversation with Rhonda, I had marveled at my own detachment from the feelings within the words.

Well, why wouldn't I? The relationship was over and this belabored processing was tiresome. A fleeting thought had come to me that perhaps I was angry and hurt. It had taken all my control to conceal from Rhonda that I'd heard she was already involved with another woman. I absolutely did not want her to know that this news bothered me.

It was all history, now. I let the small paned window bear the weight of my forehead.

"When is it all too much?"

At first I felt startled to hear my voice in the room, but I continued, "I wonder at what point you realize you no longer have the resiliency to enter a new relationship? Maybe I've reached that place."

Later, it was with an echoing loneliness that I carried my coffee into the living room. In an effort to compel myself into a better mood, I dialed Victoria's number to ask how events progressed with the horse.

"Just a second, Jane." Laughter followed, and the sound was indulgent. I could hear her speaking to her daughter, "No, Jackie, you can't wear shorts today." I heard one long wail, "But Mom!"

Again to me, "Velma's no longer . . . at least, she agreed to sell the horse to me. Delivery Sunday around noon. Beth, here's your lunch. Don't forget your math workbook. She didn't like you, though."

"Our mutual dislike society. That's okay. Well, I hope you can live with this horse, Victoria. Cribbing is such a filthy habit, and other horses learn it easily."

"Look, Jane, I don't really care if Nutmeg learns it. He's twenty-nine and it would probably do him good to learn a new trick."

The front door slammed and I knew Victoria's children were running to catch the school bus.

"The timing is wonderful because the following week, I'm on vacation from the college. Spring break. You and I can go on wonderful long rides together."

"Yes, all of one mile before Bent Jamball lies down in the middle of the road to take a breather." Then I reminded myself to go easy on Victoria; it was new love, after all.

"Oh, Janey." Victoria couldn't help laughing. "She is in pretty sorry shape. Listen, Velma asked if the mare would board with you and seemed relieved to hear she wouldn't. Odd, isn't she?"

"I'm glad the horse is going to leave her ranchette and come to live with you. I'd have the vet there waiting with shots and a worming syringe if I were you." Boy, do you sound dreary, I told myself.

"Dr. Wilson said he'll come over as soon as the mare gets here. Gotta run. Talk with you later."

"I wish you'd try Doc. Burns. He really knows horses and Wilson should've retired years ago."

"Maybe I will sometime. 'Bye."

My hand had the receiver halfway to the cradle when I heard Vic's voice say, "Are you okay?"

I brought the thing back to my ear and lied, "Sure thing."

I had goofed off long enough. Relationship stuff had taken up too much of my life lately. I decided it was time to get some work done. Going into my study, I switched on my lime-flavored iMac computer, and polished up my article for the *Brattleboro Reformer*, due tomorrow. It dealt with the recent upsurge of horse theft in New England, and

FRANCI McMAHON

was intended to alert horse owners to the possible horror of coming home to an empty paddock.

I planned to devote the remainder of the week to an article I had under contract with the *Chronicle of the Horse*, a magazine published in Virginia. This piece would be about the growing insurance market geared to wealthy show horse owners. There seemed to be too many horses dying from accidents with payoffs in the sixty-to one-hundred-thousand-dollar range not uncommon. Although premiums were high insurance companies were getting nervous.

When the phone rang Sunday evening, I had my feet on the leather ottoman and was deeply into an old Katherine Hepburn movie, my fantasy heartthrob. Regretfully, I pushed the pause button, only to find Victoria in a swivet. I turned the television off.

"I've been waiting all day for the mare to be delivered. No show, so I called Velma." Victoria's voice was a flat-line of fury. "She's not bringing Jameel. She said she could get more money for her later. I offered more, but she refused. She can't do that, can she?"

"Guess she did," I said on an exhale. "I'm so sorry."

"I thought I would get her out of there, that she would be happy with me." Victoria's voice hovered on the edge of tears.

"I know. It's tragic she can't be with you, cared-for and loved. Maybe some other kindhearted person will buy her." I paused to think of something to offer my friend. "Let's trailer over for a ride in Pisgah State Park tomorrow. We can take a lunch. There's still some miles left in your old gelding."

"If I can catch him. He's perfecting the art of avoidance." Vic sighed. "Thanks, Janey, I'd like that. In fact, I need to."

An awkward silence hung on the line, neither of us knowing where to go from there.

"How're things with Rhonda? They seemed pretty shaky last — "

"It's over. She moved out."

"I'm so sorry. I thought I heard something in your voice the other — "

"I don't want to talk about it."

"That bad? Well, say, I saw your article in the *Reformer* yesterday. It was really good, Jane. I didn't know Foxmeadow Farm's Castle Top was stolen. He was their best open jumper. He had to be worth at least fifty thousand. Any idea what happened?"

"Looks like maybe these show horses are taken by someone who can outfit them with new identities, then resell. Not much overhead involved. Seems to be a recent dump of 'new' high-class horses on the market, especially from the West."

I paused, reluctant to pass on the piece of information which had left me sick when I discovered it. "There's also an increased disappearance of the back yard horse population. The price of canner horses is way up. The average horse brings about eight hundred for meat. It's not clear yet if there's a connection, but huge meat-processing ships, the same ones which were once used for whales, are off the West Coast. Those boys are filling a whole lot of cans."

Vic sighed. "I hope Jameel doesn't end up in a can."

"She won't. Not without a lot of up-to-date paperwork on Velma's part. A freeze branded mare won't get past the inspectors without that."

4

The day dawned crisp and cool. Birds sang exuberantly, sexy and playful with each other. I dropped the horse trailer ramp so Victoria could unload Nutmeg.

"I'm glad it's sunny. Winter was too long this year." Victoria set the saddle on her gelding's back.

"Yeah, wasn't it? I'm feelin' wild and woolly and itchin' to ride. Yahoo."

Victoria teased, "Lookin' fer some dogies to herd, girl?"

"Figured I'd herd you."

Victoria flashed her blue-eyed grin. "I don't herd so easy."

I had to laugh then. "No, you don't. Never did."

Pisgah State Park, crisscrossed with trails, was easy to reach across the river in New Hampshire. Spring was the best time to ride the trails before the dirt and mountain bikes roared at breakneck speed around the blind turns.

My usual riding consisted of practice for the many shows I rode on the New England circuit. Victoria considered riding in a ring the height of mind-numbing boredom, and loved the excursions that my horse trailer made possible. I found myself looking forward to these rides too. They made for a sloppy horse and rider, though, and I really needed to cut them back.

After a couple of hours meandering through the woods we came to a log where we could eat lunch. The view looked a little too much like a postcard of New England.

With some curiosity, Victoria opened the saddle pack holding our lunch. She knew my housekeeping and home-making skills were underdeveloped. In this case though, I'd had time to stop by the Putney Market to pick up an elegant lunch. Victoria arranged the meal between us on the log with squeals of delight.

"Oh! French bread rolls from Hamellman's Bakery! Ummmmn, Brie — and let's see what's in this little package. Smoked trout. And these pastries!"

We munched quietly side by side, admiring the distant view of Chesterfield. The tiny white church spires pointed into the sky.

Victoria rested back against the log. "Rhonda gave me a smile a blow torch wouldn't melt the other day when I ran into her in town."

"Oh, Lord," I said with lively drama, raising my hands pleadingly toward heaven, "give me strength."

"Jane? Are you all right?"

I shrugged but suddenly couldn't meet my friend's eyes. I swallowed a few times trying to force the dry French bread down my gullet.

After a moment Victoria suggested gently, "Don't you have some kind of process in Quaker Meeting for problems in relationships?"

I coughed once before I could speak. My face, I knew, was a livid red, from the hacking, obviously. "Yes. It's called a Clearness Committee. Comes out of Ministry and Council. The idea is to help you reach clearness about a troubling aspect of your life." My eyes felt sort of slippery and couldn't meet Victoria's. "But, you know, they aren't called to work out how your toothpaste tube gets squeezed. Or rectify a two-sponge system in the kitchen."

"Is that all you think of the relationship with Rhonda?"

Why was Vic being such a pain in the ass? "It wasn't one of my major relationships, if that's what you mean. And no, I wouldn't ask Friends in Ministry and Council to convene just to help me sort out the mess with Rhonda."

"It isn't that you're shy of approaching them because it's a lesbian relationship, is it?" At my negative shake, Victoria continued, "I remember you talking about how pleased you are with the process around gay and lesbian Friends. So, you've just let it fall apart on its own?"

"I guess you could say that. There wasn't much glue." Even though I was glad that Vic cared enough to push me, I couldn't help responding flippantly. "It's over, Vic. Gone. Done. Hasta la vista. Besides, she's already found a replacement."

"No!" Victoria was so genuinely shocked for me that I nearly burst into tears. "That's terrible! What a creep."

My voice was on the fritz again, that dry bread had rasped my throat. "Oh, she's not that bad. I didn't give her much."

"Well, from a purely selfish position, I for one, am pleased to have you back without any wires attached."

"Me, too." My smile was sweet and true. "I've missed our impulsiveness."

We hugged tightly. "Me too."

Then Victoria laughed, patting me on the back. "We have to be spontaneous because neither of us can plan worth a damn."

I tried to nod even though my chin was wedged against Vic's shoulder. I filled my lungs with a slow breath, let it out in a long sigh, then pulled away.

Victoria looked around, "You know, we can't be far from Velma's place. Why don't we just ride by and see if — "

"Sounds like a lead balloon idea to me," I interrupted, wanting to squelch this idea quick.

Staring out over the sunlit farm country, Victoria said, "I woke up in the middle of the night. Couldn't get back to sleep, you know? I worry about her, standing in the mud, going hungry. I remember how many nights last week it rained. Hard. All night."

She pushed her hair behind one ear, eyebrows lowered. "It was a real nightmare, one I couldn't brush off and say, oh, that's only a dream. When I called Velma and she told me the deal was off, I asked her to reconsider. She said the mare was gone."

"Did she say who bought her?"

"Velma wouldn't answer any questions." Victoria looked at the water bottle in her hand.

"It's hard to believe the woman would turn down a sure sale." I said, packing things away. "Let's hope the mare went to someone who feels the same way about her you do, or at least someone motivated by a desire to rescue."

We had only been back in the saddle for a short time when I felt Dusty's body go tight with tension. A horse will hold its breath and get ready for that old dependable, flight, at the first warning something is amiss. If it hadn't been for this slight transition into full alert, I might have fallen off when he spun around. Ears pricked, nostrils flared, he let out a blast of air to clear his nose, then backed nervously.

Nutmeg pawed the ground, digging up clumps of pine needles.

Victoria asked, "What is it?" as she watched Dusty raise and lower his head, trying to get a fix on what frightened him.

"Something sure has them spooked. Will you hold him while I check it out?" Dismounting, I handed the reins to Vic. I walked off the trail in the direction of Dusty's focus.

I nearly tripped over the body. Looking ahead through the trees I hadn't noticed how the russet pine needles camouflaged it.

Franci McMahon

"Oh, no." My breath formed the words. I steadied myself against a white birch sapling that swayed sickeningly from my weight.

The corpse's fine honey-colored hair fanned out across her neck, legs flung in a last attempt to run for her life. Her mouth was slightly open, the lips pushed out of place by a branch, which lay underneath.

Unable to stop myself, I reached to feel for a pulse, certain it would not be there. A last gesture honoring the passage of life. As I knelt I saw the bone splinters showing white, like crystals on her forehead.

Victoria's insistent voice came to me through a numb membrane. "Jane! Jane, what's going on? What is it?"

"It's Jameel." I rose to face my friend. "She's been murdered."

The horror at my feet was too much. Somehow, I wanted to shield Vic from the sight of the mare. I moved to block Victoria's view with the knowledge it was pointless. Victoria jumped down from Nutmeg, tried to lead both unwilling horses forward, gave up and tied them to a tree. She advanced, not her usual graceful self, crashing through the undergrowth.

Quickly I moved forward to put my arm around Vic. I took into my own body the shock hitting her. I turned my stunned gaze back to the corpse and the stark white bone slivers exposed between the once expressive ears. My scalp crept as if they flowered from my own skull. The cold edge of a shiver moved down my skin and into the pit of my intestines.

"How do you know it's her?" Victoria finally asked, staring at the little shelves of scissored hair on the mare's belly.

I looked at Vic in disbelief. This was first-class denial. If the evidence of my barbering didn't prove to her this was Jameel, then the freeze brand would. I reached down to move the mane away from the brand. But there was nothing there. The killers had cut off the hide carrying the brand.

The skin over my jaw and skull felt as if it had instantly shrunk three sizes. Saliva flooded my mouth. Damn. I was going to puke. I bolted behind a tree and was wretchedly sick, then eased my shaking body down onto a stump.

A humming sound came to me, which I identified as Victoria, doing her wordless, reassuring singing for Jameel. A lament for the mare.

Elbows on my knees, face in my hands, listening to the soft keening, I tried to make sense of this death. They got rid of her rather than sell her to Vic. They weren't going to get away with it, I swore to myself. But why kill her?

Leaving the chestnut body lying in the pine needles, we mounted our horses. I tied my red bandanna high on a tree limb to mark the spot for the authorities.

In Chesterfield, the constable seemed impatient when we explained the death of the horse. "This was your horse?" he asked briskly.

"No," Victoria answered. "She was a mare I had hoped to buy."

"Where's the owner? It's his job to fill out a property damage report."

"This murder wasn't property damage," Victoria snapped, her eyes flashing.

"Murder!" he sputtered. Unable to keep the fine line of civility intact any longer, he openly laughed. "Lady, we call it murder when it happens to *you*, not your pony."

Next, we called the State Police from the phone booth in the small village but found a bored voice on the other end of the line. "We won't use our detectives to investigate the killing of pets. No way. Now, if the owner files a complaint — "

I slammed the phone back to its cradle, then stepped out of the booth. We stared at each other scarcely believing that all this was really happening.

"What will we do now?" Victoria looked forlorn. Tears welled up in her eyes. "I can't bear to think of her lying there. It's barbaric, you know?" She fished a Kleenex from her pocket to blow her nose. "It's horrible to know your red handkerchief will be the only marker for her grave. And that her murder is not significant."

The silence of our drive home was ended by Victoria fiercely asking, "Why would she have done that? It had to be Velma, you know?"

"Yes. I've been trying to grasp what and who could be behind this, too. It was a senseless thing to do. But there must be sense somewhere." I could not accept that it would never make sense.

Later, as Victoria unloaded Nutmeg, she declared, "I'm calling Velma."

I shut the horse trailer door on Dusty's separation anxieties. "Don't, not yet. I know you're upset, but I want to, well, have some time. They killed that horse so you couldn't have her. And they took the evidence of her brand so she is untraceable. There's a reason for that."

We faced each other, silent. Large tears slipped in a quiet shimmering path down Victoria's cheeks. Someone I loved was hurting and I had an awful suspicion I was the reason.

I held my arms open for Victoria, then rocked her. "People can be so unspeakably cruel, Vic."

When I arrived home I climbed into the hayloft, opened the big loading door, and sat there with my legs dangling into the open air of the paddock. The crunching sounds of hay being masticated rose to my ears in a reassuring concert. This was where I had retreated ever since I was a little kid, whenever knowledge of evil, or cruelty seemed more than I could bear. The simplicity of these warm vegetarian beings took some of the edge off what the higher life form, Homo sapiens, could do.

Steadied, I tried to focus on the awful death, knowing there was much to sort out. My mind lightly touched on, then recoiled like a glancing stone from the memory of the mare's skull violated by, what?

A hand held a hammer, brought it down with enough force to reduce that quick creature to crushed death.

Leaning back against a broken hay bale, its sweet aroma enfolding me, I let the sun try to warm my body. I understood my mind could only handle this in pieces, touch and run, like some children's game.

Weeding through the jungle of my emotions to find a motive for the horse's murder, I couldn't get out of the thicket. Logic, usually such a simple tool, failed me utterly. You don't destroy a horse worth hundreds of dollars on a whim, or because you don't like the friend of the person who wants to buy your horse. And you certainly don't cut out a piece of horsehide to conceal its identity without some really compelling reason.

I realized that if anyone would resolve this it would be the two people who cared about Bint Jameel.

"Okay, let's do this ABC." I spoke out loud, firmly, trying to direct my errant brain. The mare was murdered to cover up something. Safe to assume, right? Right, then, what?

The image of Velma's broad torso, hands hanging motionless at her side filled my mind. Or had it been her husband who had wielded the hammer? I got up and began pacing, talking aloud to help myself stay focused. "Wait, I've got to go back to the beginning. Why did Velma refuse to sell the mare to Victoria? Perhaps I was too mouthy and curious and she had something to cover up. And why didn't she send the mare to the canner instead of kill her? Because she got scared and knew that canneries check things like brands and demand papers. What would push that horrible woman into backing out of a sure sale?"

I stopped. "Jameel had to be stolen. That's it!"

What were the names of the previous owners? I remembered it was a couple. I tried to imagine the registration papers fluttering before me, but couldn't pull them from my memory. Victoria could. Once she'd seen something, she never forgot.

I climbed down the ladder, startling the horses out of their late afternoon nap, and dashed for the house.

Michael answered the phone on the third ring, just before the answering machine would have clicked in.

"Sorry, Jane, she's not here. She took the kids to gymnastics, but should be back in about an hour. I was really sorry to hear about the horse. Sounds like an altogether ugly experience."

"Yeah," I agreed. "I think one of the hardest parts was the official indifference."

"I'll have her call when she gets back."

In the woodshed, I loaded my arms with apple wood, then went into the study to build a fire. "I need some cheering up," I told Bugs, who was ensconced in my favorite chair. The fireplace wasn't often used; it was an inefficient heat producer but an excellent source of cheer — exactly what I needed now.

The moment the flames had begun curling over the logs, I realized how cold I had become, down to the bone. Tea would help.

Returning from the kitchen with a cup of peach tea, I scooped my kitty off the chair, then sat holding him warm against my chest and buried my nose in his fur. There is nothing in the world like clean cat smell, especially when the puss has been sleeping in the hay. His ears tickled my chin and I felt his rising purr through my own rib cage.

My mind turned like a homing pigeon to the recently published article on horse theft. Was there anything in it that could have sparked Jameel's death? The timing was beyond coincidence. Gently, I displaced Bugsy from my lap. At the filing cabinet, I rummaged for a copy cut from the newspaper.

Front and center on the Local page: HORSE THIEVES LEAVE MANY LOCKING THE BARN DOOR TOO LATE — the editors' regrettably clever title choice. Underneath, the bold byline, JANE SCOTT. Hard to miss. I read it from the viewpoint of a stranger, one who might have panicked, knowing I was on the scent.

First, as was expected by the newspaper, I had established the economic loss. This was an overview, bringing to light the number of horses — close to 350,000 each year, nationwide — killed solely for human consumption, at a value of $147.5 million. These figures did not represent the horses from America sold to Canadian meat packers, or those rendered for fertilizer and pet food. While many of these were unsound or old, a large percentage had been stolen.

Then there was a sentimental slant on a local level: "When Mary Dodge came home from school last month, she discovered that her little pony, Freckles, had disappeared . . . "

I sobered when I thought of what it would be like if Max, Victoria's daughter's pony, were one of the statistics. And theft was the easiest thing in the world to do. Most horses were unwatched and would walk up to any stranger who offered a bucket of oats.

Now, carefully, I read the part about identification. I'd written about how hard it was to identify horses lacking a permanent brand. How many fifteen-hand bay horses with a left rear sock were there in the world? Thousands and thousands. And greys. A grey horse was anything from pure white to iron-dappled grey, but the registration paper always said grey. Period.

Hot iron brands were the easiest to alter. European horses were often branded on the shoulder with a symbol representing the stud or breeding farm they came from. Horses in the American West were marked with registered brands of the home ranch.

Racehorses wore a tattoo on the inside of the upper lip, made with purple ink. I'd seen my share of smeared and unreadable tattoos. Theft was not the only reason. Sometimes an also-ran unable to get out of the starting gate had his number messed with to prevent his illustrious lineage from being discovered. Then the horse could be dropped into the paperless oblivion of the hunt field or 4-H horse shows, and no one would know if, say, it was a son of Secretariat.

Freeze branding was impossible to change. The symbols representing numbers were designed to be unalterable. Only about one-fourth of eligible horses were branded in this way, though. And it was possible to brand an unmarked horse, then sell it with forged papers. The new owner wouldn't discover the fraud until applying for transfer of ownership, or to register a mare's offspring. Most foals had to be blood-typed for registry. What an unwelcome piece of information to be told by the registry officials that your new mare had died three years earlier or the blood type was totally wrong — suddenly your horse was worth considerably less than you paid for it.

One of the newest means of accurately recording a horse's identity was photographing the hair whorls. Like fingerprints, no two were alike. Few people used this method, and once again, it was usually long after the sale that any deceit was discovered.

The space age way to identify your horse was so new almost no one thought to look for it. It was a microchip the size of a rice grain, implanted in a ligament in a horse's neck. An electronic scanner read the horse's breed and registry number.

By the time I reached the end of the article I had no doubt that Victoria's connection to its author was the cause of Velma's backing out of the sale, and this was the reason for the mare's murder. Velma had to be in deeper than the theft of this one mare.

I stared into the flames in the fireplace, feeling sick. I was to blame for the mare's death. Because Vic loved her and I loved Vic.

I tried to return my focus to the tragedy. Motive was all-important. Okay, money was easy; there was lots of it in the show world. What else?

Looking to the bank of blue rosettes on the wall and the silver trophies, packed tightly into a cabinet, flickering with reflected firelight, I knew. They were trinkets, really, but I well remember my own surge of desire for them, especially when first showing. The desire had lessened now, but it was embarrassing to admit the pleasure winning still gave me. And I was not so naive as to be unaware of the lengths to which competitors would go for trophies, nor the prices they would pay for show horses that could get them. If a horse couldn't cut the mustard, well, then get a new one that could. If money was tight, why, perhaps the disappointing horse could have an accident.

Every place I turned in my research I'd found an ugly underbelly to the show world; horses which could be stolen for hire or "the Sandman" who could put your horse to sleep in a way to pass any veterinarian's inspection. In short order the money from insurance would pay for a new and better horse. One that could win.

Pressing my cheek to Bugsy while I stared at the bright flames, I felt a growing certainty that the theft ring was connected to the insurance fraud bunch.

Had Jameel been stolen by arrangement once she had stopped winning? A break-in staged at the same time could be the reason why Velma had her papers. This could also be why her papers had never been transferred, and seemed to be the only logical explanation for Velma's actions. She couldn't be the brain behind the crooked horse business I'd written about. She didn't seem sharp enough, nor definitely was her husband. Too bad she was ignorant as well. She hadn't known what the freeze brand was until I pointed it out to her. Without papers skinny Jameel wasn't worth the meat price, and if she had gone to the canners they would have kept a record of her brand.

Velma could be a small cog in the ring who got a little too greedy, decided to do a bit of direct selling, got scared, then tried to cover her tracks.

Or the big boss had caught Velma trying to undercut the company and taken the matter in hand. I'd bet on this scene; he kills the horse and removes the brand evidence to stop the paper trail on the mare. He would figure Velma's heavy-handed greediness could put the whole operation at risk.

Yes, most probably Velma was small potatoes.

I wondered who the big boss might be. Possibly some-one whose line of work would normally take them around to posh horse farms. A feed salesman, or blacksmith. Now that was good. Someone who could wield a crushing blow with a heavy blunt instrument.

I shivered, put another log on the fire, and sat back down trying to reassure Bugs I wasn't going to leap up again soon.

A blacksmith seemed likely, since he went to each of his clients every six weeks to nail on steel shoes or reset slightly worn ones when the hoof outgrew the shoe. He would pet the dog, know where the doors were, the light switches, what the routine was. Owners or grooms would invariably chat at great length while a blacksmith worked. The new horse in the barn, what the green hunter was do-ing. "Four feet two yesterday without pecking a rail," and if they ran out of things to say about their own horses, well, there was always the competition. "Doug Emery's sway-backed grey gelding took the blue at Bennington Saturday. Don't know what connection he had with the judge that made him pin Doug's horse over my Princess."

I did that, too. At times even felt silly because I yakked on about the horse show gossip ad nauseam. Blacksmiths were like bartenders; people poured out everything to the quiet bent-over back and the steady rasp, rasp of hooves being filed. Often an occasional grunt was all that was needed to keep the talker primed. I didn't even need that.

I had an idea and once again stood up. Bugs stomped off to find a more reliable couch, his upright tail held straight as an exclamation point.

I got a big map of New England out of my desk drawer, and pinned it onto the cork bulletin board. While I waited for my computer to warm up, I dug out a box of red push-pins. After getting my iMac to sort all the theft victims by location, I placed pins in towns nearest the thefts, one red pin for each horse. A large egg-shaped pattern developed around southeast Vermont and another small nodule, thick with pins, surrounded Woodstock, Vermont. Woodstock had more expensive horses per capita than any area outside of Middleburg, Virginia.

And they were insured.

The phone's ring startled me. For a moment I couldn't remember why I'd asked Victoria to call.

"Oh, yes. Vic, do you remember the name of the owner on Jameel's papers? And where they lived?"

"Robert and/or Barbara Phillips, Woodstock, Vermont."

"And/or?"

"Can I help it if I remember it exactly? What are you up to, Jane?"

"Just a couple of ideas," I responded vaguely.

"Jane Scott, if you're planning something, you had better include me," Victoria said fiercely.

"I don't really know enough yet, but I'd guess Jameel's death is connected to the theft ring, and maybe my article set off her murder. In fact, I know I'm sticking my neck out, but I'm certain of it."

"Count me in," Victoria said. "On whatever you're plotting."

"Can you come over tomorrow?"

"Yes, after two."

As I grabbed a packaged dinner from the freezer and put it in the microwave, it dawned on me that locating every blacksmith in the theft area would be difficult. Very difficult.

I remembered how Buster had acted the day I'd seen him at Velma's. He was such an odd man, but actually, underneath his roughness I'd always thought him tender and caring. With a sinking heart I realized he'd never seemed so antisocial before that day.

I pulled back issues of the *Equine Journal* off my shelves to look up blacksmith ads. Settling into the soft chair, I put my feet up on the ottoman, and placed the magazines in my lap. Swiftly, my eyes again skimmed the symbols of my show ring victories, this time with revulsion. What had it cost the losing competitors' horses for me to win?

The beep of the microwave told me it was time to eat. What do you do with trophies, like stuffed deer heads, when you no longer want to look at them? I decided that tomorrow I'd put them away in a box.

The day had gone on too long. An hour later, crawling into bed, I began to weep as soon as I lay down. I was fairly sure that my tears were for the mare and not the unutterably lonely feeling that had swept over me.

5

I couldn't just sit around and do nothing. Sunrise found me on my pawing, ear-flicking horse.

The sun caught the red bandanna waving in the harsh, angled light. The area seemed empty, forgotten; no bright plastic yellow tape proclaimed this a crime scene: POLICE LINE DO NOT CROSS. There were no black and whites with revolving blue lights on their roofs. No uniform motioning me on, keeping me from loitering. Which I was doing now.

Reluctantly I dismounted and tied Dusty to a tree well off the trail. This time I had come prepared with halter and lead rope.

I knew it was crazy but I felt a need to look for some clue to the killer, such as an I.D. bracelet or dropped wallet complete with driver's license.

When I reached Jameel I was sickened to find that scavengers had already been working on her flesh. Where her skull had been crushed was the most violated. At least Jameel's animal non-status with the authorities had saved her from the rending indignity human bodies must suffer under autopsy. Perhaps going into the earth and the stomachs of birds and animals was not so bad.

Averting my eyes from the mare, I circled to check the surrounding underbrush. As I searched, the sensation of being watched grew and soon I couldn't examine the ground anymore because my eyes were constantly occupied elsewhere; over my shoulder, checking a flash of movement behind me. Frequently I stopped to listen.

I jumped, heart pounding, when a blue jay landed beside me, scolding me for trespass.

"A little edgy, aren't we?" I tried to slow my breathing.

Well, it was no small wonder. Being near the aftermath of another person's inner poison was unnerving, to say the least.

I came across the imprint of an unshod horse hoof in the soft ground. Tracking backward, I found that the mare had come through the woods, not by way of the trail. I wondered if the killers had no idea how near they were to the main trail.

The tracks led to the hill directly behind Velma and Chuck Smith's. Why was I not surprised? A recently mended cut in the fence told of its use as a temporary gate.

Squatting behind a large rock I watched for signs of intelligent life. "This place could be teeming with Velma and Chuck and still not qualify," I muttered.

The barn. What was in there? With a sinking feeling I knew there was only one way to find out.

I remembered a summer at camp when I'd crouched in just this fashion. Three girls had breathed heavily, giggling behind me. It was the greatest Kitchen Raid of the camp's history. And I had been the leader, entitled to the pick of the take. You can do it again, I told myself. So what if it'd been over fifteen years ago?

My body wasn't as supple as it had been, I admitted when I finally stood.

After going over the ancient barbed wire fence, I crept up a little closer. The red truck and horse trailer were gone. The sun radiated from the hillside, birds flew without a care, no one walked from house to barn, no radios could be heard. Probably just a lot of filthy stalls in that "off limits" barn I figured.

Dispirited, thin horses lounged around, about the same number as before, none worth stealing, in my estimation. I crept closer.

Not watching where I put my feet, I turned my ankle on a loose rock and swore softly. A handsome black head shot out of the nearest barn window to look at me. "Well, hello," I whispered to the curious equine.

Checking the end of the barn furthest from the house trailer, I found no door or window. No windows on the road side either. I wasn't going in through the door, I decided. Too risky, and too close to the trailer, even though I couldn't remember a dog living with Velma. Aside from her husband.

Under the inquisitive horse's head I vaulted up to the windowsill. From there it was a short leap to the floor of the stall. As soon as I landed on the squashy, urine-soaked saw-dust I regretted my choice of stalls. But then, they were probably all this filthy.

The horse, into whose living room I'd jumped, had its ears ironed flat, and was pounding the muck in the stall with one shod hoof. There was a great deal of muscle behind that steel.

"Easy, girl, I apologize for dropping in on you like this." I spoke in my best horse calming voice. The mare was not convinced. Her considerable teeth flashed in a way that sent me groping for the latch and through the stall door in a flash.

From the safety of the far side, I studied the mare. Her ears lay flat back and she shook her head sideways while pounding the mire of her bedding. The stink of ammonia vapors nearly gagged me. She was too big for a Thoroughbred, not only tall but also massive. A double antler had been branded on her left hip. She was a Trakehner, one of the Warmblood breeds, often used in Olympic-level equestrian events.

Standing in the half-light I could see four gorgeous, shiny aristocrats staring back at me over their stall doors. One of the horses reminded me of Castle Top, stolen not too long ago from Foxmeadow. Without a doubt, the barn contained way more than the value of the entire farm, including Chuck's red toys.

It was also obvious that they had been here for at least a week without turnout, judging by the fact that they were jumping out of their skins. No one was putting out any energy to clean the stalls, either. Instead of the lovely mixture of hay, horse, and straw aromas usually found in barns, the air was almost too thick to breathe. I felt especially sorry for the roadside horses; they didn't even have a window to stick their heads out of.

I doubted these animals represented Velma's effort to interest her husband in the world of horses. It occurred to me that they must be waiting for the right time to ship them. I walked down the aisle to get a closer look at each horse. They couldn't be going far if they hauled them two at a time in the scarlet wonder. No. Velma and her husband might believe they wouldn't be noticed and remembered in their rig, but the brains behind this ring of thieves would know better. A van would probably come for all of them at once. Those big commercial horse transport vans that move down the highways all the time. I counted eight stalls, and knew there must be a van on the way.

Three stalls stood empty, but as I entered them I found them waiting with filled water buckets and hayracks. It wouldn't be long before they had a full shipment.

Even though I wished I could spend more time looking for distinguishing marks on the horses, I decided to make a speedy exit. Finding a friendlier horse with a window, I entered his stall. Stroking his urine-soaked neck I saw again the famous Trakehner brand on the muscled hip.

I easily vaulted to the windowsill, hesitated, carefully looked around, and dropped to the ground.

The knowledge that the horses would be shipped soon, and that the people responsible would tone down their activities in my area afterward, filled me with a sense of urgency.

When I got home I called my blacksmith, Buster Wilde, to make an appointment as soon as possible. I'd yank a shoe, if needed, as an excuse to get him there. I had to pick his brain. Someone was altering brands. An ironworker was the perfect person to make branding irons. Right?

On Tuesday, Victoria showed up at two o'clock. "What will I do now? I don't want to look for another horse. That's what Michael said I should do. I picked up the paper this morning to read the livestock ads but I couldn't get past the rabbits. Catherine told me about three nice horses to go see, but I think you're the only one who understands. I can't do that for a while."

Silently, I poured coffee into a green-lined mug and set it near Victoria's hand on the kitchen table. "I understand. Question is, do you want vengeance? I know I can't deal with the idea of whoever killed her, the person behind this, not paying. Not very Quakerly, am I? 'Revenge, she cried!'" lifting the coffee pot high.

Victoria smiled dutifully at my efforts to amuse her.

Serious again, I continued, "I can tell you, this Scott is going to see that they don't get off free." I took a sip of coffee, eyeing Victoria over the rim and saw her eyes pick up a pulse of blue ocean current.

"What have you got in mind?" she asked casually, setting down her mug. I'd phoned her last night to tell her what I'd found. She wasn't surprised.

"Those horses I saw in Velma's barn waiting for shipment represent big business. I want to stop it. But I'm really conflicted about whether to suggest to Foxmeadow that Castle Top may be at Velma's. It might alert somebody responsible for the gelding's theft. Maybe even Foxmeadow's trainer. Whoever's behind this must be someone who gets around to all the farms, or at least to the cream of them. He could be a blacksmith. Come here and I'll show you my map." I walked off down the hall, pulling Victoria by her hand.

The map on the corkboard bristled with red pins and sparsely scattered black ones. Victoria, her nose six inches away, read the small towns. "Tell me what the colors mean," she demanded without taking her focus from the map.

I explained that red represented horse thefts, black, of course, the blacksmiths.

"Why just those?" Victoria asked, standing up straight and looking at me. "Didn't you say it could be feed merchants, veterinarians, someone giving lessons? Like Sally Swift."

"Sally Swift would hardly go around bashing horses over the head. She's pushing eighty-five years old." At Victoria's exasperated look, I said, "All right, let's give trainers orange, for enlightenment, veterinarians green for healing, and feed stores yellow, for growth." I must admit, I was delighted with my cleverness.

"It won't hurt to mark some of those horse deaths with big insurance payoffs. Like Charisma or Rub The Lamp. How's white for each suspicious death?" Victoria pulled open my desk drawer looking for colored pins, but shut it rapidly when she spotted the chaos within. "I can't imagine how you work in this environment, Ms. Scott."

I smiled benignly, opened the same drawer to remove a box of pins while watching her face the whole time. "Is this what you were so rudely looking for?"

With a grin, Victoria snatched the pins. "Okay, get out the telephone book," she ordered. "We'll start with green."

Victoria shoved a pin into Brattleboro. "Dr. Wilson, sweet old man, it can't be him. Here's Doc Burns. Who else is listed around here? Oh, yeah, there's that new horse vet just joined the Hamp-Mont practice." She stuck another green pin into the board.

Eight green dots on the map later, I commented, "With you helping this is going much faster."

"Seems terribly slow to me," Victoria responded. "Look, can't we just ignore all the recently established people? Someone would need deeply rooted connections to pull this off. You know, rubbing elbows with all the underbelly slime bags?"

"I agree. Let's cut to the obvious."

"Maybe a few phone calls can help. Leila Martin has that training and show barn in Woodstock."

"Great idea. Leila knows everyone in the upper echelons of the horse world. And makes sure everyone knows it."

"I have a meeting at Dartmouth College tomorrow. I'll try to go see her. She doesn't know me that well, perhaps that'd work to our advantage."

"Sounds like a plan."

Victoria glanced at her watch. "Look, why don't you pick Jackie up from school and give her a riding lesson? She's been bugging me for days to ask you. That'll give me time to work on this. The next thing we need to do is weed through our list to identify the hottest suspects. You know — means, motive, opportunity."

A couple of days later, Victoria and I stood at the gate watching Jackie turn her pony, Max a Million, out after a lesson.

Victoria said, "I met with Leila around noon at her barn. I just said I wanted to look into lessons for my daughter."

"Great!" I watched Jackie come up to the gate carrying the pony's bridle. "You've both mentioned Max's head-tossing as a problem. I don't think it's got anything to do with your hands, but I like it, Jackie, you looked to yourself first. Your hands are quiet and kind. No, I think his teeth may need some work. Does he drop grain as he eats?"

Jackie's blond eyebrows shot up. "How did you know?"

Victoria's ten year old daughter was a small copy of her mother, except for her nose. She lacked the distinctive beak that Victoria probably hated as a child but which as an adult put her ahead of the pack. Jackie's nose was cute and slightly upturned. She hero-worshipped me, something I secretly adored. The time would surely come when Jackie would see that I'm a flawed creature like everyone else. In the meantime I basked in the light of Jackie's eyes.

"Probably Max has some sharp edges worn into his teeth," I said as I opened the gate for Jackie. "As he chews they cut the insides of his cheek. This makes his mouth very sensitive and uncomfortable when he chews his oats or holds a bit."

Jackie looked with sympathy at Max, happily trotting away. "I hate going to the dentist."

I turned to Victoria. "Don't you think it's time to try Dr. Burns? Dr. Wilson's probably turned his attention to North Carolina and his golf game." Jackie snickered as I continued. "He should have noticed this pony's teeth before they got this bad. You can feel the places where his molars need rasping," I offered Victoria.

"No, thanks," Victoria said, lifting one lip a little. "You convinced me."

"You'll like Dr. Burns. He's a true horseman and a real charmer. As a matter of fact, one of his Thoroughbreds just had a foal. We could all go by after school later this week, meet him and see the foal."

6

On the way to visit Dr. Burns, Victoria told me about her encounter with the trainer, Leila. "It was funny. When I asked if she'd had any experience with stolen horses, she said no horse under her care had been, nor did she know of any. She was very clipped. Then I asked what you suggested, about those three colic deaths in her barn. She got snappish, asked was I there to arrange riding lessons, or to pry into her business."

"Who for, Mom? Me?" Jackie asked, her face appearing between the seats.

"Well, sort of." Victoria flicked a glance at me. "I was looking into it."

"I don't want to take lessons from anybody but Jane, Mother."

"Of course not." Victoria took one hand from the steering wheel to pat her daughter absently, then spoke again to me. "I've never been a member of the horse show world, so I probably don't come with the proper credentials."

"No. You don't, I'm happy to say. There's an ugly side to it which seems to be getting more vicious all the time."

"I never paid enough attention to see how the horse business has become big time money business. Leila told me she had horses in her barn worth over sixty-five grand. I got this tidbit before I started prying."

"I think the money's attracted a different kind of owner. They aren't horse people — they're buying a commodity. It's a tight circle, though. I think, Vic, the people who make large sums from horse deals are a select few. And they must be willing to do whatever they feel necessary to maintain a high profit margin."

I glanced in the rearview mirror, checking to see if Jackie would hear what I wanted to say next. I needn't have bothered because Jackie boogied on the back seat, ears clamped to a set of earphones

"It seems whoever's behind this must have deep connections to the inner circle. I've heard one particularly disturbing story about someone on the United States Equestrian team. He set up four of his horses' deaths by electrocution. He was indicted last month."

"No . . . " Victoria drew out the word.

"Yes. When the vet came to certify cause of death for the insurance company, it looked like classic colic. Sweat from pain and an impacted bowel."

"If more than one horse died that way, why wouldn't the insurance agent get suspicious?"

"A veterinarian has to certify each death before a single penny is paid. But when I was doing my article, I wondered that, too. I called them. I was told a horse must be valued over seventy-five thousand before they investigate. It costs too much money otherwise. Of course, they have the option of not insuring for that owner again, but it usually isn't the same owner who has the repeats. It's the trainer or barn who calls the Sandman. People in the inner circle can contact him to have a horse destroyed."

"A horse hit man. How can people arrange their horse's death before the insured period elapses?" Victoria asked with revulsion.

I agreed. "They can claim the loss of value on their taxes, too. Also, there's a triple-dip aspect to this business."

"I'll take a guess. A horse dies or disappears and insurance is collected, then the still-living horse is sold, either with a new identity, or for meat."

～♋

Dr. Burns loved giving tours. Six feet of hearty goodwill, he moved with an easy relaxed grace soothing to both horses and people. Broad-shouldered and nearing fifty, he was a handsome man. Red hair matched up well with his considerable energy. His deep-creased smile showed large, somewhat triangular teeth. The tweed Ralph Lauren Polo jacket seemed tailored to his shoulders. Gucci shoes disclosed a streak of vanity lurking within. A huge hand with freckles and curly hair on the back grasped Victoria's fine, long fingers easily.

Jackie was delighted to be lifted to the top of a stall door. From there she had a better view of the mare and new foal within. He balanced her with one hand and gestured with the other. "What do you think, Jane? I bought the mare . . . " He related a long complicated story about acquiring this mare, bred to one of the nation's top stallions, for a song. I'd heard many such stories, but they were always amusing and, I suspected, often true.

Meanwhile, we watched the week-old foal negotiate the twelve by twenty-four foot, golden straw-lined box stall, palatial by any standards. Instead of a chandelier hanging from the ceiling, there was an infrared lamp, just in case Junior got a little chilly. The mare's black, dappled coat glistened in the slanting light from the stall window. Occasionally, she buried her muzzle in the corner hayrack, chowing down aromatic alfalfa hay. Upper-crust living in the equine world.

I could tell Victoria and Jackie were won over. As we toured the farm, Dr. Burns kept up a constant flow of jokes and stories while a current of Gordon Setters flowed around his feet.

"The foals are over in that pasture, Jackie. Run on if you like. We'll catch up." Dr. Burns motioned ahead.

Then I wondered, "Where's that old mare you bought last year? The one bred to Seattle Slew?"

"Oh, that mare. After I weaned the colt, she was down the road."

I stopped dead in my tracks. "What do you mean? I thought you'd turn her out with other . . . " My voice trailed off.

His smile couldn't overcome the coldness of his words. "Jane, if I kept every old, broken down . . . "

The outside bell for the telephone rang, interrupting him. "Just a moment," he said, ducking through the tack room door.

I could see him lift the receiver of the wall phone, lips moving briefly, then he set the receiver down hard. As he passed through the door, he appeared to adjust himself, as one would straighten disarranged clothing.

"We don't want to take up your time. You've been so generous." Victoria was almost apologetic when she asked him to come by to file the pony's teeth.

Dr. Burns waved her concern away. "So, do you ride?" he asked Victoria in a way that would make most women run out to buy the first available horse or sign up for a series of a dozen lessons at the nearest hack stable.

"Oh, yes," Victoria said quickly. "I have an old gelding I'd like to retire. I thought I'd found the right horse to replace him but she . . . died." She glanced at me, unsure of how much to say. I tried to subtly shake my head, but she didn't catch it.

"Oh?" His deeply sympathetic face invited openness. "What happened?" He unwrapped a menthol cough drop and popped it into his mouth.

The story leaked out, no geysers or gushes, just trickles of information. Before either of us were aware of it, the whole story of Jameel lay there, exposed and raw.

Dr. Burns' compassion, his sympathetic expression and sounds had urged us on. Then, with his tongue, he tucked the cough drop into the side of his cheek so he could speak. "I know you feel bad about the mare, but if I were you, I'd drop it. You don't want to call attention to yourselves."

"You mean . . . " Victoria watched her daughter reaching through the rails to scratch the foals. "We could lose our own horses?"

"Why didn't I think of that? How stupid of me." I had known it, but not known it. I felt one of the setters lean against my leg and absently stroked its head, receiving licked fingers in exchange. I was imagining Moonglow lying in the paddock with splinters of bone pushing through her forelock.

"That was a great article, by the way. What are you doing next?" he asked while unwrapping yet another menthol drop.

"I'm finishing up one now on equine insurance fraud for the *Chronicle*. Wednesday, I'm doing my last interview in Woodstock." I was pleased with his interest.

"Oh? Who with?" We were at the car and he pulled the passenger door open.

"The trainer of Belgium Waffle. You remember, he was one of those horses killed for insurance. I'm surprised he hasn't been indicted yet." I got in the car.

"Oh, yes," Dr. Burns said. The car door closed amid Victoria and Jackie's thanks for the tour. His hand rested on the door frame, and he protectively pushed the door lock button next to my arm.

In the car driving back, both Jackie and Victoria raved just a bit too long over Dr. Burns. I felt troubled about his lack of loyalty to his older mares, so didn't feel engaged in his fan club.

After Jackie had been dropped off at a friend's house, Victoria got more specific. "Don't you think he's sexy?"

"Yes, and no. I can see that he must be, but not to me."

"You two would make a perfect pair," Victoria persisted, eyes front as she negotiated the dirt road. "Now that he and his wife are divorced, he's a great catch."

"There's something you're forgetting, Victoria." I couldn't believe this subject was being trotted out again. "I'm a lesbian. There's a saying, 'Don't try to make me straight and I won't try to make you queer.'" Even while I said it, I knew that I was being too severe. If only straight people had a clue how boring this was to deal with.

But instead of being offended, Victoria shrugged. "I'm sorry. At times I think life would be easier for me if you were straight. Michael doesn't say anything, but he's a little uncomfortable with our friendship."

"Sexuality isn't something you adjust to suit other people." I rested my forehead on the side window glass to watch the rushing scenery. I thought of other straight women friends who hadn't been able to take the heat of a friendship with a dyke. They would get questions from friends or business associates like, "Why do you hang out with her?" Would Vic pull away, now? Could the friendship we began as children adjust to changes? My stomach tightened and I felt a little sick at the thought of not having Victoria in my life. I always seemed to lose the ones I love.

She had known from the first, perhaps even before I had, that I liked girls instead of boys. I'd always been the classic tomboy.

Right after I first came out, telling everyone I knew, I noticed many of my friends leave by degrees, all the time claiming that my lesbianism had nothing to do with their busy lives. It was just, well, that they were so very busy.

For years I'd avoided friendships with straight women because they so often seemed to lead to pain. It was a challenge for me to risk these crossover friendships. Even now the usual reaction was, "That's just fine, but don't make a pass at me. I'm happy with my husband or lover."

How could I explain to them that my sexual orientation did not turn me into a predator? Was Victoria any different? I knew she was, but I was scared.

A few months ago, something had happened that I hadn't shared with Victoria.

Catherine and Victoria led the local 4-H Club; arranged guest speakers, the yearly horse show, etc. They asked me to speak on "Schooling the horse over jumps." For some reason, Victoria hadn't been able to attend; maybe it was that time when Jackie had the flu.

Catherine's house, the site of that week's meeting, was at the end of a long driveway so hellish that it always dampened ideas of a spontaneous visit. After the meeting, I overheard a discussion between Catherine and one of the children, to the effect that the girl's mother wanted her to be driven to Catherine's neighbor's house, where she was visiting.

Of course, I piped up with, "Oh, I'll take her. I'm going right by there."

I got my coat. A strange, evasive silence met me as I turned back. Everyone seemed frozen in a tableau. I said to the girl, "Well, get your coat."

Abruptly, Catherine took the receiver down from the wall phone, dialed a number, "Tell Mary no one is going past . . . " The way Catherine had been hunched around the phone made it hard to hear her clearly.

Again, I stupidly said, "But, Catherine, I'll take her," before the repulsive chill of understanding drenched me.

I left in a hurry. From that day on I hadn't felt comfortable around Catherine. In fact, I despised her. Despised the whole stereotype that if a woman loved other women, then she must also be a pedophile.

Perhaps some day I'd tell Victoria that story. I wasn't quite sure why I hadn't yet.

I snapped back to the present as Victoria said, "Listen, Jane, your friendship means more to me than protecting Michael from a little discomfort. Besides, he's a big boy."

I turned to her and smiled, but perhaps something cautious showed in my expression.

"Really."

"Thanks."

Deep within I knew that true belief in what Vic said would come through her actions.

Changing the subject, I asked, "What did you think of Dr. Burns' warning? We could push these crooks and end up with our own horses stolen, or worse."

"I think he has a point. The idea of anything happening to one of our horses is really horrible." Victoria drove into my driveway and let the car idle.

"This is something we should make a careful decision about, Victoria. It's risky." I got out of the car, then leaned on the edge of the open window. "Let's get together soon, to talk about how much involvement we want in this thing."

"I'm wanting less all the time. Let's just leave it to the people trained to deal with it."

"Unfortunately, I haven't seen much enthusiasm on their part." I pushed myself away from the car and turned toward my house. Scout ran up, wiggling her hard, wirehaired body, happy to see me.

7

Rhonda surged into my dreams to send me thrashing in my sheets. Opening my eyes, I felt completely awake. On the way to the bathroom I remembered the phone ringing twice in the night. When I picked up the receiver all I had heard was shallow breathing, then the dial tone. My head throbbing, I tossed down two aspirin.

Buster Wilde, the blacksmith, was due late morning. I decided to take a long ride before removing Dusty's shoe. I hated to pull a perfectly good shoe, but otherwise there would be no excuse for me to call him, and I needed to question him — discreetly, of course.

Once again, I dialed the number obtained from Woodstock information for Jameel's former owners. After days of automatic answering devices, the velvety "Hello?" made me scramble.

Disjointed at first, my story finally became a coherent whole.

Barbara Phillips' response was almost detached. "Yes, the mare was stolen. We collected on the insurance months ago. A few things were missing from the house as well, including her registration papers. What makes you so certain this was our mare?"

"She'd been freeze branded and your name was on her papers. I saw them in Velma Smith's hands."

"Quite frankly, we had that mare for sale for nearly a year. The market is down. After she was stolen it was a relief to get full value for her. Where is she now?"

Given her detached air, I gave her high marks for at least asking this question. Perhaps she did have some feelings for the horse, but I wasn't ready to hit her with the answer just yet. "Do you mind if I ask what price you offered her for sale?"

A long silence preceded Barbara's answer. "Sixty-three thousand. That's what we gave for the horse. My daughter didn't want to show saddle seat anymore. She wanted an Eventing horse, and good ones are rather dear."

As if sixty-three thousand wasn't. Barbara had snapped her last syllable off as though realizing she'd said too much. Now was the time to answer her earlier question.

"You asked where Jameel is now. Your daughter's horse was killed, her skull smashed, her freeze brand cut away to hide her identity." I let this sink in.

One lone word came over the wire, "No!"

"Yes, Mrs. Phillips. I know who was involved in Bint Jameel's theft and destruction. Would you like to report it?"

The silence on the line lengthened.

Barbara Phillips cleared her throat, and said, "No, Ms. Scott. And I would appreciate if you don't meddle. The matter is finished."

"Barbara, I'm just trying to find out who killed her." I was speaking into a dead phone.

I stared at the telephone receiver. Jameel had been an avenue to a better horse for her daughter. The child's attendance at Pony Club rallies and Events would not only open doors socially for the daughter, but also the parents. Paying to have Jameel stolen would pave their way to a brighter financial future with better business contacts with the wealthy and connections to eligible young men for her daughter. I sighed, then walked slowly out to the barn.

The Phillips were poisoned. Poisoned by their own toxic greed and gut-swelling desire for fame by way of their horses. Bint Jameel had been a victim who now ran with a herd of disposable horses whose hooves made thunder only in the heavens.

Even though I knew why people wanted the evil stuff, it still baffled me why they let money influence the fiber of their lives. I'd seen it too much. I was sick of discovering that women who I'd thought loved me were in love with my money. I was a stranger to them. I hated the money paid out to me after my parents death, tainted money, stained with their blood.

A few years ago I'd tried giving it all away, but my dear parents had worried some man would try to marry me for my money and tied it up. I wished I could lead a normal life.

Dusty shoved his nose under my arm after I slipped the bit into his mouth and drew the crownpiece over his ears. "I'll never sell you, Dusty, even if you can't win at the shows for me anymore."

I thought, some creatures are warm while others have hard spirits. Rhonda seeped into my mind. I couldn't remember a time when I felt cozy with Rhonda. My strongest sense of my father was the feel of the cloth of his shirt against my cheek, and his loving warmth.

Yearning rushed through me, with a power so strong it seized my core in a tight clamp. Would I feel that way again?

It had been too sudden. How could they be alive and calling me from London, to say they would see me soon, and then, simply gone?

Quickly, I gathered the reins and closed my legs against the barrel of the horse.

Dusty cantered up an old logging road to a high hay field. My forehead cooled and I steadied with the movement of the horse.

Reaching the far end of the meadow we came to a halt and I gave my gelding a shove at the crest of his neck, his cue to graze if he liked. I sat with one leg cocked across the saddle. Dusty's head disappeared toward the grass and his barrel's wide expansion and slow narrowing told of the deep breath happily taken. Such simple creatures. So easy to love.

～

Believing we would be back to the farm well before Buster would arrive, I was surprised to see his new 4 by 4 truck, complete with blacksmith shop under the truck cap, parked in the driveway.

Emerging from the barn as I rode up, he wore a slightly guilty look on his bearded face. "Thought you might be in there," he mumbled.

Undoing the buckles that held the English saddle on Dusty, I said, "You're a little earlier than I expected."

It was at this point that the memory of why he was here rushed into my brain. Damn! I hadn't pulled the shoe! Frantically, I tried to think of an excuse for setting up the appointment.

He opened the back of his truck, removed a welded frame, then placed it on the ground. He easily hefted an anvil, then plunked it onto the frame. His shoulders bulged, forearms stretching the flannel fabric tight; his wrists had long since popped the buttons at the frayed cuffs. He wore a wide black leather belt threaded through the loops of his jeans, clasped by a no-nonsense buckle he must have made. His skull was broad, his eyebrows making a sizeable windbreak across the forehead, bushing out over the green eyes. All of his hair was black and curly, even on the backs of his fingers. In the summer it sprang out from his chest, straining for freedom from beneath his white undershirt.

As he buckled on the heavy leather apron he said, "What's the trouble? A cast shoe, you said? I was just here two weeks ago."

"Loose! I think one of Dusty's shoes is loose." Pointing, I said, "This one. I thought I heard that hollow clunk of a loose shoe."

I blushed like a mating Scarlet Tanager. "Here. I'll lead him for you."

After watching with thick eyebrows shot forward, Buster picked up each hoof. "There's nothing wrong with this horse's feet."

Effortlessly, he reloaded the anvil, stripped off his apron and put his hand on the door handle. "I'll send you a bill for mileage. And my time."

"Of course," I said as innocently as I could muster.

Rats, what a fiasco. I casually asked, "When you were at Velma Smith's the other day, why did you pull out when you saw me there? Not very friendly." I smiled.

Buster tugged on his door handle. I backed off as he mumbled, "I figured Mrs. Smith was busy." He entered the cab, then slammed the door.

Through the truck's open window I tried another tack. "What did you think of my article in the *Reformer*, the one on horse theft?"

"Didn't see it." Avoiding my eyes, he started the truck.

He was lying.

⌒

That night I tried to reach Victoria to tell her about my conversation with Barbara Phillips, and the encounter with Buster. The answering machine dutifully took my message.

Wednesday started early and crept by, dragging its minutes. The drive to Woodstock seemed long. The interview with the man who rode in shows and trained for famous owners dragged. Other than his canned speech about the high-class horses and their owners, he remained persistently nonverbal. He was handsome, but was either lacking in brains or purposely obtuse, I couldn't tell which. Every word that deviated from his planned line had to be pulled from his mouth in a manner rivaling a dentist's technique.

Finally, I decided to cut to the chase. "Belgium Waffle was insured for sixty-eight thousand dollars, but after suffering a stroke, he was suddenly worth a whole lot less. He conveniently died before the end of his insured period. What do you have to say about that?"

His charming smile became wooden, his eyes busy.

I said, "Belgium Waffle, Rainman, and Rub The Lamp were shown by you, and all died of colic in your barn. I've heard that electrocution is suspected in their deaths."

"Oh, I hear the telephone ringing." He smiled graciously as he slipped into his office. The lock clicked on the office door as I tagged after him. End of interview.

On the two-hour drive home I wondered how much I could tell of what I knew in my article. The people I would write about held enormous power. Would the truth ever reach print? Editors wielded their red pens with one ear toward their lawyers. And yet people had a right to know about the filth I'd uncovered, and I was sure it represented only a hint of what was there. I'd write the whole story and not do my own censoring. Yes. The *Chronicle of the Horse* was in the center of some of the wealthiest horse country in the world. They would want to alert their readers.

Were the responsible crooks one huge network or different regional organizations?

I was tired and relieved as my headlights lit my own driveway.

The relief didn't last. There were no welcoming neighs at the sound of the familiar Toyota engine. The paddock gate stood wide open.

8

I hit the brakes hard. It was pointless to go into the paddock to look for them, but I did anyway. Of course they weren't there. I knew it by the silence, the absence of their spirits.

My narrowed gaze moved along the dirt of the driveway and found the signs — the wide tracks of a livestock truck. My horses hadn't pulled a springtime escape frolic. They had been stolen.

Galvanized, I sprinted for the house. They would go to a slaughterhouse for sure. A blind mare and a lip-tattooed gelding? No doubt about it, smearing the ink of his tattoo was child's play.

Flicking on my computer, I once again called up the article which I now wished had gotten a rejection slip. Under "research," I found my list of the New England slaughterhouses.

As the printer typed off the list I switched on the message playback of the answering machine. Dr. Burns' voice first: "Hello, Jane, I'm heading out your way and wondered if you'd like me to bring spring shots when I come. Well, if you aren't home . . . can do it another time. So long." I clicked the mouse to put away the theft file as Victoria's voice came on, very scared: "Max is gone. What have we done? Oh, God! We've pushed these people too far. Call me. Oh — just in case he just got out of the pasture we're going to drive around and look. Nutmeg's there but he's so hard to catch." Click. The tape ran on with other messages, but I was too frozen to make any sense of them.

Max, too! I thought of Jackie.

I began dialing the numbers. Over and over I repeated the same question. "Hello. Do you have two grey horses brought in today? Thoroughbreds. A blind mare and a gelding? Also a chestnut pony, right hind sock and a star?"

At each bored denial, I would say, "There's a five-thousand dollar reward for their recovery." That usually perked them up, brought out the pencils and prompted requests for my phone number.

Arriving at the one who said "Yes," I nearly fell off my chair.

"Are they all right?" I croaked, my voice rough with fear.

"Yeah, sure. We don't start work on the shipment until the next morning. Who are you, lady?"

"I'm their owner. My name is Jane Scott."

"The owner signed them over this afternoon."

"Who?"

"Just a minute, let me find it. Jeezem Crow, what a mess. The guy who runs this outfit has gone home." I could hear papers rustling. "Says Jane Scott. Somebody steal your horses, Ma'am?"

"Sure did. I'm coming down for them right now. I'll be there in a few hours. What's your name?"

"Jake. Look, I can't release them without you paying what we paid. I'll need to see some I.D. Later, you can talk to my boss."

"How much? It'll have to be a personal check. The banks are closed."

"Right. Eight hundred each for the two horses and one ninety-five for the pony. Bring proof of ownership."

"I can bring papers for my two, but the pony belongs to the daughter of a friend. I have no proof for him."

The pause on the other end of the line made my breath go shallow. I couldn't leave him there.

"You said five thousand?"

"Yes." I breathed easier.

"No problem. Ask for me when you get here." He gave me directions through the Back Bay area of Boston.

"Listen, Jake, thanks."

Quickly dialing Victoria's number, I was forced to wait restlessly for the fourth ring and Jackie's recorded voice asking the caller to leave a message.

"I've found Max. He was taken with mine to a slaughterhouse in Boston. I'm going for them now. I'm guessing this is a diversion to keep me away from Velma's, and they're planning to ship the horses tonight. I won't get back till midnight. Call the cops. Oh, it's four-thirty now."

It only took a second to retrieve the horses' registration papers from the file drawer, five minutes to change my clothes, ten more to hitch the 4-Runner to the horse trailer. I was out of the house and tooling down the Interstate within half an hour of locating the horses.

The slaughterhouse was in the heart of the stockyards, warehouses and many dark abandoned buildings near the harbor. Taking the canvas bag holding halters and lead ropes from the passenger seat, I walked in through wide swinging doors, across recently hosed-down concrete. Even though the weather wasn't warm yet, I struggled to keep from gagging on the stench of blood and offal, the contents of intestines.

FRANCI MCMAHON

A worker in the act of hosing scraps of unidentifiable debris from the floor around the walk-in coolers directed me to the office. Jake, a gawky college kid, relishing the role of temporary boss, had his feet on the desk.

He checked my I.D., glanced over the horses' papers, and listened to me explain the situation about Max as I wrote out the hefty check.

"Have them fax a copy of proof of ownership. For our records."

"Do you know the people who sold my horses to you? They must be regulars."

"Yeah, they are. First time I've handled the deal. We get shipments of 'bout ten to twenty horses a week from them."

Calculating the weekly proceeds from slaughter horses came to about eight to fifteen thousand dollars a week. I'd called at least a dozen slaughterhouses in New England. This calculated to earn from meat horses for the thieves between ninety-six thousand on a bad week, or two hundred thousand on a good one.

I handed him one check for five thousand dollars and a second one for sixteen hundred and ninety-five dollars. The larger of the two he folded a few times and stuck in his shirt pocket.

"What did they look like?"

He hesitated. I prompted, "The woman stocky, short, and middle-aged? Sort of bull dog type? Her husband . . . "

"No, no," Jake broke in. "She was a looker. With it, ya know? Clothes, makeup, long black hair, done up in the back. Tall and thin. She ordered her helper around. Looked like an old, pudgy ex-jockey."

This image of a short plump man didn't fit, nor did the woman, but there had to be some connection to Velma. "Were they driving a red horse trailer?"

"Naw, a four-horse van. Kind of a greenish color with black trim."

"What was the license plate? New Hampshire?"

He shifted some papers. "You'll have to ask my boss. It's his business and he might be mad if I talked about his clients. He'll be in tomorrow at seven." Shoving the wheeled chair back to the wall, he stood. "Follow me. I'll help you load 'em."

He led me down a long shed-row. Barrels of offal stood at regular distances along the wall. A metal track ran the length of the ceiling, clusters of metal hooks hung ready for the morning. A large truck pulled out, air brakes hissing.

Jake walked along a narrow corridor, his long-legged stride passing endless small pens holding four or five horses each. "I think they're at the end," he said.

Between the boards, I could see curious eyes of horses watching us walk by. What brought a horse in any legitimate way to this end? They were so helpless in the hands of people. I wondered what a typical pen held, so I peered through the boards at the horses waiting for dawn. A large bay stood on three legs, its right front knee the size of a football. A very fat pony with long hooves laid its ears flat and rushed at me. I stepped back. Two others were thin, backs hunched in pain.

They had probably been sold at auction; the used car lot of the horse world. The packing plants were the wrecking yard.

I thought of the horses I knew, thin from neglect and harsh use. Or, like the pony, sour and mean from disuse.

"We are the killers," I said in disgust.

Jake, further down the aisle, said over his shoulder, "Huh?"

"Nothing."

The full trumpet of Moonglow's neigh cut above the other stockyard sounds. She had recognized her person's voice. I ran the rest of the way.

All three of them were in a small pen. A fourth horse, snaking its head out and down, ears flat, tried to claim room. Dusty used his body like a linebacker between the strange horse and his blind mother. They moved as a team hitched together, Moonglow pressing her whole body to the familiar presence of her son. Max huddled, a small brown satellite to their movements. Moonglow's ears swiveled like a radar receiver, listening for the sound of my voice.

"I'm here and I'm going to take you home." I reached my hand through the boards for the mare to get my scent.

Setting the canvas gym bag on the ground, I handed Jake a halter for Max. "This should fit the pony. Actually, it's Dusty's baby halter." My voice box clamped shut when I said that. I pressed my eyes closed, afraid the relief at finding the horses safe would embarrass me with tears.

When I placed the halter on Dusty, he put his head under my arm, eyes under my armpit and let out a deep sigh. It was something he had done since he was a foal. He had such simple faith that I would take care of him.

Leading them down the aisle, trying not to meet the eyes of the horses on death row, I thought, What if I'd let mine down?

Loading went smoothly. Max stood crosswise in the front, happily catching the rain of hay from the net above.

It was midnight when I dropped the ramp in the driveway to unload. I jangled from caffeine.

"You can stay here tonight, boy," I told Max, turning them all out with huge piles of hay. In the garage I found a chain and padlock and locked the gate. The inane headline of my article flashed across my mind like the messages in Times Square: HORSE THIEVES LEAVE MANY LOCKING THE BARN DOOR TOO LATE.

I wondered if everything was over at Velma's. All wrapped up with Velma and her cohorts in jail.

I dashed into the house. Border Scout followed me, wriggling her hard little body with joy. I reached down to pat the dog's wiry hair and without formality, she flipped over for a stomach rub, feet waving in the air.

"You haven't had much attention today, have you, Scoutie? Well, it'll have to be later." I headed for the telephone and dialed Vic's number. Still the damn answering machine. What should I do? I'd have to drive over to her place . . . or should I go straight to Velma's? Maybe they were all still there, mopping up.

Throwing the closet doors wide, I asked the smiling dog, "What should I wear tonight? Shining armor or formal black?"

She wagged and panted.

I settled on a black turtleneck covered with a dark blue sweater and midnight blue Lycra riding pants. I laced up black sneakers. Relief must have loosened a screw, because I put a hand behind my head, and spun in front of the full length mirror.

"What the well-dressed horse rescuer is wearing this season," I said pompously to Scout.

The temperature was dropping fast, so I grabbed a down vest then ran for the study. Adding a notebook and pen from my desk, I shoved them into a vest pocket, and my wallet in a rear zippered pants pocket.

At the rumbling growl rising from my guts I realized I'd missed dinner. No time for that. At this rate, I'd be lucky if I caught any of the action.

9

My Toyota jolted over the ruts of an old logging road, the best hiding place near Velma's farm for a vehicle. The track forked; one leg led back at a different angle, toward Velma's. With the headlights turned off, I nearly drove into a tree. I sucked a breath of air through clenched teeth. A twig scraped along the door sounding like fingernails. I remembered I'd have to back up out of here, thought I'd gone far enough, and cut the engine. The silence was spooky.

I didn't want to barge in on the police. Perhaps they waited, hidden in the bushes, for the thieves to show up.

As I stepped down from the cab a branch sprang back from the truck door, whipping my face. I stood with open hands holding my face, trying not to whimper. Welts would rise before long. I shoved ahead. Deep ruts made by the log skidder slowed me down. Each foot had to find a solid place before putting weight on it. Saplings brushed my body and cobwebs touched my face like ghost breath before I came out at the dirt road leading to Velma's.

A car's headlights sliced the dark behind me. I dove for the ditch, lying as flat as I could. The car hummed over the hill, not turning off the main road. But if it had I would have been seen. I sprinted to the bend in the road where I could see Velma's farm.

The lights seemed indistinct, but then I'd never seen the place at night. A shadow bent the lights. It was a man leading a horse in a small circle to quiet it. Then I saw what blocked the light; a huge horse van. It was parked parallel to the road with its side ramp down, hidden from my view.

Why weren't the police moving into action? I should be able to spot somebody. Then I realized why I'd seen no cars hidden on the side roads: there weren't any. My message hadn't gotten through.

Threading my way closer through the brush across the road, I felt elated that I'd gotten here in time. Another hour and it would have been a dark farm on a back road. At the least I could get a license plate number and see who was involved.

All of the light and action was on the other side of the looming horse transport. It was risky, but I'd have to get nearer.

Peering through some wild rose brambles, which cost me plenty in scratches, I couldn't see a company name printed in bold letters on the side of the van. Just grey paint, and some faint messy areas, which looked as if they had been painted over. I crouched for a moment, gathering myself, then moved swiftly across the road and under the snout of the engine.

I took the notebook from my pocket and with pen held between my teeth, rubbed the grime away from the license plate. Like Vermont's tag, this one had mountain peaks at the top. Montana! A long way from home. In bold print I wrote, 51T831. A rush of high country wind brought my hair on end. As I suspected, this was no local business.

Footsteps crunched over gravel toward me. I dropped flat to the ground and scooted far under the van. The horse being led must have shied, knowing something lurked beneath the van. The man swore and I could hear the snap of the lead chain, twice.

"Ho, you wild cat. Velma, ya gotta let these damn horses out once in a while. How the hell do you think we can haul them clear across the country when they're so wound up?"

"These horses can jump any of my fences, Frank. So mind your own business."

I listened to this disembodied conversation and as the voices faded off, wriggled closer to the ramp. Above, the sounds of pent-up energy, flowing from restless hooves — lots of them — made me all too aware of the imminent departure of the van. I guessed they were trying to load the last horse.

A surge of claustrophobia licked at my edges. I fought away the knowledge of the enormous tonnage of horse van looming above.

"Whoa, damn you!" The chain snapped again.

Lying just back of the light and behind the loading ramp, I inched forward. The most visible thing about the horse struggling at the end of the lead shank was its white nylon halter; the rest faded into the night behind. The only black horse in Velma's barn was the Warmblood mare who had not welcomed me into her stall.

The big black mare circled, plunged as far from her handler as possible. A man — one I hadn't seen before — tried to hold her, repeatedly snapping the lead line attached to a chain passed through the halter rings then over the horse's nose. Four other sets of feet stood still, waiting for the man to control the horse. How was I going to recognize anyone if their boots were all I could see?

The fuss with the horse was over her refusal to have protective shipping bandages wrapped on her legs. Two front legs were wrapped. One hind leg was only partially done; the elastic roller bandage trailed behind the mare as she circled.

Frank's voice again. "I thought we gave you money for another set of Velcro-closing shipping boots. I'll never get these wraps on her hind legs."

Velma muttered a lame excuse. The mare laid her ears flat and renewed her efforts to rid herself of the hated people. She kicked out viciously, then reared, one front leg wrap unraveling to wave in the air. Again the mare spun around, flinging the thin man out to the end of the lead rope. She struck out with her front legs and connected. He fell to the ground, groaning, two feet away from me. Our eyes met like headlight beams on a dark highway.

I was moving crab-wise towards the far side before he found tongue to call the others. Pairs of feet circled the van, cutting off my escape.

Maybe I could find a recess in the undercarriage I could pull myself into and they might think I'd slipped away. Chunks of greasy dirt fell on my face as my hands tried to read the metal. The heavy, rank smell of oil and grease promised fresh-aired freedom. I tried the wheel-well, but no, it wasn't the right shape.

Flashlight beams swept the sandwich of dark between the earth and the metal hulk. Shadows from the tires crossed back and forth.

"Come out from under there," someone yelled. Whispers. Crunch, crunch — sounds came from the gravel as they got into position. The flashlight beams sniffed like bloodhounds.

Light caught my pupils, blinding me.

"There!" Behind the five white disks I knew there were eyes staring at me. "Get the hay hooks."

Waiting only long enough to hear one set of footsteps fade, I made a break for it. Rolling fast, I shot out on the side I guessed they wouldn't expect me to take, toward the barn, and beyond to the woods trail. It was good strategy, except

I came to the barbed wire fence more swiftly than I remembered. I hit it going full speed. My clothes caught. I struggled but the material was tough. "Always buy the best quality," Mother's voice came back to me. A high tense wail escaped from me, halfway between a scream and a laugh. I yanked at the clothes, praying for them to rip. The stampede of feet thundered up the hill.

Countless hands seized me, roughly yanking me off the wire fence. A sound of tearing clothing followed and with a strange detachment I focused on the shreds of material waving on the barbed wire line.

Before my vest was pulled up over my head, I got a glimpse of Velma's victory smile. Someone held my arm out at the elbow. I kicked and squirmed. For an instant I saw light from the barn backlighting two hands. They were filling a hypodermic syringe.

10

Something stabbed my left cheek. I shifted my head seeking a more comfortable place, and heard the same rhythmic thrum as the blood pounding through my temples, accentuated by regular "blups." This wasn't a dream — or my bedroom. The sounds and smells weren't right. My brain staggered in a foggy moorland mist and my eyes didn't want to open.

Then it came to me: I'm on the train with Aunt Belinda, with a crashing headache. It's our yearly excursion to the north of Scotland. Last year's salmon fishing trip had brought pink-fleshed fish steaming to our plates.

Bits and pieces of recent reality mixed with brooks and moors and the thin line of the fly rod. The images leaked in as blue water runs, as brightly colored feather and fur flies, skipping along the surface of my memory.

My eyes opened. They didn't focus well. I blinked a few times, and reality crashed in like a freight train, not some excursion tourist transport. The pillow under my head was straw, and this wasn't the train, it was the horse van.

The sharp spears of straw pushing against my cheek interfered with my shaky ability to concentrate. When I tried to brush them away, I discovered I couldn't move. A rough canvas and wool horse blanket secured me as tightly as a cocoon.

Bunching my shoulder muscles, kicking my legs and fighting to free my hands earned me meager information but it wasn't worth the pain from the ropes cutting into my wrists. At first, outrage only made me fight harder. I spent a short time going berserk, then with sweat beaded on my forehead and the rest of my body feeling slimed with it, I stopped fighting. Sweat, clammy with fear, crept down between my breasts like insects with tiny feet.

Rough wool rubbed my chin and lower back where my turtleneck had been rucked up. A black horse stared at me from an uncomfortably near distance. The horse's forelock fell over one purple-brown eye, and I was drawn into the depth of its examining stare.

Through the lifting fog came an image of large hands filling a hypodermic syringe, silhouetted by the barn's lights. Barbed wire had torn the skin on my thigh and the cord tying my hands down to my thighs, crossed over the cut.

I raised my head to look around. My traveling companions gazed back at me. Eight curious and concerned equine aristocrats, just as I had figured there would be, haltered and chained to their padded stalls.

We were all captives.

I'd been in some fixes before, but I wondered how I would get out of this one. My head dropped back heavily to the straw. Something squished and I knew my hair had horse manure staining it from auburn to dark brown.

In order to function to free myself, I needed a freer spirit. Reaching for my Quaker foundation, beyond the terror I felt building inside, I took in one long slow breath. Then another, and flowing in with the air I brought the light to center myself.

The webbing surcingles, sewn-on straps to secure the horse blanket on a horse, were buckled around me, parachute cord trussed me up like a neat package. Delivery destination appeared to be Montana. Would they let me live? How much did they think I knew? Probably more than I actually did.

We headed west, where my body could be dumped in a remote mountain gulch. By the time it might be found by some elk hunter, I would be hard to identify. A full-fleshed memory returned; the carcass of a Rocky Mountain goat I'd come across on a hike in Glacier Park. What was left of it, anyway. Grizzlies, mountain lions, and maybe even wolves had scattered the parts everywhere and polished the bones. A scrap of white woolly hide remained. I remember being transfixed by the whiteness of the bones lying on the flower-covered mountain slope.

Or would they do something to my body, like they had done to the chestnut mare?

Squeezing my eyes shut, I held my breath and rocked back and forth. The image of the mutilated horse was slow to leave.

I had cared about her. I had been responsible for her death by probing too much.

Panic nibbled at me. Then reason left me, and I thrashed around on the floor. The horses snorted, threw their heads and stamped their front feet. Finally, I lay exhausted in the center aisle, my wrists burning from the pain of my useless contest with the rope. The Warmblood mare's regular pawing matched the pounding in my skull. Get away get away get away.

I raised my head, a strand of straw sticking to my cheek, to look at the big mare. Glossy sweat, sheening her coat to ebony, made me worry. This horse should have a sedative.

Slowly, so as not to disturb the horses, I rolled over to my place by the wall. Lying on my back, I looked at the mottled ceiling, the windows framing the first light of day.

FRANCI MCMAHON

Felt the early dawn air, cold on my face, and was glad for the warmth of the horse blanket. Though I wished I'd had a choice.

"At least I have company," I spoke to soothe the horses, who were still alarmed, and perhaps, myself as well. "I know I look weird but I'm a human."

I heard the access door to the driver and groom's compartment open with a bang. There must be an intercom for the groom and they had heard me talking to the horses.

Helplessly, I watched the reedy man Velma had called Frank load a syringe, give the mare a shot in the neck, then with the same needle, jab me through the layer of horse blanket at my shoulder.

Much later I awoke feeling like a ragged piece of carpet. Opening my eyes, I saw light entering the small windows from a different angle. My vision fractured and wavered. A surge of fear rose, tasting bitter in my mouth.

Why hadn't I been killed yet? Deep within I felt surprise that I'd been able to wake up, was still a viable part of the world. I knew one thing. If there was a way to get out of this mess, I was going to find it. Talk my way out, or fight my way out.

How could I escape if I was kept drugged? Fighting the restraints only made my wrists burn and throb, and a sticky sensation, which must be blood, had emerged after the last time I'd struggled. The constant roar of road, reaching me through rubber tire tread, made sound a crude thing. My body could get no rest from the heaving, jiggling floor. The inner tissues of my mouth and throat felt sharp, as if sand-coated. And it was wet under me now. I suppressed a whimper. I'd pissed my pants while I was unconscious. How demeaning.

My mind ran unrestrained, flickering from one thing to another. My horses; were they all right? A yearning to be held, even by Rhonda, flashed through me. No one's arms had ever held me as close as my father's. Close without violating me.

Too many of the women I'd loved had been terribly breached by a father's twisted sexuality, that betrayal the ultimate loss of a parent. At least I could feel deep sadness and longing for Spencer's touch.

∽

Toward evening, the van stopped. I faked stupor. With clanging booms the big side doors opened, ramp lowered. Dry air sucked the humid, manure-heavy stench out, and replaced it with a faint hint of diesel fuel. I heard the horses being unloaded and risked opening my eyes. A postage stamp view through the open door was all I got of a flat horizon, the sun slanting through the boards of an arena fence. The pop of a lunge whip told me that Frank was chasing the horses around. With a sigh of relief I gathered that the stop was only to exercise the horses.

I wondered what day it was. How much time remained before we reached Montana? If Montana was this van's destination. Had I been two days on the road?

The horses were reloaded, carefully backed or led into their cleaned stalls lined with padding, a short chain snapped to each side of the halter. A chest bar was dropped into place on the horses facing me, and a rump bar secured behind the four round hindquarters of the others. Ramp raised, doors shut and bolted.

The grey metal whale continued on its western journey, carrying an assortment of unwilling Jonahs. I got used to the roar of passing semis, wind currents buffeting us and the small whine of passenger cars surrounding us like pilot fish.

Every time I tried to think about why the thieves had brought me along, my mind would hit a brick wall, and all thoughts would scatter into flying parts. Images of Streetwise, the young Thoroughbred whose leg had been broken with a crowbar to collect the twenty-five thousand-dollar insurance money, shot into my mind.

Was I all alone in this?

Why hadn't Victoria, and maybe Michael, met me when I got back from Boston? I knew they were frantic with worry about Max. It didn't figure. I tried to remember if I'd left Bugs and Scout in the house. Of course, Bugsey could use the cat box, but Scout must be feeling about like I was right now.

When the drivers stopped for dinner, the connecting door opened on a full fledged argument. I heard fragments, "she's just going to die anyway . . . if you won't give her water, I will . . . just try it bud."

Very interesting, I thought. They're fighting over me.

After the door closed behind Frank, I eyed the horses enviously. The sound of powerful teeth slowly grinding corn and oats into mush made my mouth water. Delicate velvet muzzles caressing the water before sucking up long draughts made me painfully aware of my own dry throat. I experienced vicariously the swallowed water shooting down the horse necks. For the first time in my life, the sounds of horses eating were not soothing to my spirit.

Darkness blended the shapes of the horses, the grey Anglo-Arab the first to fade into the grey of the walls. Was this the close of the third day? Trying to piece together the passage of time, I grew frustrated and gave up. There was no way to know. One thing I knew for sure, it would not be much longer before those crucial sphincter muscles would give up. For a while now, I'd been fighting the knowledge that there was no way to avoid this problem. Except by escape.

The regular blip of tires on highway seams became the running beats of hooves on dry, barren ground. Tall pillars of red rock swept past. Turquoise sky made stark outlines of trees. A horse moved beneath me, running without restraint. The dark mane lapped my face like seaweed blown on the wind. A taste of salty sweat entered the edge of my mouth. I ran my tongue across my lips, savoring the salt and seaweed tang. My fingers twisted into the horse's mane. No reins led back to my white knuckled hands. The horse ran, breath coming in pounding gasps, ribs expanding and contracting beneath my legs. If my grip loosened, I knew I would slip to the ground.

The mare turned her head at an angle to see me. We recognized each other. The black Trakehner kicked sideways, lowered her head and bucked.

I looked earthward. The rocks, sinister and ragged, would kill me, or shred me into tiny pieces. The mare gathered herself for an enormous leap; we rose together into the blue sky among the fluffy white clouds. No, they weren't clouds, but floating white shirts. Bright green grass waited far below to catch the suitcases falling slowly through the air. Their contents rained down: shampoo, hair dryers, ties, paperback novels and underwear. A pink plush bunny rolled through the air, its ears flopping forward, then back.

Burying my face in the warm, sweaty mane, I yelled, *Take me home!* My heels drummed against the sweat-slick hide.

There was no way to reach through the horse's terror. I was an incidental passenger, with no control over her direction.

I wondered if the mare was my own fear. If I could ride her out of this place, I would not be brought back here again, and again. The memory could be left behind, this vivid place where the plane had crashed.

Crouching low into the horse's neck, I wedged my elbows against the mare's shoulders. Warm sweat covered the side of my face and entered the corner of my mouth.

11

The reality of waking was more disagreeable than the nightmare. The urine came first, a not too unpleasant flood. The rest I could no longer hold back. It was trapped inside my Lycra riding pants, a slimy lining which filled me with shame. The smell seeped up, escaping the top edge of the horse blanket. Not a pretty package.

Dark was nearly complete. Even the small windows of the van showed no definition. Mixed soft sounds of horses, the halter rings jingling against the snaps, were the only proof that I wasn't alone. Sighs from close by and straw-stirred shifts of weight became my frame of the familiar. Faint shapes of horses were moving shadows, chestnut and grey.

At least these horses were probably going on to different lives, with new identities. I wished them well while wondering what had been decided about my own future. Tingling fear swept along my skin leaving behind prickles of goose bumps.

The dream returned in total, visual clarity, along with the powerful feelings. Memories lived always inside, with a reality so vivid there were times I'd thought I was there with my parents when the plane had gone down in the beauty of rural Scotland.

Later, on the anniversary of the crash and whenever magazine and television gorehounds wanted a story, the tragedy over Lockerbie, Scotland would be shown again. The images were too vivid. It was as though I had witnessed the crash.

One photograph, in particular, I'd studied until the magazine fell apart. It had been taken from the air, and scattered far below were the remains of the airplane and its contents. I endlessly searched the wreckage for my father and mother, knowing they were there somewhere.

During their visit to Aunt Belinda, I had stayed with Victoria and her family. In fact, had begged to stay with Vic. I had been on other trips to Scotland to visit relatives, suffering in ladylike dresses and drinking from fragile teacups. At seventeen I couldn't bear it.

The universe had jogged the night I heard on television the plane went down, and I waited with certainty for official word of their deaths. Mrs. Branch tried to talk me out of the belief my parents were dead, but I knew she was just trying to be kind.

No one could have suspected that I felt responsible for the plane crash. Somehow I believed that if I'd only done something differently, the crash would have never happened. I should have been there, too. I believed Fate had not held my parent's deaths in the original pattern of the cloth. It must have been I, by not going, who altered the warp.

Now, I must do it right. Did the nightmare show me a way to ride the fear out of me? Stay with it and not get thrown? Out of the unknown darkness I gathered light into my heart and held myself there.

FRANCI McMAHON

Not long after dawn the van stopped again. Frank came in to feed and water the horses. "Christ, it stinks in here!" he said as he entered through the groom's door. He looked down at me, stepping back.

"What's the matter?" a disembodied voice yelled.

"She shit herself. I don't want this stink in my van. Maybe it's time to get rid of her," Frank responded.

"No way," I heard from the man in front, much to my relief. "Give her some water for Christ's sake."

Get-rid-of-her echoed in my skull, bouncing off the hard inner walls. Talk. It's important to let your captors know you're a person.

"Please give me water," I begged. "Can't you untie me so I can clean up?" It was unreasonable to feel so embarrassed for having soiled myself.

"You know our orders," Frank said to the man up front. Doggedly ignoring me, he portioned out the horse feed. While they ate he shoveled up manure, occasionally glancing my way. I watched while he neatly spread clean straw over the lightly limed floor, and thought, would this man be my murderer?

When finished he left for his own breakfast at the café, which I was all too aware of. I'd read somewhere that odors were made up of tiny particles of airborne substance. I wasn't much of a carnivore; however, the flecks of bacon floating into my nostrils made my mouth get ready for the real thing. Molecules of French toast made their way around my nose hair, then went into lungs instead of stomach. I wanted to say, hey! Wait a minute, you've taken a wrong turn!

This atomized version of breakfast was being sent courtesy of the kitchen vent fan. An image of a glass of water formed. The kind of glass thoughtlessly plunked down on each table. Tiny machine-made ice cubes floated, and then someone picked up the glass, leaving behind a wet circle.

Eyeing the big Warmblood mare, I said in a hoarse whisper, "You're going to have to share your water."

The mare shook her head, laying her ears flat back at the sound of my soft voice. "Whether you like it or not." Silently, I added, I hope.

Wriggling around to face the mare, I thought, I have to call you something. I watched her closely, trying to get a sense if she was truly vicious or just too long confined.

"I rode you in my dream. I will ride the dark of night and make you my friend, Night." While I was softly speaking the mare eased, ears flicking forward.

"Okay, Night, here it goes."

I rolled into the stand stall, almost under the mare's front legs, parallel with the chest bar. Night was so surprised that she stood, ears pricked forward, with only a snorting blast from her nostrils to punctuate her reaction. Acting before the mare could decide on a course of attack, I jammed my feet against the stall, walking my back up the other, far enough to hook my chin over the chest bar.

By then, Night had recovered her initial amazement enough for one solid bite. Fortunately, she only damaged the horse blanket. It almost seemed she bit out of fear at my vision of loveliness.

While the mare sorted out my presence I got my face into the rubber bucket and drew in long swigs of water, as much as my stomach could hold. Rearing back from the pail, I was glad horses were such tidy drinkers. There were no long ropes of tacky saliva to contend with, as there would have been if dogs had been helping themselves from the same pail. A few small, hay leaves floated serenely on the surface.

Night started her restless pawing which threatened my legs, even wrapped in their cocoon. She shook her head, rattling the chain tie-ups. I dropped to the floor to undulate, like a large caterpillar, back to my unorthodox home along the wall.

A smile traced my lips as I lay with heightened awareness, feeling water flow into all my parched cells. In spite of my hunger, the need for water had been greater. I fell asleep. It was the first undrugged, natural sleep I'd experienced since my Montana holiday began.

Much later in the day, after hours of exhausting muscle-vibrating, bone-shaking jolting, the van stopped again. One thing I'd noticed was that there were a lot less semis and cars traveling the same highway.

Tendrils of airborne food particles entered the van to torture my gut. This diner had an efficient exhaust fan, too. A hollow rumble issued from my body.

The interior door abruptly opened, and Frank entered. I caught a glimpse of the dark-haired driver rising from behind the steering wheel to stretch. Why was he keeping out of sight? Obviously Frank would like some help. He wasn't showing himself to me for some reason. Because they knew I'd recognize him? Or perhaps be able to describe him later because of an identifiable mark?

While Frank went stolidly about his horse care duties, I gave my imagination free rein. What would the driver look like? A scar on his face? Mechanical hand? Harelip? Or an accent connected to a specific region. Irish? Arabic? That black curly hair . . . Oh. I sighed when it hit me. Buster.

Before I parted company with this hell hole I was going to find out if the driver was Buster. Or not.

Near my head water hissed into a bucket. Using the hose from the supply tank, Frank topped up each bucket, moving through the narrow space without looking at me. After feeding the horses hay, he portioned out grain made into a hot bran mash. There wasn't a horse alive who'd turn up its muzzle from a mash. Me either. The door slammed shut.

Move over, I thought, now a very aggressive caterpillar. Without delay, I performed the same maneuver I'd done for water. I shouldered the mare away from the mash. Wolfing it down, I discovered bits of carrot and apple in it. My face was covered with food by the time I sank satisfied to the floor.

A rending sound of the blanket, torn by something, caught my attention. Examining the stall edge, I spotted a bit of loose tin, sharp and standing out from the side of the stall.

They should nail that down! A horse could get . . .

That's really sharp!

Struggling to my knees, I backed up to the edge of the stall. Pushing the surcingles against the sharp tin, I sawed at the ties that bound me. After what felt like eons, one of the straps frayed and snapped. The cost to me was one bite, mildly felt through the thick canvas. Understandably, Night was beginning to resent my pestering her and stealing her food.

The next time the van stopped, I'd moved into a different relationship with my captors. Trying to maintain the same act, begging for the same basic care they so willingly gave the horses, I suppressed the elation I felt at being ignored. I absolutely didn't want another shot of sedative. I backed against the wall, hoping neither Frank nor the mysterious driver would notice the frayed ends of cord. And I craned my neck to see into the driver's compartment each time Frank returned to the front.

Some of the haze caused by hunger and thirst lifted, leaving my mind clearer: my actions became stronger, more coordinated. I was going to escape. Somehow.

After a time, Night accepted my presence, although she was still watchful of her evening feed bucket, which included a bran mash. I was relieved that the drivers were aware that mashes reduced the risk of gastric upsets, since colic was the number one killer of horses. So, although it was only a once-a-day feeding for me, it furnished a cooked cereal, somewhat chewy, laced with carrots or apples and sweetened with molasses. Great stuff for an otherwise starving human.

FRANCI McMAHON

My mind skipped all over the place while I patiently sawed at the restraints. I watched the door against the horrific possibility it would open while I was doing this. I fretted that we would arrive in Montana too soon. Or, too late. Ideally, I should make a break at a place unfamiliar to my kidnappers, where there might be people around. I didn't want it to be on their home ground. Each time the van's brakes were even touched I tensed, ready to drop and roll.

I'd been genuflecting in front of this horse long enough. Wouldn't these cords ever break?

Then, carelessly, I cut my wrist on the metal. "Aghhh," I cried aloud, unable to stifle it. Almost immediately the latch on the groom's door was thrown. I dropped and rolled.

"What's going on in here?" Frank came through the door fast.

I let out what I hoped was a convincing moan. My eyes were closed enough to look through the lashes.

"Need any help?" a deep voice called from the front. Was that Buster's voice?

"No," Frank replied. His feet shuffled near my head, then toward the horses. I opened my eyes to slits, and suddenly, chillingly, between his legs, I saw a red scrap of canvas horse blanket dangling from the stall edge. My blanket. A few drops of bright blood painted the surface. My blood. My eyes became attached to the scrap. It was waving like a miniature bullfighter's cape.

Quickly my gaze moved to his boots. I groaned softly. Don't think about it, I ordered myself. Your energy will draw him.

"Can't you give me water? Are you trying to kill me? I don't know what this is all about. Please let me go," I whined as convincingly as possible.

He took a step toward me. It might cost me a kick or another injection to distract him, but I must.

"I don't like doin' this." He was standing so still.

His feet wore leather packer boots. I focused on a scrape near the toe.

"Somehow I got in over my head," Frank whispered so softly I almost didn't make out what he said. A candy wrapper floated past my eyes. Half a Mounds bar was shoved into my mouth. His boots stepped back, then turned for the door.

Dessert! Ah.

The driver spoke indistinctly. Frank responded, sending chills into my core. "Yeah, where did he think we could dump her body? Alongside the interstate? Killing horses is one thing — I'll deliver the package but he . . . "

The slam of the metal connecting door put an early period to his sentence. It couldn't be any clearer: these guys had been instructed to kill me. A sliver of hope lay in the fact they had chosen to disobey their boss. But I couldn't bank on any help from them to escape, or on their continued defiance of the head honcho's orders.

The candy had a bitter taste. However, the fact that Frank hadn't noticed the red flag was total luck. I would have to be more careful. I retrieved it with my teeth, then, with my nose, made a place for the cloth. Carefully I pushed straw over it, just like a dog with a cherished bone.

FRANCI McMAHON

12

Snow-capped mountains rose above the restaurant roof at the breakfast stop. The large side door stood open to air out the van while Frank moved around tending the horses. I couldn't take my eyes off the towering snowy peaks. I was running out of time.

After the van rattled over the cattle guard, then made the huge circle of the on-ramp, I thought, we're definitely in the open range land of the west. Where else are cattle guards located on interstate ramps?

I went back to work with a vengeance. Over and over I squatted, straight-backed, toes pointed slightly out, bending my knees in an exact duplicate of a ballet position. The memory returned of my mother informing me that dancing class was essential for a young lady's future. I stifled a tense laugh, realizing it was the truth.

In the midst of this trip down memory lane, the surcingle snapped; the red sheath slipped softly to the floor. I felt like a newly pupated butterfly. Didn't smell like one, though.

Night snorted and laid her ears back. I kicked the canvas trap away, then went to work on the single cord holding one hand. This was a little trickier, as a careless stroke could cut me, and my wrists were in borderline condition already. I was nervous about what damage Night's teeth could do to me without the canvas shield. Fortunately, I stank, making Night back away, nostrils flared. The mare's purple-brown eyes followed my movements.

The van slowed, crossing the cattle guard at the off ramp of the Interstate. I froze. The whine of gears climbed once again as they negotiated a long uphill on a secondary highway.

The cord frayed, then broke. I spread my wings, reveling in the unrestricted movement. Without further ceremony I grabbed up the horse blanket, stuffed it with hay and arranged it next to the wall. With increasing urgency I rummaged through a trunk looking for some kind of weapon. It contained more rugs, leg wraps, halters, lead ropes. An idea formed. I took out two of the lead ropes.

The van slowed to a stop, then maneuvered backwards.

Clipping a lead rope to each side ring of Night's halter, I then crossed the ropes through the mare's mouth. I chose Night, not because she might be the easiest to handle without a saddle or bridle, but because Frank seemed afraid of her. I scrambled onto the restless mare's back fighting a wave of dizziness, hunkered down, and grabbed the mane in one hand.

Waiting for the familiar sounds of ramp dropping, door opening, my breath came in short gasps. Three different voices — all men's — came indistinctly to my ears. That rumbling speech, was it Buster's? They seemed to be arguing.

Once the interior of the van was flooded with sunlight, I reached down, pulled the pin holding the chest bar in place, and kicked the mare hard.

FRANCI MCMAHON

Just as eager as I for freedom, the mare left the van in a pounding leap that took us past recoiling men, down a chute into bright sunlight. The startled shouts felt explosive. I tried to catch a glimpse of the driver and the stranger as we shot past the three men. All were a blur. It all happened too fast.

Night galloped to the center of the rodeo arena. My heart sank. Ahead were high wire mesh fences strung between poles top and bottom, built to contain bucking horses and Brahma bulls.

The sweep of bleachers rose in a wall on the right, a maze of corrals to the left. Behind me the van blocked the unloading chute and the only gate. In front of me, beyond the fence, stood a large white barn with red trim and lettering reading, *Jefferson County Fair and Rodeo, August twenty-four.*

Dragging on one lead rope, I got Night to circle toward the maze of corrals. Must be a gate in there somewhere, I hoped.

A bullet whistled by, evidence of its passage a small bright red spring of blood immediately in front of my eyes. The bullet had nicked the mare's crest, blood springing through the mane at the top of her neck.

This was an old wild horse catching technique; if the shot was right the horse was stunned — wrong, it was dead. Or were they simply trying to shoot *me?*

The mare slid to a halt, planting her hind feet in the soft dirt. At first I thought we were going down, then Night spun around to tear full speed for the other end of the arena. When I realized the mare meant to jump the rodeo arena fence, I tried to aim her at the one place which seemed to lead to open field. The woven wire fence came toward us fast.

I sure as hell hoped this horse could jump. If not, I'd be looking like a waffle. What if she was a dressage horse who'd never stepped over a rail?

A piece of the top pole burst into splinters to our right as the mare lifted off the ground. She sailed over the top, neatly tucked, in a manner to make any open jumper proud. I hung on like a cocklebur, the original Velcro. When the mare landed, we nearly parted company, but Night immediately gathered herself for another leap. A pole gate rose solidly ahead, separating the rough and ready rodeo arena from the rest of the fairgrounds. We flew past an assortment of buildings labeled Flowers and Crafts, 4-H barn and Livestock, then over another fence.

Now we galloped across a vast field, surprised Black Angus cows watching our progress. While Night plunged on, going over or through anything in her path, I tried to get my bearings.

The horse was running full tilt toward a paved road lying down a bank on the left. A broad valley stretched out ahead, encircled by a mountain range. A small town spread lazily in the center of the grassy range land. Behind, on the left, lay the rodeo grounds. A brown truck slued its way across the parking lot, shooting gravel out from under the tires. It turned in the direction of the paved road and in a moment we would ride right into their waiting arms. I had in mind finding a house with a telephone, or missing that, a cop in a car.

I braced my knees against the mare's sides and hauled on the right rope while I pushed with my left heel. It worked. The mare turned to gallop toward a mass of mountains with one snow-covered hump in the center. A dirt road lay at a right angle ahead of us. With sickening fear, I realized a barbed wire fence, largely invisible, ran along its edge.

Not again, to be caught on the wire! I drew back on both rope reins to slow Night, then managed to guide her in a circle.

Making certain she saw the fence, I then circled Night again, asking this time for her to jump. A spring of joy lifted my heart as the mare leaped over the fence. In a few short

FRANCI McMAHON

strides, we came to a fork marked by National Forest signs. Night was traveling too fast for me to read the signs or even attempt to choose a direction. Taking the left fork, we raced up the dirt road leading into a narrowing valley, green with grass, and not one house.

Foam from the mare's mouth flew back in tiny white clouds catching on her mane and my hands. Blood ran along her crest, mixing with sweat to sheen her neck. The musky scent of the horse filled my nostrils. I worried about Night's back becoming too slippery for me to stay astride.

The dream in the van returned, freshened by reality. I fought the images away.

Just before we rounded a curve in the road, I glanced over my shoulder. The brown truck followed, probably half a mile behind. Since I saw no cop cars or houses sheltering telephones I knew I must leave the road. The choices were between a steep bank leading to tall timber on the left, or the exposed pasture beyond a marshy stream on my right.

It had to be the timber.

I slowed the mare to a trot, then sent her up the bank to find her own way while I hung on. Surging forward in pounding leaps off the hindquarters, the mare dug her way upwards. As the roar of the truck neared, we entered the timber.

Knowing the driver of the truck would be back, would see the marks where the horse left the road, I urged the fatigued mare on. Night had received minimal exercise for quite a while, cooped up in that miserable barn at Velma's, but she must keep going until we were safe.

Unlike Eastern forests, there was little underbrush in these mountains. We needed to get far away from the road to avoid being seen, to find footing Night wouldn't leave tracks on.

A trail opened up before us. I didn't know, nor did I care, what animal had worn the path. We took it at a trot onto the uphill section. It threaded its way through lodge pole pine, low brittle branches making me dodge constantly, then around huge boulders, always up. When the mare slowed, I had to kick her sides, now slick with sweat.

Then her hoof slipped on a rocky section of ground. She almost fell to her knees, nearly jolting me off her back, but Night managed to save herself from falling.

I allowed her to stand and rest a moment, while sifting for sounds other than Night's labored breath. Sitting still for the first time since we left the van, I became aware that my whole body trembled. I looked at my hands, white-knuckled, curled around black mane and the two lead rope reins, and felt the energy drain out of me.

Slumping forward onto the mare's neck and shoulders, I rested my cheek against her damp hair. Without this mare I never could have gotten away from those men. I found myself moving into a soppy place of gratitude, and sat up. Fear and the goal of escape had been an ever-present companion for days. It would be too easy to allow myself to be seduced by relief before I was safe.

Night, rested, moved up the trail on her own.

The trail ended abruptly at an open stretch of grassland. I halted Night at the edge of the timber and listened. Again, the only sound was the heavy panting breath of the mare. Gradually even this faded and I heard nothing but the sound of silence, of an earth undisturbed by human beings.

A breeze brushed its soft way through the branches near my head and caressed the young grasses in swirling, spiraling waves, making patterns for an instant only. Pine needles filtered the wind into song.

Sleep elbowed its way into my brain. I shook my head to fight it off, then asked the mare to keep going. Can't sleep yet. Later.

I did not even see the small brown rabbit that suddenly decided to leave the bush under Night's nose. The horse leaped a good six feet to one side, dumping me to the ground. It was a long way down, and it hurt.

Night snorted, trotted a few steps away, looked back, then cautiously walked back to me. The mare shook her head, spitting the lead ropes out of her mouth.

Was she readying her mouth to get in a good chomp on me?

But the mare lowered her head to my face, distended her nostrils and softly her warm breath washed over my cheek, fluffing my hair. After this farewell Night turned in a balanced pirouette and cantered away.

"Bye, my friend. Have a good life among the wild horses."

The landscape became much emptier as the departing hoofbeats of the mare faded away. I rolled into a fetal ball, hugged my knees, and waited for the pain to ebb. Listlessly, I watched the sun change its angled light. Mule deer came out of the timber near me, snorted their curiosity, then moved away.

❧

I awoke to the sound of crunching steps near my head. Night! She'd come back. My eyes opened, but instead of hooves I saw two cowboy boots, scuffed and worn. A dog's low growl made the hair on my neck stand.

"Are you hurt?" A woman's voice, deep and rich. "Go back, Skip. Do you want a hand?"

With effort, I rolled onto my back. Towering above me was the real article: a cowgirl complete with batwing chaps, Stetson, jeans jacket and, nonchalantly held in one hand, a rifle. There were creases around her eyes, shaded by the hat brim. Her nose was freckled, her mouth wide with full lips. Her short sandy hair stuck out stick straight below the Stetson.

"What's your name?" She flared her nostrils. "Gal, who-ever you are, you stink."

"Were you in that brown truck?" I asked suspiciously.

The response was slow to come. "No. I came by geld-ing. Maybe you'd like to tell me who you are? I'm Miles."

"My name is Jane Scott, and believe me, I am not in this condition by choice." A wave of shivers shook me.

"Well, that's a relief to hear," Miles said with a small lopsided smile. Her face grew serious as she studied me. "I imagine you have a story to tell. Layin' here ain't going to get you cleaned up or warm, though. Come on."

I flopped around on the ground trying to find the strength to push myself to my feet. In the end, Miles had to lay her rifle down in order to get me up. She helped me with a certain degree of gentleness, though it was clear she didn't want to get close.

I dazedly looked around. A very intent Australian sheep dog watched me from a half crouch. Her blue eye seemed particularly suspicious, the brown merely wary. Immediately behind the dog stood a solidly built red dun Quarter Horse. Dropped reins ground-tied the animal. A smaller chestnut gelding waited quietly with his reins tied to the dun's saddle horn.

"Hop on the sorrel," Miles said, motioning to the small horse.

"Why do you happen to have an extra horse?" I asked, not quite ready to trust her.

Her blue eyes caught my cautious ones in a frank gaze. "Long about dinner time, this horse turned up outside the horse corral. Big, well-bred animal. Black. Didn't look like somebody'd been out pleasure-riding on the mare. I penned her at my ranch."

"She's okay, then?" I smiled with relief. "She was my fellow prisoner."

"After some fellows showed some curiosity about the horse's rider, I decided to backtrack the mare. You coming with me? Or do you want to spend the night out here?"

Her strides were firm; each heel striking the ground made a separate sound. Miles slid her rifle home in the scabbard, then leaned against her horse, waiting.

"Sure, I'll follow you." Anywhere, when you sweet talk me like that, I added with a private smile.

I shuffled up to the sorrel horse, then grabbed the saddle horn with one hand, the stirrup in the other. I sagged weakly into the horse, my cheek resting against the basket-weave tooling on the leather fender. I seemed to have reached an impasse.

Miles waited. Eventually, seeing no action, she walked around her horse and lifted me, gingerly, into the saddle. She looked down to see if any of the unthinkable muck on my legs had transferred to her own clothes.

"Sorry," I said. "It's disgusting, I know."

"I'll dig out the saddle soap tomorrow."

I nodded, but in a spasm of exhaustion the nod became a lurch.

"Hold onto the saddle horn," Miles said, mounting her own horse.

"That's not done," I said, somewhat arrogantly.

"Hey, girl, you think I'm goin' to pick you up twice, you're mistaken. Hold on to the damn horn. This is not some show ring. It's a rough ride to the ranch and it'll be dark before we get there."

I suspected my smile had a drunken quality to it.

Miles neck-reined her horse for home, said, "Stay back" to her dog, then nudged the dun into a jog trot. Skippy brought up the rear. When the sorrel lagged, Skippy closed in, crossing back and forth behind the horse's heels.

Miles led us between and around huge gray boulders, haphazard monoliths strewn over the mountainside. Long shadows gave them a lurking appearance. We traveled on grassy, overgrown dirt roads that I later learned were Deerlodge National Forest access roads.

We came to a barbed wire gate where Miles dismounted. I looked around at the valley formed by two mountain ranges. It was the most beautiful place, in a quiet way, I'd ever been to. A widening V of grassland, radiant from the setting sun, gently rose on either side, then changed to a darker green of pine meeting a hard-edged, purple-lined sky. As Miles closed the gate after me, the skyline finished devouring the sun. On the far side of this valley, near the dark line of trees, a small cluster of lights emerged. Not many. Certainly not a village. Except for headlights which broke the horizon at the far end of the valley, they were the only lights I could see.

"Come on," Miles said. "We're too exposed here."

I thought: this woman knows I'm in danger.

She jumped into the saddle, leading off at a lope across the broad expanse of grass toward an indistinct line of trees. I felt fear return again in a rush.

Arriving at the sheltering trees, we watched a search-light rake the grassland. The truck didn't turn into the ranch driveway, but continued on in our direction. The search-light moved ahead of the invisible truck in huge half circles. A small band of antelope were caught in the beam, held a moment while they bounced to attention, then were left alone in the gathering dark.

"What do you know?" I asked Miles in a low voice. A sunset glow on the far line of mountains was the only light. Her face was hidden.

"I know you're in serious trouble."

"I was kidnapped in Vermont by some horse thieves."

One nod came from the hat brim. More silence followed and I understood this was her way of digesting information.

"Long way from here. Norburt, my brother, saw the black first, called me over to look. We couldn't figure out where she came from, but it was for sure a valuable cayuse. She was a pistol to catch, so we lured her into the barn with some grain and got her shut into a stall. No sooner than we had got her caught than this truck drives up. One guy in the cab, one in the bed, and he had a rifle. I didn't like the look of them. Red in the face, urgent, trying to be polite. They asked if either of us had seen a girl on a black horse."

FRANCI McMAHON

From the cover of the line of brush and aspens, we watched the truck turn around. This time it entered the driveway and headed toward the ranch.

"Norburt said 'No,' then I could hear him take a deep breath to go on, so I told him to go check the biscuits."

I could hear a soft laugh. "He looked at me pretty funny, knowing I didn't have any biscuits in the oven, but he went. I told those fellas that they were barking up the wrong tree. I hadn't seen anyone. As soon as they drove off, I figured I'd take Skip here and backtrack the black horse. Skipper can find any stray — best cow dog there is."

It was my turn to laugh. "I beg your pardon. Are you saying I'm a cow?"

Low laughter returned mine. "While I was getting the horses ready to look into the matter of a riderless horse, I told Norburt if those fellas showed up, not to tell them anything." Very solemnly, watching the headlights join the sprinkle of ranch lights, she continued. "I hope they don't give him any trouble."

I could see the silhouette of the cowgirl's hat turn toward me. "They claimed you stole that horse."

"Yes, I did. I stole a horse they had already stolen — in order to escape from them. You're right. It's a story, and a long one, that I'll willingly tell you." My teeth involuntarily chattered.

"Let's work our way down this drainage. Keep close to the trees and brush."

Hearing the truck engine start up again in the wide quiet, seeing the bright lights slice the dark in a huge circle as the truck turned in the yard, we halted the horses and waited. As the truck met the end of the driveway, it stopped for a last sweep of searchlights.

Suddenly, Miles hissed, "Down, Skip." She must have noticed him out in front, trotting for home. Just before the lights reached the dog she crouched, her highest point the two round tops of her haunches. The light did not pause, but ran on fast over the ground.

Once the truck had left the valley, Miles led us to the gate at the road and we loped the horses down the long straight road to the ranch. Another dog barked as we neared the barn. One porch light came on, softly illuminating a one-story log building, then a screen door banged.

A voice called from the bunkhouse porch, "Sis? That you?"

"Yes, Burt. I saw those guys come here again. What did they say?"

"They want that girl. Do you have her?"

"Yes. I hope you didn't tell them anything."

"No, I did what you told me. She all right?"

"Weak. Been through a hard time, I'd say."

"Hello," Norburt said in my direction as he stepped off the porch to the dirt. "Give you a hand with the horses?"

"No. Thanks, Burt. That's Okay. We can handle them. We'll talk about this over breakfast."

Norburt stood in the weak light of one bare bulb screwed into a socket on the porch ceiling. His sandy hair was neatly parted on one side, face in shadow. His arms hung at his side, hands heavy. A blue heeler leaned against his leg, her mouth open slightly, tongue shiny.

Miles led me past the bunkhouse to the barn where electric lights glowed softly. She unsaddled, then turned out the horses while I waited for her, unable to do anything but prop myself against the tack room doorway.

Returning with rubber boots in one hand and some lumpy thing slung over her shoulder, Miles said, "Here. Strip off and put your clothes in this feed bag. You can wear these overalls into the house, they're clean. I keep them around for calving." Miles watched me fumble with the fastenings of my clothes a moment, then said gently, "Need some help?"

Nodding with relief, I let my hands drop. I swayed each time Miles pushed against me in the slightest way, undoing

FRANCI MCMAHON

a button, or pulling the sweater over my head. In the end Miles lifted me up and carried me to the house. God, she must be so strong. I rested my forehead against the corduroy vest, felt the wool flannel shirt beneath, and closed my eyes.

In the kitchen, Miles propped me against the counter and ran a glass of water. As I watched the water rise to run over the rounded rim, I felt thirst catch up to me. She waited while I drained the glass then, without ceremony, picked me up and carried me to the bathroom. I never thought of resisting. In fact I was beginning to like being hauled around, taking in her special scent, feeling her strength.

Sitting me on the dropped toilet lid, Miles turned the bath water on full blast. She rummaged in the wall closet, emerging with a packet of bath salts, which she poured under the faucet. A light, steamy, balsam fragrance filled the room. Kneeling in front of me, Miles unfastened the overall's snaps down the front, only once shyly meeting my eyes.

"Come on," she said, holding her hand to steady me as I climbed into the tub. A long soft groan escaped my lips as I slid under the waves of hot water. Miles soaped up a wash cloth, then scrubbed my limp body everywhere.

"Good thing I wasn't rescued by some cowboy," I said, and she laughed a little. I appreciated the impersonal quality of this woman's ministrations. She could have been scrubbing a grubby little kid. I drifted, sleep dragging at me, pulling me under its safe waters.

Miles made me sit up so she could wash my hair. Tenderly, she scrubbed the shampoo into my caked hair. It took three washes to get it clean. Finally, she stood me in the tub and played the warm water from the hose all over me, for a final rinse.

"You've got a few bruises here. Welts on your face look pretty tender. And your wrists look like something's been gnawing on them." Miles held them under the light. They oozed blood. She blotted them dry, and applied ointment and gauze bandages to my wrists and the slash across my thigh.

Later, I found myself tucked into a bed made up with flannel sheets. I sank into sleep before the down comforter had been pulled up over my shoulders. A delicious, cared-for aura held me as warm as the down.

13

The clatter of dishes and the aroma of cooking food brought me awake. My eyes traced the map of Africa stained in light tan on the ceiling. The wallpaper displayed its once fresh yellow roses, tied with faded blue ribbons. A heavy, dark wood dresser, filmed with dust, sat like a bulldog on the wall opposite the foot of the bed, whose bedstead was probably crafted by the same Victorian maker. Filmy, pale yellow curtains drifted on the window.

Obviously the guest room. I sat up, then dropped my feet to the round braided rag rug positioned on the pine floor in just the right spot. As I stood, the white flannel nightgown unfurled to cover my bare toes. I paused, supporting myself against the bed while a fog of dizziness passed.

The click of dog nails crossing linoleum came to my ears, then Skippy poked her head around the door frame. We stood eyeing each other, then Skippy turned, clicked her way back to her spot where she collapsed, hard bones announcing her arrival.

"You up?" Miles called from the kitchen.

Curious to see my cowgirl rescuer in the daylight, I walked into the bright room. "I guess you could call it that." I rubbed the hip which had landed first in my fall from the horse.

Miles smiled in a friendly way, then faced the stove again. "You've got a whopper of a bruise there. Sit down. I didn't know if you're a vegetarian or not, so I didn't fry up any breakfast meat."

"I'll eat anything, right now."

She poured coffee from a blue Agateware pot into a red mug. Glancing at me, she asked, "You do take coffee, don't you?" At my eager nod she continued, "Lot of people don't drink caffeine now. I can't get started without it."

She set the mug down near me, then went back to the stove. "Sugar and cream are on the table."

"I'm surprised you are aware of those issues." I said pouring a slug of cream into the strong coffee.

Miles turned slowly, rested her hips against the counter and folded her arms. A disturbingly amused smile flicked across her mouth. "Oh? Being a redneck, and all?"

Oh, now I'd offended her. I shifted in the chair. "I thought those were more — umm, city concerns."

"You know, I may live on a ranch but that doesn't mean I have my head in the sand."

"I'm not. A vegetarian I mean. I drink coffee and eat some meat." I watched the annoyed woman turn her back on me to put some bread in the toaster. A feisty woman, this rancher. "Guess I did stereotype you. Sorry."

"We can all do that."

The coffee was pure ambrosia. I sipped while I took pleasure in watching Miles' purposeful movements. She had a well-weathered look; seamed creases fanned out from the corners of her eyes, fine lines traversed her forehead. Her face was tanned and covered with freckles. A narrow, shiny, white scar ran from her right cheekbone to the hanging oval of her ear lobe. Large-knuckled, long-fingered hands with broad white palms were also rusty brown. Her rolled up sleeves exposed stark white skin above the wrist joint. It appeared her hair had never seen the inside of a beauty salon, or her skin a tanning booth. If there was any curl to her almost-blond hair, it had been Stetson bent. I admired the easy way she wore her faded blue jeans, hoof pick sticking out of one hip pocket. Her high heels carried spurs but not the big, pointed, star rowels movie actors strutted around in; these were blunt. Tiny jingle bobs hung from the spurs, making music.

I wondered if a mister shared the house with this woman. I doubted it — this lady looked like a dyke to me. Then I remembered what a friend of mine who'd worked on a dude ranch in her youth had said: "The men are ALL man in Montana, and so are half the women. But they just look that way. The butchiest are married with three kids, can ride and rope, and only exchange recipes with the other gals, not kisses."

Miles picked up the skillet, snatched the toast out of the toaster with the other hand, to expertly slide the fried eggs neatly on top of the whole-wheat bread. She turned, setting it down in front of me. Her blue gray eyes picked up the angled light from the window.

"Eat this up and dinner will be in an hour," Miles said with a smile.

Lost in my appreciation of Miles, I was confused. I looked out the window at the low sun, then searched the room for a clock. "Do you mean lunch? I know some people say supper or dinner when they mean . . . what time is it?"

"You've slept the clock around, or just about. It's four thirty."

I was wide-eyed, my mouth full of egg yolk and sopped toast. I closed my eyes, swallowed, said "Wow," then filled my mouth again. A purring sound came from my contented self.

Miles ignored me while I ate. She stirred the Crock-pot stew, then rolled out the biscuits she had stopped working on when she had heard me shuffle out of bed. She dunked her hand in the flour canister to lightly shake flour over the dough and wipe it down the long plain rolling pin. I watched her cut the biscuits into two-inch circles with a water glass, then chuck them onto a cookie sheet. Then with a fresh towel she covered the biscuits and placed the pan to the back of the counter.

After topping off my coffee, Miles said, "I've got some chores to do outside. When I come back in, we need to talk about calling the Sheriff."

I nodded my head while she strode to the door, trying to force down my partly chewed mouthful. Miles took a jeans jacket off a peg, pushed one arm into it and was almost gone by the time I sputtered, "Wait! I'd like to use your phone. Do you mind? Credit card, of course."

"Go ahead." Miles settled her hat and was gone.

After tidily wiping my plate with a corner of toast and shoving it in my mouth like a feeding raptor, I carried the coffee mug in my hand to explore. The floorboards were cold, and in the windowless hallway, so was the air. In the living room a brown chair, squat and old, with wood trim running down the face of the square arms, hunkered beside a hewn granite fireplace holding a gas fixture with fake logs. Over the fireplace hung a bold watercolor painting of a bull elk lit by dawn sunlight.

On the mantle rested a plain wood picture frame holding a snapshot of Miles, minus a few of the deeper squint wrinkles, standing beside a blond woman with a hard mouth. Miles' companion didn't look particularly happy. In strong contrast, Miles radiated into the camera.

I got on with my business at hand.

The phone looked like a black daffodil, holes of certain numbers on the round dial under the mouthpiece worn thin. A pear-shaped thing with a frayed cord perched in a bracket off the side — the receiver. Was this thing functional in the modern world? Lifting the ear piece, I was amazed to hear a dial tone come out of it.

I dialed the familiar number and croaked "Hello" when I heard her voice.

"Jane!" Vic shrieked. "Where are you? Are you all right?"

"I'm all right now. It's been hell on wheels, but I'm worried about Scout and the horses. Have they been fed and — "

"Oh, for God's sake! Of course we're caring for your animals. Scout's here with us. We left Bugs at your place with food. Are you okay?"

"Yes, yes. I'm okay."

"I called the police when we didn't hear back from you, then Michael and I went over to your farm, found the horses and Max. We had to hacksaw off the chain. Five days, Jane! I've been so worried about you."

Five days. Bound and terrified. "Didn't you get my messages? The one about talking to Barbara Phillips and the one I left for you before I went to Velma's?"

"Oh, no! There was nothing on the machine."

"Maybe one of the kids erased them. Anyway, Jameel was stolen from the Phillips. Last fall they collected on a sizeable insurance claim and don't seem very willing to stir things up."

"Jane! Do you think that it might have been set up?"

"I'm almost certain of it now. Want to check it out?"

Only a brief silence came over the wire as Victoria weighed the information. "Yes. You mean call the insurance company to see if the claim was for death or theft?"

"Yes. The other message was, I found our horses. When I got back from picking them up at the slaughterhouse in Boston, I went over to Velma's. I guessed they were trying to keep me occupied while they got the stolen horses loaded and off her place. I figured you were over there already."

"So what happened? Come over and tell me about it. Or I'll come . . . "

"Don't I wish I could. I'm in Montana. And really, beyond that I don't know."

"What? Montana? How did you get out there?"

I filled her in.

"Oh, God, Jane, this is scary. Do you need money to fly home?"

"Don't worry about me, Vic. I've got my wallet. But what a story! Maybe we can get to the big cheeses by way of the little rats."

"You're not saying you want to stay on this?"

"Absolutely. This is where it all comes together, all the parts snap into place. If you don't mind taking care of my animals and keeping an eye on my farm, I'd like to stay here and try to find out who's behind this." It wasn't until I said it that I realized what course of action lay ahead. It was as though the reporter in me took over.

Silently digesting this information, Victoria took a few moments to respond. "Jane, don't do anything stupid. The police have a missing persons out on you. You'd better call them and tell them you are all right. It's the FBI now, you know . . . kidnapping across state lines. Did they mean to kill you?" Victoria's voice was thin and high.

"I don't know what their plan was. Maybe they hadn't made one yet. And you know what's really weird? According to the guy at the slaughterhouse, whoever took our horses was driving a four-horse van, and the descriptions of the man and woman don't seem to fit. Nothing like Velma and Chuck. What do you think? Short chunky man, balding, about fifty? And stylish, tall, woman with black hair slicked back in a bun?"

"Interesting." Vic gave a short laugh. "Almost sounds like Leila."

"You're right! I never thought of her."

"Wouldn't it be funny, for all her airs? I'll tell the police."

"Good. Have them check out the other slaughterhouses. The list is on my desk. What did you tell the police?"

"Everything, Jane. They found your truck on a logging road near Velma's. She was questioned, but they couldn't get anything out of her. Maybe with some new facts, they'll be able to. Can you give the police a description of the van?"

"Yes. It's fairly nondescript, though. Grey, no markings. I had the license number written down, but my little notebook got trashed. I do remember it started with a 51T."

"Well, give me your phone number there."

I examined the daffodil and read off the number. "Vic, could you find out what Buster Wilde's been up to? I want to know where he is. He could have been the driver."

"Really? You think he's involved in all this? I know he isn't very skilled in the art of conversation, but — "

"Look Vic, whoever is stealing those horses knew about my article. He lied when I asked him if he'd read it — I could tell. To me, that makes him a prime suspect."

"Do you think so? Oh, my God."

After we hung up, I sat with echoes of contact from the person dearest to me. It felt strange not to be able to mount my horse or climb into the 4-Runner for a quick visit.

That evening's dinner of sinkers and stew, as Miles proclaimed it, was an essentially silent affair. Norburt, while schooled in the rudiments of table manners, had nothing to say as he shoveled in stew and buttered biscuits. His hair was wet-combed, as I was to find it at all meals. He wore a clean shirt buttoned one button off its pair. His hands were scrubbed and looked old compared to the rest of him.

Miles glanced a quick smile at me a few times, made sure I had plenty on my plate, but otherwise left me alone. I couldn't believe how much stew I packed away. And I lost count of the biscuits.

After the last spoonful had left Norburt's plate, he used a biscuit as a sponge to mop up. Carefully, he polished the plate, then crammed the soggy mass into his mouth.

"I don't know why you call these biscuits sinkers. They're so light, if you dropped them in a lake they'd float," I claimed with a smile.

Chewing furiously and shaking his head, Norburt eventually got enough food swallowed so he could talk. "Oh, no. They would get soggy and then they would sink."

Nodding, I replied, "Yes, of course, literally." He met my eyes with a blank stare. This man had zero sense of humor.

Once Norburt had finished eating he methodically wiped his mouth, folded the napkin neatly then pushed it under the left edge of his plate. He rose, then lined up his chair a precise two inches from the table's rim.

"Good night, Sis." He nodded in my direction. "Miss, good night."

We said good night, and after the screen door closed I heard, "Murna." I could hear him happily talking to the dog on his way to the bunkhouse.

During dinner, I had begun to wonder if something was different about Miles' brother. I glanced at her.

Miles answered the unspoken question. "My brother's slow. Been that way since birth. He gets around just fine, though. After Jack and I — Jack's my older brother — after we left for college, Mom and Dad sent Burt to a training center in Butte." She pushed her chair back from the table. "They did a lot to teach him to be independent. When he came back, my parents gave him the bunkhouse as his. Took him a while to adjust to it, but it's the closest thing he'll have to his own apartment. It gave my parents some space, too. When they retired, it was an easier transition for him. He goes down to visit Mom and Dad in Arizona during the worst of the winter."

Gesturing to me to stay where I was, Miles rose from the table, had it cleared in two trips and the dishes rinsed while I sat wondering what it would be like to have an adult dependent on you. The days must get long with just her brother for company. I wondered what she did for amusement. Maybe that woman on the mantle was only temporarily away.

After the dishes were loaded into the dishwasher, Miles turned to say, "Right now, I've a mind to call the Sheriff, but I'd like to know your end of it first."

"Fine," I said. "Tell me though, is that mare safe where she is? What will happen to her now?"

"She's in the barn. The brand inspector will come for her. He'll hold a stolen horse till the owners can be located. That's the way it works here. Do you want to see her?"

"No, that's okay." I hesitated. "Well, yes I do."

Miles laughed at me; kindly, though. She handed me her jeans jacket and pointed to the rubber boots. "I'll take you out there."

The center of the log barn peaked high. Along one side were horse stalls, on the other side of the aisle, a loafing area I guessed was the calving shed. In the last stall I could hear that distinctive rustle of horse in straw.

Night's head appeared, and just as instantly vanished. Standing at a safe distance from the open top of the stall door I saw Night circle restlessly, head lowered, ears flat back.

"Is this normal? She's been pawing and circling since we got her in here," Miles observed. "There's no other signs of colic. I've been keeping an eye on her."

"She's wound up. She's one hot horse who's had a long van ride and before that confinement in a stinking stall for I'd guess a couple of weeks. Escaping from the van has been the most exercise she's had, and now she's cooped up again."

"Norburt will open her door into the corral soon. When it's full dark."

"Is that a good idea? I mean, she can be pretty fierce."

Miles smiled. "It's set up so we can open or shut the connecting door from the other side of the corral rails. Sometimes we run some rank animals in off summer range."

"Thanks for taking such trouble," I said, getting a wave of the hand from my hostess.

Back in the house we went into the living room, which had become chilly once the sun set behind the western range. Miles brought me a plaid wool blanket, then lit the gas fire. When Miles rose from her crouch, her glance seemed caught by the photograph on the mantle. Her fingers held the corner of the frame for an instant, like a caress, then she turned to sit in a chair opposite me.

An hour of talking later, I stiffly unfolded myself. "I sure would like some hot tea. I can make it."

"Sit tight. I would, too. All I've got is Red Rose and a granola one — I think it's chamomile."

"I'd like the chamomile, thanks."

Granola tea, really! I shook my head, but thought she was pretty cute.

Miles came back a short time later carrying two steaming mugs, her boots exchanged for sheepskin slippers. "So," Miles said. "What's next?"

"I want to stop them, preferably without getting myself or anyone else killed. I guess I'm like my terrier, Scout. Once I get my teeth into something, it's the devil to get rid of me." I smiled at her. "If you could tell me where to rent a car and find a good local motel, I'll be out of your hair."

"Whoa. You can use that room you stayed in last night for as long as you want." She hesitated, then continued. "You can see what kind of company Norburt is — nice enough for family, but mealtime for him is groceries, nothing else. I'll tell you honest, I'd like the company. You can use my little car. I've got the truck. Just put gas in it."

"That is very generous of you. Thanks."

"Don't you have a job, or someone to get back to?"

"I'm a free lance writer, and no, I don't have anyone special to go back for." Our eyes met, briefly.

Miles nodded, eyes playful. "We'll have to go to town to dress you decently. Tomorrow's the horse auction in Butte. We should check it out, see if there are any horses or people you recognize." She seemed unaware of her ready acceptance of the role of accomplice.

"Good idea. You're right. They would try and get rid of them. I figure all the horses on the van were stolen, either to fit existing papers of dead horses or new false identities for show sales. The chance of discovering a false identity on a gelding is nil since they'd never have any blood-typing done on them to verify offspring. The black was the only mare on the van. And she could be spayed. I'd bet the risk is too great for them to try to get the prices originally planned for them."

"What would that be?" Miles asked, sipping her tea.

"Around twenty-five to fifty thousand each."

"Who-ee. They're going to lose big bucks on this batch." Miles closed her eyes. Then looked at me and said, "Adds up to about two hundred eighty thousand, minus the black mare. I'd guess they'll try and dump them for horse meat, if they can slip them by the brand inspector."

"Yes, and they're not going to be happy about my spoiling their plans." Sobered, I reconsidered her offer to stay at her ranch. "Don't you think I might cause trouble for you? It might be better if I left."

Miles got up and moved to the fireplace to turn up the gas fire. "Out here, there's a long-standing dislike of horse thieves. Not that long ago they were considered worse than murderers and got strung up as soon as caught. Stranding a person on foot in this remote country is unwholesome business." Rocking back on her heels, Miles focused her gray eyes on my own. "So, you see, I'll help you any way I can."

"Are you married or — " I blurted, instantly blushing with embarrassment.

Miles' slow smile did nothing to ease me. "No. Never been. My partner left three years ago." She picked up the phone. "Went back to Seattle."

She dialed a familiar number. "Hello. Marge, could I speak with Lance? Thanks." Miles sat in the brown chair with her long legs crossed. "Lance. I'd like to talk with you about a bit of trouble we're havin' here. Can you come by tonight? I don't like taking you away from your family, but . . . Good. In an hour? Sure thing, see you then."

The man who walked through the door later that evening took horse thieving seriously, as well as abduction. While Miles did the introductions, I had time to study the Sheriff. Tall, winnowed and lean, he had broad shoulders and long hands with calluses, which raspingly enveloped mine. His kind brown eyes carried flecks of sadness; perhaps a piece of each time he had told parents of their son's suicide or a daughter's fatal car wreck. Later, I learned that Lance never relegated that task to a deputy.

Lance sorted out the events leading up to my dramatic entrance to Montana. It was ten-thirty by the time the sheriff stood to leave. He told us he would contact the Vermont and Montana state police as well as the FBI, and asked me not to go back home without calling him.

As she handed him his hat, Miles said, "I'd be happier if you could arrange to come get that black mare those men are lookin' for. If those boys see that horse here, they'll know I'm involved."

Lance's lips got firm. "You bet, Becky. I'll get in touch with the Livestock Inspector. Probably take the horse to the Butte stockyards till all this is cleared up. Give a shout if anything comes up. Good night, Jane," he said to me as he negotiated the door frame.

"Becky?" I said with an impish smile after Lance had left.

"We went to high school together," Miles said shyly.

14

The next morning Miles dug up a pair of blue jeans for my trip into civilization. I had to roll the bottoms into fifties cuffs and cinch a belt to its furthest hole to make the jeans a success. Topped with a rugby shirt and wearing my own sneakers, still somewhat damp from the washing machine, I was decently clothed. My credit card-loaded wallet was still zipped into my pants pocket.

As I climbed into Miles' car, I noticed the license plate on the Chevy truck. "That says 51T and then a number."

"All the trucks in Jefferson County start with that." At my raised eyebrows, she explained. "The counties in Montana each have a number prefix, followed by T for truck, P for passenger cars. The state's too big not to have some system like that."

"So, Lance knew the van had been registered in this county?"

"You bet."

We drove the long dirt road to Whitehall. The Tobacco Root Mountains, starkly white, hung like a painted backdrop at the end of the valley. Black Angus cattle speckled the green grass. Miles tuned in the country western station on the radio, contentedly tapping the steering wheel as she drove. "I need my sugar baby like the crops need the rain." Wind from the open window ruffled her blue cotton shirt. "The Fox, 99.9. From Bozeman," she explained to the uncurious me.

"Country western is not my favorite."

"Oh? What is?"

"Music with substance. Classical."

"Hey girl, country is the stuff of life. You can't get more substance than that."

Miles looked out the windshield, happily unfazed by my opinion. After a moment she flashed me an open, plain-old-me sort of smile. "You mean you haven't heard of Mary Chapin Carpenter? Everybody knows k.d. lang. She's reincarnated from Patsy Kline."

I knew she was fishing. "Yes, I've heard of her. She's a lesbian, isn't she?" I decided to meet her head on.

"So I've heard." A very faint smile rode her lips, but she kept her eyes on the road.

She was playing with me. We both knew we were lesbians. This woman had used that poker face before. And not just with cards. An easy woman to take at face value, I decided.

At Whitehall, we took the interstate west to Butte over Homestake pass. Haphazard boulders covered the mountains. It was as if all the extra rocks used in making the world had been dumped here. Many rose in narrow, fractured fins, mountain knife blades. Dropping down into the wide valley which held the city of Butte, I saw with horror the scars left from mining.

"Well, I know it looks like a mess, but really, what you're seeing here is a real improvement. Butte nearly became the biggest ghost town in America. Years ago the sky was so full of smoke from the smelters you couldn't tell if it was noon or midnight. The crap in the air killed all the trees that hadn't already been cut for mine timbers or buildings. Those little junipers you see on the hillsides are a sign of recovery. Didn't even have grass or sagebrush on them a while ago."

My jaw sagged as I stared out the car window. Miles motioned toward the chewed up hillside. "The Berkeley Pit is closed. It's filled with polluted water now. A flock of migrating snow geese landed there last fall. All of them died."

"Oh, that's awful! They're so beautiful."

"We had a hard time even getting the mine's owners to admit the water was what killed them. We held a vigil. It was like a mass funeral."

"At least it won't happen again?"

"It will. Mining is king here. We've tried to get laws passed that regulate the cyanide use and force them to clean up, but they make the rules. At least till we get through to the voters." Miles tuned in the Butte country western radio station.

Turning off the highway, we drove up Montana Avenue. Many of the buildings were boarded up or simply abandoned. It looked to me like a ghost town.

"People turn up their noses at Butte, but you know, I really love the people here. No pretensions. The Irish Catholics settled here in droves, but there's also a large community of Protestant Irish. Finnish, Croats and Chinese. They call it Butte, America, because there's no other city like it."

"Looks like the yuppies haven't found it."

"Yeah, Butte's not pretty. While you're talking with the Feds, I'll run some errands. Then we go on a clothes buying spree. Then the auction. Horses won't go through until about noon. Cattle first. We'll save the food shopping till last." Miles pulled into the parking area of a large tan complex of characterless buildings and let me out. "Pick you up in an hour?"

It actually took two hours. I had to tell the same story twice, then, to new listeners, once again.

I was fuming by the time I found Miles patiently waiting in her car with the doors standing wide open, reading the *Stockman's Journal*. She let me rant while she drove us to the store.

I didn't waste any time shopping. First boots. Nothing fancy, just good quality riding boots. Then a couple of pairs of blue jeans and some shirts.

"You'll need a hat," Miles said, eyeing my pale face. She handed me a straw western hat.

"Not my style," I said, making a face in the mirror.

I saw a green duckbill hat with stitching claiming, Some of the Best Cowboys are Cowgirls. "Now this is more my speed," I said to Miles, plunking it on my head.

"No one'd recognize you in a Stetson. You'd blend in wearing this." Miles removed the cap, to settle the straw hat on my head, tilted just a bit over my eyes.

"Yes," I drawled slowly. "Would sunglasses be too much?"

"No, I don't think so. Keep 'em simple."

From the rack I selected a pair of pink plastic shades with a cluster of cut glass at the outside corners. Putting them on my face I ducked behind Miles to look into the full-length mirror. The total effect sent me into near hysteria.

Miles wasn't far behind me. "Those are the ones," she gasped.

Of course, I bought a pair of less memorable glasses. Leaving the store Miles said, "Boy, you spent a bundle. You'll need tennis shoes, too, I expect."

"Tennis shoes? Where will I play tennis? Oh, you mean sneakers?"

"That what they call them out east?"

At my nod, she smiled, a smile that grew from her eyes. "Guess you *are* planning some sneaking around."

On the way to the auction yards I felt excitement at the possibility of finding my equine traveling companions.

Miles interrupted my thoughts. "We have time to catch lunch."

"Great." My hunger was still unsatisfied. I'd eat anytime of the day.

Miles drawled with a sly smile, "I'll take you to one of my favorite places."

I followed her across the street toward a pink stucco bar graced by a neon sign proclaiming it to be Pair A Dice.

Oh, *dear*, I groaned to myself.

The dark musty old beer smell, which always reminded me of stale urine, enveloped us at the door. I stood just at the brink of the gloom, allowing my eyes to adjust. The dark, wood bar lined one wall. A nude, painted on velvet, lay like an opal above the rows of liquor bottles.

Miles placed her elbows on the bar, right foot on a brass rail running along the bottom, then said, "I'll have a tube steak, Bob."

Looking in vain for a menu or a printed sign describing the bar offerings, I asked for one. Bob, the bartender, rummaged through a pile of old magazines and mail, drawing from the stack a stained and yellowed laminated sheet. This he handed to me. Not from around here, his expression seemed to say.

I peered down the bar into the dusky corners, choosing a grilled cheese sandwich as being the least likely to make me ill from food poisoning. When the bartender went into the kitchen to give the order to the cook, I said to Miles, "I really need to ask. Why is this," I lifted one eyebrow and grimaced, "your favorite place?"

"I've loved it from the days my dad brought me here when we came to town. Paradise. Isn't it great?" She waved her hand fondly.

The bartender placed a hot dog on the bar in front of Miles.

"Tube steak?" I eyed the ordinary cur.

The cowgirl's smile was very engaging.

❧

A maze of corrals flanked the sales building. Over the years, countless cattle and horses had passed under the auctioneer's hammer. This yard represented the backbone of Montana commerce. As I entered the building, I pushed away the thought of how many animals had ended at slaughterhouses.

Potential bidders lazily returned from lunch. The sales room was like an amphitheater with seats surrounding the pit, no larger than many a bar's dance floor. Workers were scraping the floor with a tiny tractor-like machine, which scooted around after the loose cow manure. Fascinated, I watched while they spread sawdust over the surface.

Miles explained. "See the floor? It's a weighing scale. Groups of animals are sold as lots, by the pound."

I looked at the digital number board over the auctioneer's booth. My enthusiasm faded. "Let's go outside till it's closer to sale time. Let's look at the horses in the pens."

High-railed catwalks led above the corrals. Miles and I took the stairway up to get a better view. It was a city of horses. Every color, every size, from kids' ponies to giant Belgian workhorses. There were even some mules. The livestock milled about in small groups, enclosed and sorted into tiny corrals. One thin chestnut horse rested its head on a top rail as if gazing longingly at the grassy foothills.

I stopped, studying one corral. Yes! Those horses were familiar. I grabbed Miles' arm. "Look! There." I pointed. "That pen. The one with the chestnut, and two dark bays."

"Oh, yeah. You recognize them?"

"Can't tell from here, but they could be."

"Let's get closer."

Then I saw someone in the crowd I knew. "Buster!" I shouted.

I leaned far over the railing and called again. The man, dressed in a tan jacket, appeared to walk faster.

"That's my blacksmith in Vermont. That clinches it."

We struggled through the tail end of the crowd. Retreating hats and jackets, so many wearing tan Carhart jackets, bobbed down the wide aisle. I pushed through the crowd reaching a sturdy, dark-haired man in a canvas coat. I placed my hand on his sleeve. "Buster! What are — "

A strange man turned with a puzzled smile on his face, blue eyes instead of brown, a gap in his teeth. "Well, honey. Do I know you?"

He was similar. Same height, hair color. "Sorry. Thought you were someone else."

"Too bad I'm not, lady." His smile suggested he could fill in for Buster.

I rose on tiptoe to scan the rest of the crowd. Another black-headed man in a tan jacket went through a door into the auction house. I'd reached the wrong guy.

Miles said, "Lots of men in tan coats around here. Those Carharts are favorites. Let's get a seat." She headed for the door leading inside.

"That was him. I know it. Wait, I want to check those horses out."

Running down a cross aisle, I found the horses on that side had already been hazed into a chute leading into the auction barn.

"Let's go inside," Miles said. "Loose horses go through first."

"What do you mean, loose horses?" I turned to her.

"The ones that haven't been broke, or are old. Or broke down . . . " She avoided my eyes.

"Hey, I'm a girl. I can take it. You mean they're going to the slaughterhouse, don't you?"

At Miles' short nod, I said, "But if those horses are the ones I think they are, we better get in there."

Miles picked up a bidding number. "Just in case. Once I missed a great buy on a little cutting horse."

Inside, smoke hung in a blue mist near the ceiling. Men, sitting in their regular seats in the front, smoked cigars. Cowboys dangled cigarettes from their lips by the spit on the paper. Of the few women, most had two or three kids with them and it was clear they were interlopers. While no one could say that the men weren't gallant, leaping to their feet to let the women pass to empty seats, it was clear it was a man's world.

The first horse ran onto the penned floor with panic in its eyes and burrs in its mane and tail. It spun, looking for escape.

"Never had a hand laid on it," Miles whispered near my ear. "Probably stolen off the Pryor wild horse range. Illegal, but at today's meat price, for many people it's worth the risk."

The horse sold for eight hundred, and was quickly herded through the "out" door as another equally frightened creature suddenly found itself on center stage.

"Pisses me off." Miles slouched low in her seat. "Ain't a damn thing you can do about it either, since they don't carry a brand. The BLM ought to round up the wild horses every three years and brand them. That would put a stop to it."

"Sounds to me like quite an undertaking," I said, really liking the fact that Miles cared. "What's the BLM?"

"The Bureau of Land Management. They ride herd on the herd." She smiled at her own joke. "I'd volunteer for a roundup. I'll bet lots of ranchers would. Hell, it could be sold as an event. Get some Dudes to pay to join us and it wouldn't cost the government a red cent."

While we talked, other horses were prodded and spooked in one door, out the other. Horses with no more usefulness to people — old, lame or rebellious. The line of grim cigar smokers in the front row bought them all.

And then a seal-brown gelding trotted elegantly through the door. His nostrils sifted the air calmly, gentle intelligent eyes examined the crowd. This horse was accustomed to an audience. Number thirty-two had been chalked in yellow on his hip.

Most everyone sat up, alertly. The last time I'd seen this horse, he was groomed to perfection. Burrs, tangles, and dirt did not in any way disguise his worth.

Our eyes met and I nodded.

The bidding started immediately. The knackers in the front row led off, others cautiously joined in. Bidders who wanted the horse to ride were slow to part with their money without knowing whether the animal was there because it had a vicious streak or some other invisible problem. Spotters facing the bidders caught the slightest nod. Quickly the price rose to nine hundred dollars, then hung for a brief minute. The auctioneer's voice ran on like water over tin cans, then snagged. Slam, the hammer fell. "Lot number thirty-two, one thousand four hundred, buyer number sixty-two."

My eyes searched the audience for the buyer, then something in Miles' face caught my attention. It was a tiny smile in the wrinkles of her eyes.

"You?" I whispered.

"Nice horse."

A few more classy horses went under the hammer, but I couldn't be sure about any of them. It was much harder to recognize my traveling companions than I thought it would be. I wrote the hip numbers on a scrap of paper. They seemed to be picked up by people scattered throughout the audience. Four, all together, that might have been on the van.

The mood changed to a festive air when the first saddled horse appeared. A big Paint mare did pirouettes on the floor. The sale barn employee showing the horse ran his hand down her rump to the tail, dismounted at a sliding stop, picked up a front, then hind hoof, took off his jacket and flapped it all over the mare to show how solid she was. She sold for four thousand three hundred in about two minutes.

The line of canner men stood, slowly moved up the center aisle to pay for and load their purchases.

"Is there any way we can find out who bought those horses?"

Miles nodded, rising. "They'll know in the office. Half the buying and selling happens out in the parking lot, though."

Talking men gathered by the glass window of the cashier. They fell silent as we approached, tipping their hats. One said, "Ladies."

Miles seemed undaunted. "Hello, boys. Not a bad bunch today."

Eyes averted, they murmured agreement, waiting for their turn at the glass window, checkbooks ready.

When it was Miles' turn she slid her number forward and asked, "I'd like to know who bought these horses." She turned to me holding out her hand for the slip of paper with hip numbers.

The clerk, flipping through file cards, said, "One thousand four hundred."

"Who was the seller on this horse?" Miles asked casually.

"Not from around here." The cashier turned the card to examine it more carefully. "Tall feller. Name's Jim Turner. From Billings."

"Oh, is he black-haired? I may know him."

"It was pretty busy when he came up, hon. I think he was blond or somethin', but I can't really recall."

"Could I have his address? I'd like to find out if this horse is broke," Miles said, her eyes intent on the check she was filling out.

"Sure," the clerk responded obligingly.

FRANCI MCMAHON

"And if it's not too much trouble, could you give me those other buyers' names and phone numbers?"

"No trouble, honey. It's slowed down."

We waited for her to fill in names and addresses on our list.

"I'll pick the horse up this afternoon."

"Fine. Give the yardman this slip."

"Bonanza!" I said after we cleared the door.

Miles, delighted with herself, winked at me.

"Where is he?" I asked. "Let's go look at him."

"Better not. We don't want anyone to know I bought him. Mosey on over to the car with me, madam, and we'll go grocery shopping." Miles had a recently-swallowed-canary look about her. "I'll call Lance and see if he'll ride back with me later to get the horse."

"I'm sure the horse's owner will reimburse you. That is, if we ever find out."

"Oh, I'd have done it anyway. Something about this horse I like. Couldn't see it go to the killers. If it can be identified, it'll be tangible evidence of theft. I'm guessing the branded horses are hidden till all this cools off. They must be scared. This one ran the canner line because he's slick."

"Slick?" I asked, clipping on the seat belt.

"No brand."

Ah, yes, I thought. Did this mean they would kill Night if they could? Cut away her double moose antler brand?

15

While Miles unpacked groceries, I donned my new clothes, then waded into the kitchen through a sea of floating brown paper bags.

"When is that brand inspector supposed to pick up Night?"

"I'll call Lance to find out what he's set up." Miles finished stacking cans onto a roll-out shelf.

"If that guy was in fact Buster, he's got to be staying someplace around here." I asked. "Do you know anybody who could be mixed up in illegal horse dealings?"

"I'll think on it. I've been figuring, if anyone asks, you're the hand hired on for summer work. Might be smart to pick another name."

"Right. Good thinking. Guess I'll take my mother's name, Hannah."

Miles' face shut down. Quickly, she stooped to sweep up the empty bags. "Do you mind picking something else?"

"Of course not," I answered. "How's Sara, then?"

FRANCI McMAHON

"That's fine. Well then, Sara." She cleared her throat as she stuffed the paper bags into the space between the refrigerator and the counter. "There's a couple of ranchers that come to mind."

"Oh?" I said, studying Miles closely. I was willing to bet that Hannah was the name of the blond-headed grump in the photograph.

"Yeah. They deal in horses. We could go visit and have a look-see. You could try out your new sneakers." She grinned at me.

"You mean drop in on them . . . as in have coffee and donuts?"

"Perhaps not knock on the door."

"Sounds like a great idea." I liked her assertive approach.

Miles turned to the wall phone and called the sheriff's office in Boulder to bring Lance up to date.

After the conversation she reported to me, "He'll send Deputy Bullock to meet me at the stockyards. The mare won't be picked up till the day after tomorrow."

"I don't think she's safe here, not for that long. We've got to move her someplace else."

"Can't be helped. No reason for you to come with me to Butte."

"Won't you need help loading him?"

"The yard man can help me, if he's a problem. You could stay here and — "

I jumped in to state firmly, "If you don't want me to go, that's different. I can understand you might need some space, but I hate it when other people make decisions for me."

Miles rocked back on her heels. "Whoa there. I don't mean to run you. Just thinking that you might be recognized at the yards and figuring to — "

"I don't need protecting."

"You a feminist?" Miles asked playfully.

"I most certainly am." My shoulders squared, my knuckles rested on my hips. Was she really not a cute, charming cowgirl, but some conservative misogynist?

"Hey, ride easy. You can go wherever you like, lady."

"Good. Then I'm coming. I'd like to see that horse close up. Do you have a padlock for Night's stall? What if someone tries to take her while we're gone?"

"No one could get close enough to that cayuse to steal her."

"You don't care about her. She's just another horse to you." Anger sparked through me, then a surge of tears.

Miles laughed. "Aw, come on. You riding the white pony?"

I frowned at her. "What do you mean?" Then I got it. "You mean a Kotex? As in, on-the-rag?"

Something danced in Miles' eyes.

"Oh, that's disgusting," I said, but I laughed. "I'll bet it is my time."

As I laughed, I felt a surge of fluid slip out of me. Hot, wet. I ran for the bathroom.

I found a herd of white ponies in the bathroom closet.

As I came out of the house I saw Miles backing the truck up to her gooseneck trailer.

I decided to pay a quick visit to the mare. She flattened her ears when she saw me, moving to the back of the stall. What was it about this nasty-tempered equine that I liked so much? I flipped a section of alfalfa hay into the manger. She looked good.

I heard an impatient truck beep. "Gotta go!"

⟨∾⟩

The deputy waited in a patrol car near the front entrance of a parking lot congested with people leading horses.

"Deputy Bullock," Miles said, as we approached the parked car, and introduced us.

The deputy unfolded herself from the seat while straightening the brown and green uniform. Her brown eyes were serious, in contrast to her frivolously yellow curls dancing in the breeze.

The yardman escorted a buyer from the maze of corrals with the correct horse. When he turned, Miles held out the purchase slip.

Taking it, he read the number. "Oh, that one. There's a problem here. The horse died half an hour ago. One minute he was standing there, next time I passed the corral, he was dead as a doornail. Heart failure." He handed the slip of paper back to Miles, taking a side glance at the deputy. "Go to the office. They'll give you your money back."

Miles' fingers held the small piece of pink paper, fluttering in the breeze. Her eyebrows drew close together. "I want to see the horse."

"Yes!" I butted in. "Where is he?"

"I don't see why. We had our vet check — "

Deputy Bullock stepped forward. "This horse is part of an investigation. Where is it?"

The yardman led us into the empty corrals. The seal brown gelding lay crumpled along the back wall of his pen. He looked so much smaller lifeless.

At the gate Deputy Bullock reached for the latch before Miles could open it. "No one goes in here," she said with authority. "How many people have already walked into this corral since the horse was found dead?"

"Well, me. And two of the boys who work here. And the vet."

"Could you ask him to come here? As fast as he can. What's your name?"

"Marty O'Neil." He sauntered away.

Pulling a notebook from her shoulder bag, the deputy made entries, then carefully opened the gate. She stood just outside examining the powdery ground, churned up and too dry to hold any footprints. What she did find was the pink sleeve for a hypodermic needle. This she picked up with tweezers and dropped into an evidence bag.

I watched her work with growing respect and a sense of alarm. This horse had died from a lethal injection, I was almost certain.

The law officer reached into her bag for a camera. From every angle she photographed the surrounding ground, and the destroyed horse. The veterinarian arrived, agitated. He seemed to be fresh out of vet school.

"Officer, why do you suspect foul play?" He launched into copious technical jargon trying to justify his earlier diagnosis of heart failure.

Deputy Bullock held up her hand, fingers spread wide. "This means nothing to me, sir. What I do need is a blood sample. I found a hypo needle sleeve in the dirt and I want to find out what this horse was given."

The vet looked shocked. "I didn't give the horse anything. It was already dead when I got here."

"Somebody did. I need the blood now, before it coagulates too much to draw into a needle." She handed him a blood kit sealed in a plastic bag.

Silently, he obeyed, found the vein on the side of the neck and managed to fill the syringe. Deputy Bullock gave him a form to sign while she initialed the seal on the evidence bag.

When it appeared everyone was readying to leave, Miles said, "I know this horse is slick, but is there any way to check him more closely? Maybe for a micro chip in the neck tendon, or something? Do you boys have a scanner?"

My eyes snapped to attention on Miles. This gal is sharp, I thought.

Marty didn't know, but said he'd ask.

"We could use some help turning him over to get at that side of his neck," Miles said.

"Rope!" They all looked at me. "It'd make it easier pulling him over."

"Right. Marty," Deputy Bullock said, "get some of your boys, will you?"

Straining together, on ropes tied to the horse's legs, we rolled the twelve-hundred pound animal over. Once the halfway point was crossed, he came over with a crash, his legs landing with a sound like falling firewood logs. On the side of the horse's neck a small neat patch had been cut away. It was filled with dirt.

The auction yard workers had the air of being unshockable — they had seen about everything. But Deputy Bullock's face showed horror and Miles sank back on her haunches, knuckles sinking into the dirt, and swore.

I remembered Jameel.

Deputy Bullock took photographs, knowing that the horse would never be identified now. These negatives would only bear witness to the waste of this horse's life.

Solemnly, we filed out the stockyard gate. The trailer seemed particularly empty driving home; even Skipper's warm hairy body, curled sleeping on the seat beside us, wasn't much comfort.

When Miles pulled up beside the barn, I jumped out to help unhitch. The daylight shining through the stock trailer slats brought home the reality of what had happened with a force which brought a solid kick in my guts. My throat closed painfully.

Miles stood down from the truck, letting Skip jump to the ground. "Evil business," she said, sympathy in her eyes. "Deputy Bullock told me she'll take the blood sample straight to the lab in Butte herself. Lance will call us when they know what killed the horse."

"This has got to stop." I turned, running my fingers through my hair, sweeping it back from my forehead while I brushed away the tears. I paced to the rear of the stock trailer, looking through the slats to the barren interior.

Miles picked at a small fringe of frayed cuff on her sleeve. She looked up. "That experience — seeing that gelding lying there — left me scared. I'd hate to see anything happen to you, is all."

"Yes. Warnings don't come much clearer than that. You know, I don't think the Butte Stockyard is the healthiest place for Night. Isn't there another place to take her? Some back forty or something?"

Miles stood quietly thinking. "I know of a hiding place."

I got the creeps then as she lifted her eyes to the low hills behind me, vigilant, like a hunting dog checking each sagebrush and tree for irregularities.

"We're being watched." I said it flatly.

Miles nodded. "Twice now I've caught a flash of reflected light. Off a gun or binoculars, I don't know. After dark, I'll go."

I considered this. "I want to go with you."

Miles shook her head. "We need to divert attention. I'll ride away while you and Norburt walk around with flashlights. Shout to each other a lot."

"That's good." I smiled at her.

"I'll call Lance."

I studied this rancher's strong back as she made for the house, and slowly nodded.

~❧~

We had hours to kill before night fell. A good time to call Vic and bring her up to date.

I asked, "What can you tell me about Buster?"

"His wife called to cancel. He's got the flu. Anyway, not being here wouldn't prove anything."

"Look, humor me, will you? Find out if he's around."

"All right. I'll tell you who isn't in town though, Dr. Burns. His head groom answered the phone. Seems he's out west."

"He always goes to the yearling sales in Kentucky. That's west to a lot of people."

"You know, I heard the ugliest bit of gossip yesterday. Nora Curtis said that Dr. Burns was on the verge of bankruptcy. You know Nora, she works at the bank."

"Nora has no business talking about his financial condition. Besides, he told me he bought a condominium for his ex-wife, a new car, and settled a monthly allowance on her. He said the whole thing pushed his retirement back ten years."

"Oh. Well, I just thought I'd pass that on to you."

"Really, Vic, you needn't have." Trying to soften the moment, I added, "It's not relevant. If he's in temporary difficulties, why, he makes a good living and matters should be cleared up soon."

"I picked up your mail and there's a letter in here from Rhonda. Do you want me to send it out there to you?"

I frowned. "I guess so."

"Are you and Rhonda still processing the end?"

"We've been processing the end ever since we started. It's funny, Vic, but I don't think we ever actually *had* the relationship."

"Maybe I shouldn't say this but, Jane, I never liked her very much. You seem to attract social climbers like magnets. Are you sad?"

"I guess I haven't had time to figure that one out. In some ways I am. Perhaps I got involved with Rhonda because I knew it never could go very deep."

"That's an odd thing to say. You mean you were lovers with her because you didn't love her?" Vic gave an incredulous laugh.

"Guess I thought I wouldn't get apprehensive about Rhonda leaving." I gave a bitter laugh.

"Remember Andrea?"

"Andrea!" I shrieked. "I'm not like her!"

We giggled, willfully interrupting each other, touching the deep connections we shared.

❦

After dinner, I went out to the barn to pay Night a call. And, I think, to reassure myself. The barn was dark and cool, light showing in dusty horizontal beams through the cracks between logs in the west wall. I noticed Miles had brought in a few horses. One black, one white, and a loud paint perked their ears at me over stall doors.

Night greeted me with ears flat back. She jutted her nose out, teeth glinting in the barred evening light. I saw a small bay mule now shared her corral and stall. The mule focused adoring eyes on Night.

"Same as ever, unfriendly beast," I said to her. At the sound of my voice, her ears shot forward. A soft welcoming nicker came from her sleek dark body as if from a living drum.

"Night! Are you all right? You act like you just recognized me." An answering smile came straight up from my heart as I reached a cautious hand out for the mare to smell, then stroked her neck.

Perhaps it was the activity that made the difference. Night pushed her muzzle through the poles along the top of the stall. Hesitantly, I opened the stall door and went in. The mare didn't crowd me or even flick her ears back. Under Night's belly was the right spot for my fingernails. Her lips flopped as she nodded her head to the motion of my hand.

Warm horse aroma reached my nose and as I placed my forehead against the mare's round barrel, I could feel the slow, deep breaths. So alive.

I went to the tack room to select a dark leather halter for her. I fastened the brass buckle to a secure fit on her head.

"You'll go to a safer place tonight. Miles will take you there," I said, straightening a small wind twist in her mane.

16

Norburt cleared the table after dinner, while I washed dishes. He was awkward around me and nearly dropped a handful of plates, blushing furiously after he had saved them. I smiled warmly at him, trying to put him at ease. I think I made his discomfort worse.

Miles placed a box on the table. "We have to do something until dark. Would you like to play a game with us? Norburt likes this one where you stack blocks then take turns pulling one out, without toppling the tower. Jenga, it's called."

"Would you play with us?" Norburt waited, lips parted for my answer.

"Sure. I've played that before. It's fun."

Norburt eagerly took his regular seat, then sprang up to pull out my chair.

Miles began setting up the game. "Burt, pour us some lemonade, would you?"

"Okay, Sis."

By the time each glass held pink lemonade, poured to the exact same level, Miles had the tiles stacked tall in the center of the table.

I was surprised to discover that Norburt was very clever at choosing which block to remove. He glowed with pride every time he managed to entice a block from the stack without reducing the tower to ruin. Finally the tower fell when I removed the wrong tile. Norburt bounced in his chair, tickled it had been me.

Miles leaned back, rocking on the rear two legs of her chair. Her arms crossed over her chest. An expression of deep contentment covered her face, and the fan of wrinkles at the corners of her eyes deepened.

I said, "You're good at this, Norburt."

"Thank you. Miles taught me." He sat erect, feet flat on the floor.

The chair's front legs hit the floor. "Jane and I want to play a hide and seek game, outside with flashlights. We need you to help us do it well. Before the end I'm going to take that black mare away. I'll be back later tonight."

His face glowed with anticipation. "Oh, that sounds like fun."

"You can use my big flashlight. The one that flashes red. It's in the truck. I'll go get it." As we had planned earlier, Miles left the house to saddle her horse.

When Miles returned we turned off most of the lights, then stepped off the porch into the darkness to take our places. The dogs quickly got into the spirit of things. Murna's earsplitting bark had supercharged Skip, who couldn't understand why I was lying on my back in the driveway. When she came to investigate, I tucked the small flashlight in her collar and let her go. She tore around in large circles until it fell out and she kept running. I slipped between the barbed wire strands, walked into the pasture and picked it up.

We all got carried away, until I heard the soft thud of hooves on grass and the pit of my stomach fell away remembering why we were here acting foolish. I jumped up and ran to the barn. Norburt joined me and we took the white horse and the spotted Paint down the driveway in the opposite direction Miles had taken. Norburt waved his red flasher while making ridiculously funny siren sounds. This, of course, made it difficult to control the horses, who blasted air from their nostrils. My charge hit the end of his lead rope, nearly jerking my arm out of its socket. Whoever might be watching would surely call the nearest hospital professionals, the ones with white straitjackets and sharp needles.

I made sure Miles had at least five minutes to reach the trail in the pines before we switched off the flashlights, and slapped the horse's rumps, turning them out in the big pasture across the road. We could see them running, contrasting against the night sky for a long time.

We walked back and turned on lights in the house. All of our silly grins looked the same, except the dogs', who let their tongues roll out.

It took a while to settle down. Eventually Norburt left for bed. Miles and I had discussed how much to tell Norburt and decided it was better to keep the details from him. Miles would be sending him to their parents in Arizona for a visit until things were resolved, and I had insisted on paying the airfare.

It was the least I could do. He would fly out in two days.

I sat in the big brown chair with my feet on a red leather ottoman. Perhaps if I tried to set down events in an orderly way I'd see some pattern.

Nothing seemed to connect. What was my relationship to the people and events which had caught me up? In the center of the pad, I drew a cartoon face of myself. On radiating spokes, like a Tinker-toy, I drew other small circles and gave them names. Jameel. Seal brown gelding. Buster. Frank. Velma. I stopped. There was so much I didn't know. The driver? Had he been Buster? The Phillips' and Leila. They all had threads to me, but what connected them to each other?

The front door closed. I hadn't heard it open. What if it wasn't . . . "Miles?"

Her solid boot steps walked the hall. "I took a mule to keep her company. That molly mule loves all horses, even Night." Miles looked tired.

"Would you like some tea?"

"Yeah," Miles said, reaching her fingertips to nearly touch the ceiling. "Can't sleep yet."

When I returned with two steaming mugs, she had lit the gas fire. The flames added a certain amount of warmth to the room, but I missed the crackle and hiss of a real fire.

Miles took a sip of tea and asked, "What about your work? You said you're a writer. Don't you have assignments? Deadlines?"

"No." I found myself somewhat reluctant to explain. I struggled a moment with how much of my life to reveal. I decided that with this woman I would be totally frank. "I don't have to. I'm independently wealthy."

"Yeah? I've never known anyone who didn't have to earn a living." She was thoughtful. "Was that why you weren't anxious to tell me?"

"Actually, I *was* anxious." We both laughed. "People change when they find out I'm rich."

Miles crossed her long legs, looking me straight in the eyes. "I don't know anything about all that. This ranch is all I want, plus someone to share it with."

"You don't even have a foot on the bottom rung of the social ladder?"

"I try to keep my feet in the stirrups. That's where I want to be," Miles drawled with an amiable smile.

We'd exchanged next to no personal information, and now we both wanted to search each other for the hidden places beneath our crusts. After a long moment Miles asked, "What about family? Have you had a chance to talk with them? They must be worried."

I shrank into myself. "I don't have any."

"Don't answer if you feel I'm prying . . . which I guess I am."

Drawing in a deep breath of air, I slowly let it out. "I have an aunt I adore, who lives in Edinburgh. A close friend, Victoria. I called her. No brothers or sisters. My parents died in the Lockerbie plane crash. I was seventeen." I shifted in the chair, and felt a veil drop between myself and Miles.

Her eyes held true empathy. "That's a hard age to lose your family."

"I survived. Victoria was my neighbor and that helped. I spent part of my summers in Scotland with my aunt. She's the one who introduced me to horses. It was a good thing I had a creature to love." I bent over and unlaced my sneakers. "What about you?"

Miles sketched her past. "My folks live in Arizona now. I have — had another brother, Jack. We all grew up on this ranch. Everyone expected Jack would take over when Dad retired, even though it was always obvious that I wanted the ranch more than Jack did. I went to college in Missoula to become a teacher, but all my electives were Ag. courses. Agriculture. Dad figured me to marry. He said I didn't need a ranch or a career, just a husband. It was my Mom who told me I'd best have a way to earn a living. Just in case, she said."

Something showed in her eyes and I wondered what was coming next.

"Guess you've figured out I'm gay."

"Guess you've figured that makes two of us." I smiled broadly.

"Yes. I liked your little fishing expedition."

"Oh, you mean the k.d. lang hook?"

"A pretty out lady."

Our gaze held for a moment. Thinking of all the chance meetings of other lesbians in the most unlikely places, I also thought of the lonely isolated times in a world which took heterosexuality for granted.

"Go on with your story," I said. "Now you can tell me the juicy parts."

An amused chuckle. "Seemed pretty dry at the time. After I got my teacher's certificate, I headed for Seattle. It was good for me to get out of this valley. See a bit more of the world. Find out about vegetarians and such." She looked directly at me with her lips formed in a faint smile.

I felt myself quiver in the oddest places.

"Didn't take me long to figure out I was gay. Seattle was a hot town, great bars, softball leagues, all gay. I thought I was settled for sure with a gal named Hannah."

I said a soft, "Oh."

Miles nodded. "Then my brother Jack got himself killed going over MacDonald Pass in the winter. Drunk. Hard enough to do sober. Since my parents had already retired to Arizona, the ranch was mine. Dad had been sheriff around here a lot of years. Which made him able to retire without selling the spread. For a while there, Dad wanted it sold anyway. Figured I couldn't run it without a husband." Her face grew hot with the memory.

"You seem to be doing just fine."

Miles smiled at me. "Yeah, I am. I do substitute teaching and home-tutoring to fill in the lean times. I think the main thing that swayed my dad was that I would take care of Norburt. Jack did a lot of hanging out at bars and Burt was often left alone. He's been scared of the dark since he was a little kid. My mom knows I love him, and Norburt and I've always taken care of each other, so she helped convince Dad we'd do all right. It's not a one-way street with Norburt, you know."

Miles paused, smoothed her unwilling hair, and continued. "Burt does a fair amount around the ranch. Actually, I'm not sure I could make ends meet if I had to hire someone to do the work he does." She laughed remembering something. "He's a gentle sort. The kind of boy who'd rescue flies getting their wings ripped off by other kids."

"Yes, I can see that about him."

She smiled warmly at me. "To be frank, I wouldn't want another hand around the place unless it was female. Burt's on S.S.I. so it gives him some independent spending money and health care."

"Tell me about Hannah," I said, my gaze following the line and folds of Miles' blue jeans.

With a snort Miles firmly set her mug on a coaster. "Short and sweet. When Jack died I had to act fast because Burt was all alone. It was nearing calving time and I had to get here. Hannah thought the idea of being a cowgirl would suit her — the two-step was the rage in Seattle then. She packed our apartment and joined me a week later. Her fantasies of ranch life never panned out. Didn't seem to realize it's hard work, and plenty of it. It's the work I love, though. I'll never leave Montana."

I nodded, "You're lucky to have this place."

"A lot of the ranches are being bought up by movie stars or developers. The movie stars post no trespassing signs right away and the developers divide it into twenty acre pieces. I sold the ranch's development rights to Fish and Game. It's valuable elk wintering range. Then when I die, at least I won't have to worry about it getting chopped up and covered with houses planted thick as knapweed."

"Same thing is happening in Vermont. The price of land has gone beyond what farmers can afford. But, you were telling me about you and Hannah."

"I just couldn't live the life she wanted, city, Olivia cruises, that stuff. She was real serious about her career. That was all right with me, but she wanted me to have one. Teaching!" Miles made a disgusted sound. "Hannah never could understand that the only career I ever really wanted was running this ranch. She lasted four years. After that first hard winter, it was three years longer than I thought she would."

"I've had the same experience. Vermont looks pretty on Christmas cards but no one mentions that it's thirty below in that winter wonderland," I said with a laugh.

Miles, smiled too. "It gets pretty lonely up this way. Power would go out, and Hannah watched a lot of TV. I'd knit or fix some tack, something you can do by kerosene light. She'd pace and get mad at the power company. Couldn't do anything about it. Some winters need a bulldozer to plow that road from the ranch to the highway at Whitehall. When it's really bad, I leave my truck parked at a buddy's ranch near town and ride my snowmobile back and forth."

"Are there any lesbians around here?"

"Oh, sure. In Helena, forty-eight miles and a rugged pass away. I've got a few good friends up there and *Pride!* is based in Helena. In Butte, there's Snookum's Bar, and the gay rodeo is active there. Missoula has a large alternative community of hippies and gays. A young crowd, for the most part. I'm getting to be an old dog." Miles snorted.

I crossed my legs at the ankles and admired the woman sitting opposite me. Miles was one of those rare women utterly at home in her own body. "I'll guess you like to dance. Where do you go to two-step?"

She laughed. "You may not believe this, but about the only place I've seen two-stepping was at a women's music festival near Yosemite and at bars in Spokane and Seattle. I like the kind of dancing where you look the other gal in her eyes, and hold her close."

"Oooo baby." This woman was not afraid of being corny.

"Most of the tunes out there to dance to kind of keep you hopping, though. I bunch up with friends once in a while and head for Missoula, but it's over three hours away, and you almost have to stay the night. That's hard for me to do. There's the cost of a motel room and Norburt to consider. Plus, if it isn't one thing, it's another. Calving time is done now, next is branding and there's always sorting and moving cows for some purpose or other. When haying starts you're so tired you can hardly wait to crawl into bed at eight-thirty. Then roundup, sorting the yearlings and bred heifers and cows, and winter blasts in again." She glanced quickly at me. "I'm painting a pretty bleak picture, aren't I?"

"Actually, it sounds inviting." My gaze moved to the fireplace mantle. "Is that Hannah?"

"Right after we first met." Abruptly Miles stood. "I'll bet you're tired. I know I am. It's midnight."

"Tomorrow I'm going to snoop around. Perhaps go talk with Lance."

"Take the car. Good night."

～๑)

Breakfast dishes had been rinsed and stacked neatly. I glanced at the teapot clock, which told me eight-thirty. I looked out the window to the stable yard. No sign of anyone. I was no match for this gal.

The car keys lay square in the middle of the kitchen table.

I decided to splurge on breakfast in town.

It turned out to be a bad choice. Boulder, Montana, aka Grease City, USA, offered fried eggs, home fries and umpteen different varieties of fried pork. I had fried dough shaped in an appealing circle, and skipped the rest. The doughnut left a dark ring on my napkin.

I found Lance in the Sheriff's office behind a thick wall of bulletproof glass. The dispatch area was in the county jail. I bent over to speak through a narrow slot at the bottom of the window.

"Hi, there. Lance, do you have time to talk?"

"How's Jane?" he shouted through the slot.

"Fine." I nodded to reinforce my voice. I always found the common Montana greeting confusing, as though they were talking to someone else named Jane standing behind me.

"I'll be right out," he replied.

We sat in his cluttered office. Riot shields lay heaped in one corner. The camouflage green and brown shag carpet stored many law enforcement items, not to mention paper clips and bits of tobacco chew. On his desk, thick with papers and weighted down by his holstered gun, was a gray computer with a variegated philodendron crossing the screen.

"How can I be of help in finding the kidnappers?" I asked, and had to wait for an answer.

"We're handlin' it."

"I have quite a lot of investigative experience. Give me something to do."

Lance stared silently, and with remarkable neutrality, at a spot over my shoulder. Before he could escort me out of his office I said, "Like, who around here deals in horses? I could check them out. I'm the only one who could recognize any horses they might still have."

"If we have any horses we want identified we'll give you a call, Ms. Scott. Meantime, the Feds have taken over this case and we're assisting them."

In a courtly manner he escorted me out of his office, and again slipped behind his glass shield.

The front door whooshed open and Deputy Bullock entered the building. I noticed blue smudges under her eyes from illness or a lack of sleep. "How are you, Deputy?"

"Oh, Lord, one of the dispatchers got broke up by a bronc. Drew the wrong ride at a rodeo in Big Timber. One of the deputies is on vacation and another is at his mother's funeral in Cincinnati. I've had to do three shifts in a row."

"Ouch. I came by to see if I can help find these horse thieves."

"Did you see Lance?"

"Yes." In response to her raised eyebrows, I said, "No go."

"That figures." Annie Bullock rubbed her eyes. She nodded toward the door and we walked out of the building.

Leaning against her 4-wheel drive cruiser she drew a small notebook from her breast pocket and methodically wrote in it, ripped the page off and handed it to me.

I tucked the paper into my pocket. Smiling at the deputy I began to thank her, but she held up her fingers spread in a fan.

"Now, don't go around saying I gave you this. Keep your head down and don't get into trouble. When you find out something let me know."

Not if. When.

17

"Do you know how to get to these places?" I showed Miles the notebook page.

"You bet. Hmm, the Triple Dot. Wonder why it's on there. Jack Logan is one of the county commissioners. And Bill and Carla Peters, nice people. They deal in dude ranch horses. We can check them out after I move bulls tomorrow. You can come if you want."

"Great." Something was beginning to happen.

Later, I made a call to the Phillips' home in Woodstock. I wanted to ask some more specific questions.

"Oh, it's you again," Mrs. Phillips said.

Quickly, before she could hang up on me, I said, "Please talk with me Mrs. Phillips. If I can I'd like to stop the killing of innocent horses."

There was silence on the line, but she hadn't disconnected. Her held breath was released and she almost whispered, "I've been thinking about that mare. She was lovely. Come see me. I'll talk to you."

"Talk to me now. I can't come to Woodstock." Quickly I censored how much I should tell her. "I'm out of state on business. Tell me about Jameel."

"I've thought so many times about what you said, that she's dead, they killed her." I heard her take a deep breath. "We believed she'd go to a nice new home, and we'd get the money for an event horse for our daughter. Everyone would be happy. Leila was the contact person we were told to reach. My husband will be furious that I'm talking with you, but it's the right thing to do."

I said, "Thank you," from my heart.

⁊∾৶

By dawn the next day, moving bulls, I thought I'd never been happier. The docile, slow hulks moved at their own stolid pace. We had the pleasure of reuniting them with the cows for a summer of lust.

The horse Miles had saddled up for me knew more than I did about his work. The breeze held a cool fragrance of Douglas fir, young grass and wild flowers, and dogs ran happily doing the work they were bred for.

While Miles rode ahead to open the gate, I sat watching for bulls wanting to double back. I seriously doubted any of them would, but there could be a gay bull, I guess. The twenty purebred Hereford and Angus bulls flowed through the open gate like water through a spillway.

⁊∾৶

Before noon we headed for the Peters' place. "This ranch is a long shot," Miles said, taking the turn to Elkhorn. "It's worth checking out anyway. They deal in beaucoup horses. Lord, Skip, give me a little room to turn the steering wheel."

Skip sat between us on the wide Chevy truck seat, her weight pressed tightly against her mistress, aiming her blue eye at me. I had tried making friends with the dog. However, she quickly reverted to her usual watchful state.

"She's a slow starter," Miles said. "Can't decide if she can share me, or have a new friend. Never able to let somebody new into her herd."

"I struggle with similar issues, myself." I patted the dog's head. "Don't let anyone get too close or you get hurt. Keep it light." I think this was the first time I verbalized this concept, even to myself.

"That's a hard one." Miles looked straight ahead out the windshield.

Parking the truck at a wide place in the graded dirt road, we got out to walk up a trail made from the wear of truck tires taking the path of least resistance. Skip ran ahead.

I gestured toward the binoculars around Miles' neck. "Is that a good idea?"

"No one will wonder what I'm doin'," Miles answered. "I'm known around this area as a birder." A tumbling laugh came out of her. "People think I'm pretty weird, anyway."

"Because they know you're a lesbian?"

"No, some do, but that's not it. I'm an environmentalist. The most suspect people around here are environmentalists and animal rights activists." Miles shook her head. "This is something I've never understood. I can have a talk with Bob Evans about the wetlands near his house, or the health of the deer herd, or the way his neighbor treats his horses and dogs. We can be in total agreement. Yet red veins appear in his eyes when I use any of the buzzwords. Riparian area. Habitat. Animal abuse. Species reintroduction. I know what they are so I just talk around them. Take the wolves, for instance. His eyes actually lit up when he told me about hearing a howl one full moon night up in the Lockheart."

I smiled at the tall woman walking beside me. "Buzz words. I wonder sometimes, how they get such power. Slow down, would you?" I stopped walking, panting for breath. "Must be out of shape. Let's sit and take in the view for a moment."

"It's the altitude. Takes a while to get used to it."

We sat in the cool shade beside a tiny patch of yellow flowers.

"Tell me about the wolves. It was on TV, but I've been curious about what's really going on."

"What a to-do putting those wolves in Yellowstone caused! The cost is what stirred most ranchers up. A bundle of money was spent to transport wolves from Canada, acclimate them to their new home, and then monitor their release. We were told we'd be reimbursed for calf losses. It's almost impossible for ranchers to prove predator kills in a way that satisfies the government. Usually there's nothing to find. Just a bawling mama cow. Wolves are coming back anyway without anybody interfering. There's wolves right up there," Miles said waving a finger toward some mountains to the southwest.

"National Forest people call them the Boulder pack. We've known about them for years. Ranchers try to put in claims for lost calves, but forest rangers say it's dogs. We know better. Nearest place with a dog is fifty miles, and that's a twelve year old poodle. Evans family has run their cows in the Lockheart for, well, quite a while. Few generations, anyway. They tell a story about riding home from some doings in the winter. That's back when they lived at the original homestead. Pack of wolves followed them, getting closer. The youngest kid had an old pony, and well, those wolves were closing in. The father took the girl over the front of his saddle, tied the pony to a tree, and rode like hell."

"Oh, my God. You mean they just left the pony tied up? For the wolves?"

"Better than losing more than one horse and risking the child."

I almost heard the pony's screams and the child, held in her parent's arms, calling back. Not understanding.

"It's the way things are. Ranchers know that wolves don't just exist on coffee mugs and tee shirts. Every summer we'll lose a calf or two, or a colt, when the pups are learning to hunt and will go after anything easy. The hard part is getting the government to pay for stock losses like they promised.

"This time last year I came upon a dead elk calf. Hind leg was so neatly removed a surgeon could have done it. Looked like lion kill. I got out of there in a hurry."

"I guess that's part of the environment. The whole of nature." I stared off toward the hills holding the Boulder pack.

"Yeah. Nature isn't pretty."

A shared moment of silence ticked by as we gazed out over the rolling green hills speckled with wild flowers. White snow- shouldered Bull Mountain rose up to brush the passing clouds. The utter beauty of our surroundings sank peacefully in.

A tiny smile pulled at the edges of my mouth. "It certainly isn't."

"Not pretty." The tough rancher's eyes crinkled. We shrieked and whooped. We rolled over the grass, gasping, unable to stop laughing. My side hurt. Skipper moved away to a place where she could watch, head between paws, for this silliness to stop.

Finally Miles jumped to her feet. "We better get a move on."

The song of a lark rose from the grass nearby, heartbreakingly beautiful. We stood side by side, listening. Skippy's whine told us how long we had been silently standing there. This woman's energy seemed like an electric field, radiating to me.

Miles reached for my hands. She brought them together to a place between our bodies, gently forming a cradle. "You say you aren't with anyone out East?"

"Right," I answered cautiously.

"Then would you like me to court you?"

"Well . . . " The pause was enough to separate us. "I'm not much on commitment and I live a bit further than two mountain passes away." I turned and continued walking.

170

"You have a point. How 'bout a fling?"

I pursed my lips prissily. "You are persistent."

"Have to be. You're as light on your feet as an antelope."

"And just as spooky." I wondered at my own reluctance. What did I have to lose? I would be back in New England soon and Miles could be as emotionally messy as she wanted to be and I wouldn't be around to pick up the pieces. The easiest separation in the world; climb on an airplane.

I kept walking forward, fast. Miles caught up with me. I said, keeping my eyes focused ahead, "I know I'll start feeling close to you, then pull away. You don't need that. And neither do I. Most women I'm attracted to have an aloof side that makes me feel safe. You don't have that."

"At least you admit you're attracted to me."

The way she said it made us both laugh.

"You know," Miles said. "I've been scorched in the relationship fire, too." Her smile was far from bitter. Her grey eyes held a humor I would do well to include in my own view of life. A serious sort of apprehension dogged me, always.

We walked in the worn track of one tire, our hands meeting in the grassy middle over Skipper, who walked between us. There was something cozy and friendly about walking together. Suddenly I ached for a home with someone I loved, and for a moment a full picture of life with Miles flashed into my mind. It was way too powerful. I pushed it away with a joke. "What does a lesbian drive on the second date?"

Miles looked puzzled. "Is this a joke?"

I nodded. "A U-Haul van."

"Well, here's one," Miles said. "What's Montana foreplay?"

"Show me."

Miles rolled back on the high heels of her western boots, pushed her hat low over her eyes, and said in a voice like the south wind through chaparral, "*Get* in the truck."

My feet itched for the Chevy truck. "Don't tempt me."

"What the hell do you think I'm trying to do? Put you off?"

There was that lopsided grin again that made me weak in the knees.

⌇

The track took us along the top of a park, through a heavy stand of timber, then out once again to unhemmed blue sky. Directly below us a ranch sprawled, built over generations. A modern house had been placed very close to the original log cabin. Log outbuildings lay in haphazard relation to the corrals holding livestock.

"These are nice people who have this ranch. But you never can tell, if hard times come, who would trade in stolen horses." Miles adjusted the binoculars.

As we passed the glasses back and forth, we occasionally accidentally touched one another. When this happened we'd mutter a quick apology, or an awkward "Sorry."

Skip lay twitching in the warm sunshine but the click of a horseshoe against rock brought her out of her afternoon nap and onto her feet with a low growl. Both of us spun around, alarm and guilt on our faces.

"Oh, it's you, Miss Miles," the young cowboy, barely fourteen, said.

"Why, how's Bill?" Miles greeted him.

"Out for a ride on my birthday horse." He proudly patted the neck of stunning black and white Paint. "Looking for the eagles? Calving's all done."

"Yes. I saw a Bald Eagle flying this part of the valley last week. My fr . . . um . . . new hand here, Sara's never seen one."

"Calving?" I said. "Isn't that an old myth, that eagles eat the calves?"

"The eagles circle overhead to watch for the placentas," Miles said. Still seeing bafflement on my face, she clarified, "They eat them."

"Oh." My stomach turned.

"Nice lookin' animal." Miles stroked the gelding's shoulder. "Your dad have any good horses for sale? I've got a cousin in Denver who's looking for a jumping horse. Got to be good. He'd pay big bucks for it."

I threw her a quick glance, thinking Miles was a wily fox.

"We don't have anything like that, but I'll tell Dad," the boy said, lifting his hat to the ladies.

After he rode off, she briskly turned to me. "I think we can cross this place off your short list."

"We didn't do too well in the inconspicuous department today," I observed.

"This next place, Logan's Triple Dot, I'll guarantee you we won't be seen."

18

Norburt had come down with a cold. "I'll have to cancel his trip," Miles said. "He gets these awful sinus infections if he flies with a cold."

If anything happened to him because of my involvement in this mess, I'd never forgive myself. I was growing jumpier by the hour.

When Miles returned from the bunkhouse after putting Norburt to bed, I got this surprising rush. Quickly, I busied myself fixing dinner. "Is there someplace Norburt could stay until all this is over?"

"I think he's all right at home. Whoever's keeping us under glass is looking for the mare. And you."

This sank in like a wet blanket to my spirits.

"I've been worried about Night. Is it possible to go see her?"

Miles rubbed her face with her wide open hand, making a soft rasping sound. "She's fine."

"I'm so tense, I'd love to go for a ride. It would be relaxing and fun."

Bewilderment clouded her face. "You mean, for fun?"

"Well, yes."

"Jane, I've never gone riding just for fun. Horses get me where I'm going to do a job. It would never even occur to me to go for a pleasure ride. But, hell, girl, if you want to go, take any horse you want."

"I can't imagine what it would be like not to enjoy riding, for its own sake."

"Hey, don't get me wrong, I fancy being out there on the back of a good horse. It's more like there's always so much to do, I guess. It wouldn't cross my mind not to have a job as the goal."

I looked up from dishing out three dinner plates. "I feel bad about taking up so much of your time."

"Right now, things are coasting along between calving and haying. There's miles of fence line to check. Now *there's* where a horse is useful." She smiled engagingly at me.

The guest room had begun to feel remote and the bed larger than a regular double. I woke smelling breakfast cooking. This woman sure could get a jump on the daylight. Even now the sun was trying to rise above red and orange clouds, which seemed to pulse from the heat beneath them. Dressing fast, I made for the bathroom, and came out looking nearly as orderly and combed as Norburt.

I didn't expect to see him sitting at the table.

"Norburt flat-out refused to stay in bed. Says there's a big break in the east fence line and he'll show us. Times there's no arguing with him."

I took a chair opposite the triumphant Norburt, and Miles ladled sausage and onion gravy over fresh baked biscuits. She smacked the plate down on the table in front of me. There was a lot of breakfast on it.

"Figured we should stoke up this morning. Instead of fixing the wire, I want to replace it with jack fence. This place is a major game highway. Deer and elk, especially the calves, get tangled up in the barbed wire and die each year. Someday I want to get rid of all the barbed wire in places where they cross."

The image of animals caught in the barbed wire gripped me with horror. "Of course I'll help. But can't this wait until later?" I wondered. "We could be catching horse thieves."

The expression on Miles' face made me squirm. "Believe me, it'd take more than a morning's work if I had to round the herd up and drive them off Bull Mountain."

The work was hard. Miles cut young lodgepole trees down with a chain saw and Norburt and I limbed and notched them with an ax. The butt ends were cut in lengths for the jack legs and the tops made the long poles. We chopped notches to fit and join the two legs together, then nailed them with spikes.

By the time we finished, I decided I'd never worked this hard in my life before. I noticed Miles watching me.

Miles stepped back to admire the line of fence marching across the dip in the land. "Good piece of work."

Norburt smiled with pleasure while he tied the tools and chain saw to the rack on the ATV four wheeler.

Miles watched as he drove down the long slope. "Those things are very stable, but I still worry about him."

Her eyes met mine. "That was the hardest thing I had to learn. After Norburt graduated from Butte training center they gave us a day-long workshop on supporting his independence. I want to protect him from getting hurt, but it makes him feel so competent when he drives that thing. I couldn't take that away from him." Miles turned and mounted her horse.

"He doesn't need to feel helpless. I think you're right." I smiled at Miles. A groan escaped as I swung my leg over the cantle. My leg brushed the horse's rump and he hunched a little. I couldn't imagine getting on a horse again in three hours.

⌇

Miles drove toward Boulder. The dirt road climbed slowly to a high park, then dipped sharply down. Here, she turned the truck off to the right, crossing the grassland over a rough two-line track, to park in a thick stand of timber.

Miles sauntered around to the back of the trailer, opened the gate, and stood back. Our horses, Buck and Tiger, jumped out without assistance.

Tagging along behind Miles, riding a sure-footed mountain-bred horse, I could allow my mind to drift. The last time I came this way my exhausted brain could only focus on escape.

The metallic clink of a horseshoe on rock, a brief soughing of the pines, a far off birdcall, drawn on the air, and from under me, the squeak of leather; these sounds accented the depth of the silence.

A musky sweet smell of sage warmed by the sun, blended with aromatic alpine and Douglas fir, and the denser, darker whiff of lodgepole pine created an untamed incense. I knew there would be a time when this unique blend of scent would become a memory tag to rush upon me at unsuspecting times; at Thanksgiving when the aroma of the turkey's sage stuffing would fill the house, or an intangible bouquet on a breeze during a hike.

Bright, tiny pink wildflowers were underfoot. Shooting Stars, I remembered Miles saying. They had yellow noses pointing ahead, pink petals flying behind making them look as if they were traveling at great speed. Beneath the cover of tall timber, patches of snow increased the coolness of the shade. Clusters of huge standing boulders crowned each elevation in the land; a feral Stonehenge.

I relished the fact that Miles could ride along without constant conversation. Following her on the narrowing trail,

I watched the woman whose legs straddled the round barrel of the red dun. I imagined her hips curving around my own mouth, swinging with the horse's limber walk and my supple body. I became aware of a growing dampness between myself and the saddle. The roper's rhythmic movement, melding with my lush imagination, set my body humming.

The trail broke out of the timber and Miles urged her horse into a jog. We rode across the small park.

At a place where the trail dipped down, Miles paused for me to catch up. We let the horses blow a moment. A slight squeak rose from Tiger's saddle when he took a deep breath. The smell of horses and sweat engulfed me. And the smell of Miles. A unique blend of horses, cattle, warm leather and a very faint whiff of lime cologne. I resisted digging my nose between the flaps of her jeans jacket, burrowing into the soft small breasts. I'd better tighten the reins on my fertile imagination, I observed.

We came to an outcrop of rock overlooking the Triple Dot Ranch, and Miles hobbled the horses. She dug her binoculars out of the case and played them over the ranch in concentrated silence. She passed them over to me. "Glass the corrals on the side of the barn farthest from the driveway."

What I saw made the hair stand on the back of my neck. I recognized one of the Warmbloods. He was in a corral with the gray Anglo Arab and a couple of other sleek, expensive-looking horses. Idling in another enclosure were half a dozen blocky ranch horses. The hood of the brown truck was barely visible in an equipment bay. No other vehicles around. My guess was that the brown truck wasn't used much these days. "I'd venture to say no one's there. Take a look at that," I said, pointing out the truck to Miles.

"Pay dirt." Miles shoved the binoculars into the case and looped the strap over the saddle horn. "I'd bet Lance wouldn't have put the Triple Dot on any list. He'd figure Jack

Logan wasn't involved."

"Must have been Officer Bullock's idea." With rising excitement I said, "I want some photos. Of the horses, the truck . . . hard facts, to get a search warrant."

The number of rocks we rolled ahead of us had to rouse every antelope and bunny in four counties. No way could anyone be home at the ranch or they'd have been on the front porch with iced tea for us when we arrived. Or guns. My breath came so short from held tension that by the time we reached the rails of the corrals, I was gasping for air.

I got a great shot of the warm-blood's shoulder brand with Logan's ranch house in the distance. Miles disappeared into the barn, while I snooped in the equipment sheds.

The brown truck was there. I flipped the seat forward to find a tangle of jacks, jumper cables and old smut magazines. The glove compartment held dozens of mustard and ketchup packages and a tire gauge. Stuffed into a milky cellophane envelope were items much more interesting. An insurance card and registration papers for the truck. And, not for any Jack Logan. The listed owner was Leila M. Logan. Was this the same Leila dealing and training horses in northern Vermont? Daughter, or wife?

Folding the papers into a small packet to fit in my shirt pocket, I heard a quiet sound behind me. I jumped. Dropping the papers as I whipped around.

A barn cat eyed me warily. Before I could sigh with relief I heard the unmistakable crunch of approaching footsteps. I crouched inside the shed's wide open door and peeked around the corner.

A man was walking into the barn. A very big, muscular man. Miles had been headed for the barn when I'd come to the equipment shed.

I'd never felt so exposed as during the mad dash to the red brown barn. In the shelter of the far end, I crouched in tall dried grass and pressed my cheek against the weather-grooved fir boards, and listened.

Silence. That seemed like a plus, for if the man had discovered Miles he would most certainly be grilling her. I put my eye to a knothole and could see nothing at ground level except a jumble of pack saddles and canvas bags. However, I could see Miles high in the hay loft. She crouched in the diffused sunlight from the open loft door. Old grey-yellow hay, left over from the days before balers, covered the floor. Dust motes slowly drifted. Her entire focus was on something below.

I scrambled and found a board which had curled with the years, leaving a wide crack for viewing.

Buster! I saw him, sitting on a hay bale, deeply engrossed in scribbling in a pocket sized spiral notebook. I looked up to the hay loft again. Miles had disappeared.

Movement brought my focus back to Buster. He came to his feet, tucking the pen into his shirt pocket, and headed for the clutter of pack panniers and decker frames near me. Bending over to lift the pannier flap he froze, then abruptly stood. Standing stock still, he seemed to be examining the inside of the barn. Then he strode to the bottom of the ladder to the hay loft.

Halfway up the ladder he stopped abruptly and wiped a finger across the disturbed dust on the top of each rung. I could almost see his brain's wheels turning. He hadn't known she was up there until then. Leaning dangerously far back he looked up. I could hear him sniffing the air. Good God, this guy was like an animal.

Movement caught my attention from the far right edge of the open loft. Suddenly Miles appeared swinging on a rope into open space. The silence of her slice through the air was spooky. No Xena yell, or anything.

Her shirt flapped. Buster saw her just before she hit him at the shoulders with her extended boots. Dislodged from the ladder he fell, stunned and spread-eagled. Miles hit the ground running and I left my vantage point to race with her to our horses.

"That was Buster," I called out.

"Run. Talk later." Miles sprinted toward the hill trail. "Jane!" a man's voice called. I looked back over my shoulder and kept running. Buster stood dazedly in front of the barn. He trotted a few unsteady steps, then paused. "Jane! Jane, stop!"

Miles grabbed my arm. "Come on! He's up to something."

Part way up the rocky hillside, I heard a truck engine. This time we stopped to look and catch our breath. Buster wasn't chasing us. He too, watched a brand new Ford truck pull into the yard. Two guys got out. One of them was Frank.

A brief, shouting conversation ensued. The man I didn't recognize got back into the truck cab, reappearing with a rifle. We raced upward toward the dense pines with increased urgency.

Buster and the man with the rifle chased us. A motorcycle's roar shattered the tension and I saw Frank tear down the road. I wondered if there was a place he could cut us off.

We made it to the jumpy horses, got the hobbles off and rode the hell out of there.

19

The ride back to the horse trailer was almost anticlimactic. Peaceful, serene landscape was the backdrop for my pounding heart. We urged the horses into a steady trot.

As we neared the truck and trailer, the sound of a motorcycle engine reached us. It sounded as if it were heading toward us, then its noisy scream dipped down toward the valley.

I wondered if Frank was the rider.

Miles held up a hand. She flipped open the keeper of her rifle scabbard, pulling the grey Winchester free. Cautiously, she stepped down from her horse, circled the rig. Remounting the gelding, she said, "Tires are slashed. Let's push for home, Jane. Stay close."

Not until a good distance had been covered did Miles replace the rifle in its scabbard. Cold settled into us as we rode. Now that the sun no longer warmed the air, the patches of snow acted like a refrigerator. I felt my feet going numb.

My wristwatch said eight-thirty when Miles dismounted to open the gate. No lights winked at us from the ranch.

FRANCI McMAHON

Miles gruffly said, "Something's wrong." We urged the tired horses across the long grassy slope, driving six antelope before us. Reaching the last barbed wire gate Miles opened it from the saddle. She pushed Tiger into a gallop for home. Steam rose from our horses when they halted beside the dark bunkhouse.

"Norburt!" Miles shouted, then said to me, "Deal with the horses, will you?"

While I led the blowing horses to the barn I could hear Miles calling out. The absence of the dogs was ominous. The light in the bunkhouse flared on.

I figured the horses would be all right in a stall for a few minutes. I threw a couple of empty feed bags over each one then ran to help look for Norburt.

I met up with Miles coming out of the bunkhouse. I saw the bed sheets had been pulled from the bed and a blanket dragged out in a line toward the door.

She ran to the house. I followed her close. The kitchen appeared strangely silent and undisturbed. But there was an unfamiliar smell in the air. A male scent; perhaps shaving cologne.

We found Norburt bound and gagged in a horse stall, the last place we looked. Murna cringed against him, whining softly.

I removed Norburt's gag while Miles worked at the ropes on his wrists. His nose ran and he traced his lips with his tongue, but he was unhurt.

"Some guys came. They came into the bunkhouse and tied me up. One guy shot Skippy." He rubbed his wrists.

Miles froze. "Where is she?"

"Right over there." Norburt got to his feet.

Miles found her dog crumpled in the dark corner of the stall. Sinking to her knees, she cried, "Skipper."

The cow dog's tail worked like a rudder over the ground. A whine leaked out of her.

Norburt and I stood behind her. I felt utterly helpless.

"He kept asking me: Where's the black mare?" Norburt said.

Very gently, Miles scooped the dog up in her arms. I stood riveted, staring at the coating of blood on the straw.

"I said I didn't know, and he said he'd shoot Skippy." Norburt shifted his weight from right to left foot, then back again. "Where is she, Sis? I wish I could have told him so he wouldn't hurt Skipper."

"Burtie, you did fine. He was a mean man." Heading for the car Miles yelled, "Jane! Call the vet in Butte, Doc Keene. Helen Keene, Silver Bow Animal Hospital. Have her meet me there!"

That got me moving and I ran over to the car and opened the front passenger side door. Miles eased the dog onto the seat. Skip's head was limp, but her tail waved.

"Want me to come with you?"

"Norburt'll need the company. Just call, please."

I watched the two taillights, the distance between them shortening, then the sweep of headlights at the turn. Pivoting on my heel, I nearly bumped into Norburt standing behind me.

"I couldn't tell him." He tried to smooth his hair, big raw-boned fingers combing and combing. His agony was painful to see.

"What did the men look like?"

"I don't know. I was asleep . . . it was night. The other guy stayed in the dark. He said, I think I know where the black mare is."

"Oh? Did he say anything more?"

"Why did they want to hurt Skip if they knew where the mare was?"

"Some things don't make any sense," I said. I watched while he rocked himself and wondered if it was a shadow memory of his mother holding him.

"Skippy and Murna were sleeping under my bed. I know they weren't 'sposed to be there. Sis will be mad. Will he come back and hurt Murna? I'm scared. Tell me where the black mare is so I can tell those guys."

Gently, I held out my arms to him. "It's okay. You can stay in the house tonight if you want. Murna, too." I patted his back, then felt him pull back. "I'll talk to Miles."

Norburt said, "I'm hungry. Would you fix me something to eat?"

"Just as soon as I finish taking care of the horses."

"Oh, I can do that," Norburt said eagerly, glad there was something he could do to help. He blew his nose on a large white handkerchief.

The phone call to the veterinarian took only a moment. Helen would meet Miles at the surgery. I found Lance's home number and dialed.

My voice was shaky as I started talking. It took a few tries to get my speech to sound familiar to my own ears.

Lance was patient, stopped me a few times to get different points clear, then said, "It's hard for me to believe Jack Logan could be involved in this. But you saw what you saw."

"I agree."

"There's a hell of a lot of brown trucks in this county. You say it was registered to Leila Logan? That's his ex-wife. You're certain Buster Wilde was the driver of the van? We'll get him. He won't get out of the state, you can bet. I'll let the F.B.I. know." He was silent a moment. "So, Skip was shot. Think she'll be all right?"

"I don't know, Lance. She lost a lot of blood."

"I got one of her pups. Super dog." He paused. "Glad Norburt's not hurt. Ask Becky to give me a call tomorrow, will you? I'll send two deputies to Logan's. Now, I'm asking you to stay out of this. You might get hurt."

It was very late when Miles returned. She walked slowly across the kitchen floor in the dark, and opened my bedroom door. "Can I sleep with you tonight?"

"Of course. Norburt's in your room, anyway."

"Oh, good. He was probably pretty shook." The clunk of one boot falling from Miles' foot was soon followed by the other.

I was afraid to ask, but I did: "How is Skipper?"

"Still alive. The bullet lodged in the right shoulder. Lost a mess of blood. I'll call in the morning." The springs gave out a soft screech.

I wrapped my arms around her tight body. I stroked my warm hands over her. Miles curled against me, shivering with grief, fatigue and the cold night air.

20

The bed seemed bigger without Miles in it. Her voice, faintly audible, came from the kitchen. In the night, I had been awakened by sounds muffled into the pillow and the bed shaking. Now, I could hear Miles striding across the kitchen floor.

"She's going to be all right," Miles said, a smile of relief lighting her face. "Helen says Skip is responding really well. The biggest problem is blood loss." Miles sat on the bed, put two pillows behind me and handed me a cup of coffee.

"Working dogs are never allowed in the house or treated like pets, but somehow she just wiggled her way into my heart and before I knew it she was sleeping beside my bed." She cleared her throat. "I won't let Burt have Murna in the bunkhouse. I know he sneaks her in."

"Yes. Did the vet say when she might be able to come home?"

"A couple of days, maybe." Miles stood with purpose. "Guess I'll make up a soft bed for her in the kitchen. That rug she usually flops on is worn out."

I sipped my coffee. This never would have happened if I hadn't come here. I found Miles in the kitchen arranging old blankets. "I'm sorry this mess I'm in caused Skip to get hurt and frightened your brother."

Miles answered. "Way I see it, we're in this together. I took Norburt and Murna to a neighbor's this morning. He can stay there for a few days. Anyway, you didn't hurt Skipper or frighten and tie up my brother. The guy that did doesn't know it yet, but he just insured that I'll do my best to find him." She stood with resolve, and went to her bedroom.

"Do you know how to use this?" Miles returned, sliding a bullet into the chamber of a revolver.

"I won't, Miles."

Miles looked startled. "What do you mean, won't?"

"There's a whole part of me you know nothing about. My spirituality. I'm a Quaker. That translates to my not using a gun."

"No kidding." Miles studied me with new eyes. "The Quiet People. But you don't wear those bonnets and long black dresses."

"You may be thinking of the Amish. There are major differences. The Religious Society of Friends are fairly invisible."

"You must be quite an outcast, being queer and all," Miles said, amazed.

"Looks like your stereotyping is working, now. As a matter of fact, gay and lesbian Friends groups are all over the country, and same sex marriages are held in many Meetings."

This was a little beyond what Miles could process right then. "This means if someone was going to kill me you wouldn't use a gun? You'd just let me get shot?"

How could I explain my spiritual convictions in fifty words or less? "It's not that simple. I believe each person has an inner light which is connected to everyone else's. If one's light is damaged, all are. To kill someone who's interfering with what you want is the easy way. What's hard is to reach that light in them."

"Oh, bullshit, Jane. You'd be out to save them while I'm getting killed?" An incredulous look covered Miles' face.

"Please, Miles, it's not about saving. I don't want to defend my religious views right now. What's important is that I have a strong commitment against violence. It's vitally important to me to not meet violence with more violence."

"What about the violence done to my dog? Ah, shit." She turned to a drawer under the wall telephone, pushed the phone book to one side, and placed the gun beneath it. "If you need it, it's here," she said brusquely.

"I think I'd better leave. This has become too — "

The expression in her eyes brought me to a grinding stop. "It's too late for that now. You're going to have to ride this one through."

Caught wanting to run! I didn't like it but she was right. I turned my back on her to gather myself.

With a quick sense of shock I felt Miles put her arms around me. Meaning to push myself roughly away, I found I was melting against her warmth. Tension and fear flowed out of me to be absorbed into her corduroy shirt.

Her voice softly reassured me, "We'll get through this."

She turned to her jacket hanging on a peg by the door. "You've got a letter, here. I picked up the mail last night. Everything else was sheepherder's mail."

She handed a thick envelope to me. I let it rest in my lap, unopened. "Sheepherder's mail, what's that?"

Miles laughed. She stood a moment with her hand on the refrigerator door, thinking over the definition for a term she used routinely. "It's that stuff that arrives in your mailbox or that you send away for — catalogs, magazines, coupon books — but nothing personal. Lonely mail, brought to you by the camp tender once a month, that fills the hours when the sheep are bedded."

This was the sort of term I loved. Words that gave depth and meaning to something as common as junk mail. Turning over my letter, I saw the bright red AIDs ribbon stamp and Victoria's large, hurried scrawl. I remembered her promise to send Rhonda's letter. Dreading the invasion, I slipped open the envelope. Inside was another envelope holding three closely covered pages covered with Rhonda's tiny, controlled writing.

A cup of coffee appeared at my elbow. "Good news?"

"No. The letter is from a woman . . . " I didn't know what to say and suddenly realized it was more than over. I tossed the wadded up letter in the kitchen trash, unread.

I knew Miles watched me as she stirred the hot cereal. "Old girlfriend? Looks to me like she might have a rope on you." Miles observed with a devilish smile, one eyebrow raised.

"The separation is mutual."

"Divorce or separation?"

"I'd say a definite divorce."

With a pleased expression Miles dished up the hot cereal. "While you finish getting up, I'm going to meet with the guy from the garage. He's coming with some new tires for the truck."

"I'll pay for them. No, I insist. My treat."

Miles laughed and agreed.

"And I forgot to tell you, Norburt said he overheard one of the men claim he had an idea where Night was. He thought the voice sounded familiar but never got a good look at the man. We need to bring her back here and have her moved someplace safe."

"How would . . . Oh. This is our local connection. Jack or someone who knows me and this ranch. Yes, we'll ride up to the cabin this afternoon."

The sun shone straight overhead by the time we had the horses saddled. Miles adjusted the saddle strings holding her slicker, but her hat brim didn't quite hide the worry in her eyes. She mounted Tiger and led the way up the gulch. Reaching the narrow end of it, we climbed up a trail emerging at a huge open park.

The rugged mountains, grown with lodgepole pine and fir, filled the high view, and far off island masses of sharp white peaks held up the sky. Open grassland formed scattered changes of texture and color. In Vermont these meadows could only be formed by logging; here, they took their shape by lack of rain and the path of the sun.

I removed my jacket and tied it with the saddle strings in front. The sun beat down, dry and warm. A gentle zephyr stirred my hair. Nearby, a small gathering of aspens shook their young leaves in a breeze, like soft rain on a tin roof.

We cantered the horses partway across the park. I noticed a smile of pleasure on Miles' face and remembering her claim to ride only to do a piece of work, I yelled across to her. "You don't seem to be suffering too much on the back of that horse." Miles' eyes crinkled, "No, not too much."

Soon we came to a small log cabin, built on the edge of an aspen grove, where Miles stepped off her horse. She tied the reins in a knot around her horse's neck, removed the saddle bags, then slung them over her shoulder. She opened the gate of a pole corral and turned him loose. I followed suit with my horse.

"Prissy," Miles called. "Priss." She shook the contents of one side of the saddle bags onto the smooth grass of a second smaller pole corral. Two white heaps of oats glistened alluringly on the grass.

I smiled as the little mule and Night came scrambling down a steep hill together. Soon each munched at her pile.

"She looks okay to me," I said, as Miles closed the gate. "In fact, this may be the great summer vacation of her life."

"Yeah." Miles rubbed the long ears of the mule. "Prissy is a good baby-sitter."

Slinging the saddle bags over the cabin's porch rail, Miles said, "How'd you like to see the old mine?"

"The Lady Smith gold mine? Sure."

We walked past the corrals toward an orange dirt pile that seemed to flow out of a cleft in the hillside. She described the process as I took it all in. Trees, cut long ago from nearby, were used to shore up walls as the shaft deepened. The hole was fairly large, considering the amount of effort it must have taken to dig, and must be very deep judging by the size of the dirt piled up in a long mound in front. Miniature train tracks led from deep within to the edge of the tailings. A small ore cart lay on its side, as it had for more than seventy-five years, abandoned after its last load.

"We can go in there if you want."

"No. I don't want to go in there."

"It's real safe."

"I don't care. I feel scared."

"It's pretty spooky inside. I check the timbers now and then for rot. A few supports have been replaced over the years."

Oh, God. The idea of being inside the mine when it collapsed washed me in waves of terror.

"Did those shafts fall in on miners?"

"Yeah," Miles answered. "That's one of the black spots on Montana history. When the shaft got deep, or the gold got lean, if a miner had any money at all from their claim they would pay a Chinese worker pennies to dig for him. When the shaft collapsed, often on the person digging, the miner would dig higher up the gulch, following the gold vein."

"Disposable workers. I've read about the Chinese railroad workers and the hardships they suffered, but I never knew about the miners. Horrible."

Miles eyes were serious. "There's a lot of darkness in America's past. Maybe you could write about it, do a special article about the west."

"It might mean I'd have to fly out here to do some research."

"That wouldn't be a hardship. Unless, of course, you stayed at the Best Western."

Perhaps it was Miles' plain and un-messy vulnerability which allowed me to come and go emotionally. There did not appear to be a shred of manipulation in her being. Nor did she chase me when I disappeared into safe distance, which made it so much easier to come back.

"Well, back to work," Miles said winking at me. She took a little notebook and a silver mechanical pencil from her breast pocket. Sauntering back to the cabin she made occasional notes.

"What are you doing?"

"Oh, I'm figuring what needs fixin' and what I need to haul up here when I get a chance to do it."

While Miles made her notes, I stood back to admire the well-made cabin, logs fitting together beautifully. Each log had its notch on the underside, ensuring that moisture would shed away from the heart of the wood. Moss grew on one corner of the roof, a bright chartreuse green, and the peaked head of a metal chimney poked through the shingles. I climbed the porch's two stairs and entered the cabin to find Miles checking a food cabinet.

"We keep a good stock up here so we can stay the night on the spur of the moment."

I smiled at her and looked around. One room held the entire living area. Cabinets and bookshelves were built against the walls. A rectangular pine table and two hand-hewn chairs were set in the southeast corner beneath a long window. Near the wood cook stove were two camp chairs.

"Want some coffee before we head back?" Miles asked, putting an enamel pot of water on the stove. She laid a small fire, which added its cheering crackle to the warmth of the cabin.

We drank our coffee on the porch sitting in mismatched wicker rockers. Miles put one boot heel on the low railing, then nestled her other heel at her ankle. The sun came in bright, dancing patterns through the wind-woven trees.

A large black bird appeared, dropping from tall pines near the cabin. Landing on the bar of the hitching rail, it strutted toward us. First one eye studied us, then it turned its head to find what the other black eye saw. A goiter-like ruff under its throat and unkempt head feathers combined to give it a rowdy appearance.

"A crow," I whispered. "I've never seen one so close."

"That's a raven checking us out." Miles took my hand. "Much chunkier than a crow. This rascal must live here, sees us as the interlopers."

"We are. I'm feeling examined." I laughed.

The raven raised its head, gave out a metallic "*Toc*," hopped once, then flew to the top of a nearby tree.

Out of the blue Miles said, "It will be mighty lonely when you go."

We drew together, embracing. I nuzzled my soft downy cheek against Miles' forehead.

The kisses started with comfort and tenderness, traveling soon into quick-breathed desire. I loved the fact we could sit on a front porch, breezes rippling through our hair, tongues touching in the softest way, lips, eyelids, and know we were in the wilds, away from anyone.

It felt so good to be close and happy, pressed tight together, life and heat radiating from our bodies. It became obvious my guard had dropped. In fact had dropped out of sight. That familiar ever-present cool veil had been torn — not violently but softly — by Miles. For the time being, I would accept that, yet a rush of fear, like a tiny trapped animal ran looking for an exit.

I closed my eyes, calmed my fears and tried to stay in the here and now.

Inside, the cabin was a sauna. We left the door ajar allowing some of the heat to escape. The only sounds that could be heard were lips, tongues, buttons, and zippers. Layers of denim and flannel pooled the rug. I ran my fingertips down her ribs then cupped the round buttocks in each palm. I took a step to lead Miles toward the bed, but tripped on the jeans hobbling my ankles. I fell across the bed.

"Very romantic," Miles laughed. She helped me take my jeans off the rest of the way.

We took our time exploring each other. Damp places under the curve of breast. How the nipples sat on the roundness. The moons of the cuticles of fingernails gently grazing skin. The degree of curliness of the pubic hair. That particular smell each woman carried as her own. And the taste.

I rolled my tongue over the rise of Miles' small breast, finding the junction place of arm. I burrowed into her armpit where I snuffled, taking in the rank, unrefined incense. Traces of soap aroma lingered there, fading under her own scent.

With force, I realized how much I'd missed this realness of a woman. Rhonda had kept herself so squeaky clean and perfumed that her own flavor had been totally masked. I remembered the douche bag hanging in Rhonda's shower stall. It was put to heavy use.

I nibbled, licked and whuffled my way over Miles' body.

Miles was delighted with this robust approach. Neither of us could have been called passive. Up until the moment my mouth closed over the springy pubic hair, parting it eagerly with my tongue, it was undecided who would be first. Passion rose like fire consuming dry pine branches, and I rode the heat wave.

We never noticed the eyes watching us, round with interest.

21

The wool blanket Miles pulled over us as the cabin cooled smelled of lanolin, and warmed our bodies as if a small flock had gathered around us. Only an hour had passed, but already muffled sleeping sounds, snorts and hums, came from Miles. I lay awake studying the details of the room; the lacework of orange rust at the stovepipe junctions, a small shelf made from a slab of split wood, holding a couple of Zane Grey novels placed between *Western Birds*, and *Treasure Island*.

There were no curtains on the windows and I could see the raven pecking at a shiny button on my jeans jacket, draped across the porch rail.

The cabin was very plain and yet it was somehow easy for me to imagine myself living here a hundred years ago.

Miles stirred smoothly against my skin. I felt utterly delicious lying next to her. An open, straightforward predictable aura surrounded Miles. I suddenly stiffened, not trusting that it was real. I couldn't see any hidden dark corners in her but they must be there.

She nuzzled her face against my breast. Her scar showed the shiny path between eye and ear. Tracing my finger its length, I asked her how she'd got it.

"Back in my rodeo days, I was heading in the team roping with my buddy." At my puzzled expression she explained further. "I roped the head and my bud roped the hind feet. I rode a borrowed horse and he didn't stop as quick as I asked, so that steer ducked behind. Most horses don't like a rope under their tails. This one blew up, bucked me off right there in the middle of the arena. A razor sharp edge of his worn shoe brushed my cheek. Beaucoup blood."

Miles bounced up and retrieved her cold clothes from the floor. "Yikes, this is torture," she said, pulling them onto her rapidly goose bumping body.

She lifted the covers to shove my cold clothes in beside me. "It's warmer outside, I swear. Seems to take forever for the chill to get off these old cabins in the spring. You getting up?"

One of our horses neighed. An answering neigh came from somewhere up the hill, and that brought me upright.

"Did one of our horses get loose?" I asked Miles.

We both headed for the door, I pulling on one boot as I hopped. Miles threw the cabin door back. In a puzzled voice she said, "No. They're all here. Prissy, wait! Where's Night? She's gone."

I looked out past her. Prissy paced alone in the corral. "Did she jump the fence? Do you think — " Then I got the willies.

Miles stepped out to the far end of the porch and searched the timber behind the house. The gray in her eyes glinted like gun metal and her lips were firm. "Somebody just came right in here and took your black mare. Let's get out of here."

"We have to get Night," I said. "I can't leave without her."

For the first time I saw fear in Miles' expression. "Honey. You're going to have to."

In short order we closed the cabin and got our horses out of the corral. She opened the gate to let the mule run along with us.

"We'll get Lance to watch out for her, check the Triple Dot. You'll get her back. They've run out of places to hide horses." After a fairly lengthy pause Miles said, "They must need her for some reason, or they'd have just shot her."

"It's frightening to think somebody came that close while we were in the cabin. Making love."

Miles took me in her arms for a moment. "Yeah, I thought we were completely alone."

"The mare can be such a snake. If somebody took her for transportation he'd have to be a good rider."

"Personally, I hope she kicks the shit out of him."

The trail back led through a grove of aspens, shimmering young, pale green leaves in the sunlight. Light grey trunks seemed stark white, in contrast. At the crest of the ridge, crossing over to the dry southern exposure, the trees thinned out.

I caught Miles studying our back trail and asked, "Do you think we're being followed?"

"Haven't seen any sign." She looked at me. "Could've been anybody. Night might've jumped the fence to join another horse. Forest Service rides up here to check on the grass. They'll make you move your cows off if it gets too short." Her voice sounded distracted.

"Think it's a forester?"

"No," she admitted. "Usually he calls me first."

22

When we got back to the ranch we found Norburt and the neighbor sitting side by side on the bunkhouse porch, Norburt with his overnight bag on his lap. The neighbor rocked with his big Stetson in his lap, booted ankle resting across the opposite knee of his blue jeans. A large smile spread over Norburt's face as we rode up. His companion rose, stretched his back in an arch, put his hat on, and said, "How's Becky?" He nodded politely at me.

"Any trouble, Ned?"

"No, no trouble. Burt wanted to come home. Said he worried about you. Not even a new litter of rabbits was enough." He reached out a hand to shake Norburt's. "Come see us again, Burt."

"Okay." Norburt created an opera of snuffles and snorts.

"You're still feeling punk, aren't you, Burtie?" Miles said.

Norburt took a large, crumpled white handkerchief from his pants pocket and blew his nose. He sounded like migrating geese. His soft dark eyes looked dismally at Miles. "Yeah."

We tucked Norburt into bed.

"He's not getting much better," Miles observed on the way back to the house. "Think I'll get him in to see his doctor. God, I wish he'd stayed away. I'm scared they'll try to hurt him. Can't leave him alone again."

After making an appointment for Norburt, Miles spoke to Lance, who had nothing to report on Buster yet. "It's obvious," I said, "that Buster's been the one watching us, and now he has Night. Can't they use helicopters to spot them?"

Miles gave me a funny look. "Just think of the square miles they'd have to cover. And the expense."

∽

We went to bed in Miles' room, both of us slipping easily over the edge of awareness into our own dreams. I lay curled into the bow of Miles' body.

The morning brought us awake and instantly aroused. Long slow breaths of sleep became shallow, quick. The sound of Norburt's boots on the porch brought Miles out of bed fast. "Damn! We overslept."

"I can think of a better reason for that 'damn.'"

At breakfast, Norburt sat red-eyed and upright at the table. His hair, wet-combed and parted at the side as usual, looked orderly above his carefully ironed plaid shirt. Between halfhearted mouthfuls, he swore he was feeling better.

"Are you going away today?" he asked, looking at his sister and me.

"No." Miles handed him a glass of orange juice.

Norburt smiled and took the glass in two hands to drink.

"I've got a doctor's appointment for you, Burtie, on Monday."

Norburt asked, "In Helena? Doctor Tom?"

"Yes. I'll take you in . . . "

"But, Miles," I interrupted "Aren't you supposed to pick up Skipper in Butte that day?" I had an idea. "I could take you to the doctor, Burt. Is that all right?"

Seeing his happy smile, I realized that Norburt liked me. Well, I liked him, too.

Kindness and affection held this family together. A certain simplicity in the way they treated each other reached deep into me.

∽⑨

Dinner dishes done, I made a call to Victoria to bring her up to date. Afterwards a lonely feeling washed over me and I felt an urge to be alone. I went outside in the angled last light of day.

Homesickness tugged at me. I turned my thoughts to solving the problems I needed to in order to return to all that was familiar.

Things might be moving now, I thought, feeling excited as I walked down the long driveway. The unfettered sky was clear and bright, the shadows, distinct and long. I picked up a stone to fling at a fence post. It hit with a hollow clunk. We were going to stop those killers.

Digging like an archaeologist, I brushed off and examined all the small pieces of information. I remembered once reaching for the tack room key, kept in its hiding place nook, and suddenly realizing that Buster was watching me. Normally insignificant incidents grew new meaning.

And now we knew that Leila was involved. The coincidence was too great for it not to be the same woman as the one in Middlebury. Buster must have met her at a show. He was often the show farrier, available if one of the horses threw a shoe, mid-event. So now we had Jack Logan and a guy named Frank who also knew Velma Smith, Leila and Buster. Was Leila the common connector?

Grasshoppers clicked and flew ahead of me. I kicked a small rock as far as I could, and walked back through a cloud of fine dust stirred up by a frolicking gust of wind.

Something bright flashed from the rocks on the hill. Metal or glass? I suddenly felt very exposed.

23

The whole way down the driveway I had the creepiest sensation along my back and neck. I found Miles coming out of the bunkhouse carrying an empty tray.

"I think somebody's watching us from up there," I said, pointing as I got near. "I saw a flash of something reflecting sunlight from those rocks."

She laughed a little. "I think we're getting jumpy. There's an old dump and a lot of broken glass on that ridge."

"Now they've got Night, what else would they want?"

"You," Miles said, matter-of-factly. It wasn't said lightly. A certain tightness showed in the muscles around her eyes.

Of course the horse theft ring wanted me dead. I knew where the parts were and how they fit together . . . well, mostly. I could identify Buster.

"Whoever wants you has to come through me," Miles stated.

Her strength drew me to her. It was the strangest thing; that I, who always was the "strong" one, loved this about Miles. My guts fluttered, a smile wavered. I didn't want to fall in love with this woman but it was happening. Or maybe had happened. I thought I was protecting myself. Using an emotional condom. Must've had a hole in it, I smiled sheepishly.

Opening the screen door Miles asked, "What's the joke?"

I said to this woman, who by her nature demanded honesty from me, "I'm afraid of getting too attached to you."

Miles hung her cap on the peg by the door. She walked over to the white curtained window to stand looking out, absently fingering the open work at the hem. She let her forehead rest on the warm glass.

"What's too?"

I crossed the floor to stand behind Miles. Butting my head against her armpit, I then burrowed under it as she enfolded me with her arm. Quietly, each of us soaked up the warmth, the reassuring contact of cloth and smells of each other.

"What'll we do?" I asked, not expecting an answer. "This is painful." I squirmed out from under her arm to face her, resting back against the window frame. "I thought I was through with all this. Relationships are more trouble than they're worth."

A soft laugh, and weathered wrinkled eyes met me head-on. Miles pulled me to her, cupping my head against her shoulder with her hand. She stroked my cheek with a callused finger. "Oh, hell. We're lucky to have anything as nice as this, for however long we have each other."

I felt myself sink into this protected place, sheltered in Miles' casual strength. Yet I was aware I still resisted, trying to keep myself from feeling so safe. Like a wool rug on a polished floor, safety could be yanked out from under you without notice.

Without either of us speaking, we turned and walked to the bedroom. Lying close, we stroked each other and talked of ordinary things for a while.

I nuzzled my nose against Miles. "Whoof, now that's sweat. Oooh, baby! "

"Ladies glow, remember?"

"I was going to say you remind me of a wart hog."

Miles laughed, tickling me. "Don't like your smelly cowgirl so well today, is that it?" She jumped off the bed. "Let's take a bath."

While the water ran hard and hot into the bathtub, we stood on the white chenille bath mat as close as skin would allow.

Hands spread full out, I traveled over Miles' body. Through the skin of my fingertips and palm came the tenderness, the softness covering the hard muscles, and I smiled at the contrast to my lover's worn, exposed face and hands. These were tanned a rich brown, like supple well-used leather oiled by hands and horses and weather to its own distinct character. But the skin my hands toured was the soft, pale underbelly of a woman.

I was roused from my meditation on Miles' body by the rasp of her hands crossing my buttocks. Miles reached down to mix in cool water and throw in some bath salts.

Cool air rushed into the space where Miles had been, to flow over my breasts and stomach. Trickles of sweat ran down my sides and clung to the crease under my breasts. Other moisture traveled the insides of my thighs. Deeply, I drew in a full breath, hardly realizing my breathing had been so shallow and rapid as to leave me breathless.

Miles turned her face to me as she ran her fingers through the bath water. "Ready?"

"Oh, am I!"

Miles stepped into the water, then slid to the back, opening her legs to make room for me.

I put my hands on my hips, the lightness tinged with an undercurrent of seriousness, and said, "I can't believe that a woman as sexy and attractive as you, is hanging around in an available condition."

Miles' laugh was short, aimed at herself. "Hard to believe, isn't it?"

Slowly, I let myself into the bath, getting used to the heat by degrees. I settled back against Miles, who rested her chin on my hair.

"Of course I'm loaded with flaws. Everybody is. And I'm married to this ranch. There aren't many gals who would like to share it with me and my brother." She paused, adding, "Or who I'd like to share it with."

Her hands covered the roundness of my breasts. "Now, you are an exception. I could happily grow old with you here."

Silence held me tight. I realized whatever I did, I'd lose. It was time to build a wall around my feelings for Miles and put them in perspective. And keep them there. There was no way I'd leave Victoria, my friends, Putney Friends Meeting, the farm. Moonglow would never be able to make the move, adapt to a strange place. Move for love? Don't be a fool.

Abruptly I sat up, snatched the bar of soap and busily applied it to a washcloth. "I should be out of here within a week."

At first it seemed easy to talk like this, with my back to Miles. Yet, underneath my hard shell, I knew her face filled with pain and my own heart felt pierced. Ignoring the fact of my faulty shield, I talked on, refusing to acknowledge the harshness of my words.

"Buster has got to be a central actor in this terrorist ring. It's a simple matter of fitting the people together, and breaking the ring. When that's done, I'll go back home."

"Jane, Jane." She nudged me. "It's me back here, remember?"

The thin shell, holding my feelings for Miles at bay, cracked and shattered, the first time my shell had let me down. My weeping became overlaid by sobs. Sinking back, I let her enfold me. I turned sideways, curling up, allowing the warm water to climb up over my shoulders, wet my hair. The bath water took my tears.

She held me close, while scooping handfuls of warm foamy water to keep me warm. She petted me with the bubbles.

Softly Miles spoke. "I'll survive either way, you know. I've gotten along with my own company for years, even though I may be the world's most boring person."

She continued, quieter still, "The loneliness will come when you go. The long winters, silent mealtimes. I kid you not, it'll be hard to step back from this and wave to the airplane taking you out of my life, climb into the truck and ride home with my arm around Skip."

The bath water cooled. Miles reached up with her big toe to push the drain lever down. "But it's the way things are."

The water, slowly at first, then with an increasing rush, left the tub. Our bodies seemed to become much heavier. Miles stood, reached for a towel and wrapped me. We dried each other, still silent, and climbed between the cold sheets of Miles' bed. She drew the wool blanket up under our chins and we waited for the bed to warm.

Sadness carried over into our lovemaking. It was increasingly difficult to ignore my personal danger and eventual exit from Montana. A sense of desperation filled us.

Prairie-fire passion swept over me, then across Miles' body. I lay on top, hands stroking her shoulders, soft lips and tongue following the swales and breaks. My eyes, up close to the fine grass-hair, could see the land from a homesteader's view. A sentinel nipple rose high. The wind sighed mildly, carrying the sun's warmth. My fingers, seeking moisture, found a spring among damp, curled moss. A lark sang.

Later, as we drifted in a state of soft bliss, Miles asked quietly, "When we were in the bathtub you spoke of your blacksmith being in a terrorist ring. Did you know that?"

"Oh, I didn't mean that. I meant theft ring."

"I figured that. But didn't you say your parents were killed by a terrorist-planted bomb?"

A barely audible, "Yes," came from me.

In the long forming silence, I could feel all the heat from the bath leave my body.

"Want to talk about it?"

I shot the covers back, shoved pillows behind myself and sat up. I yanked the blankets to my waist. "I hate even thinking about it. I can't stop. I wasn't even there, but images still come to me. They died when I was seventeen."

Miles put her arm around me, and I accepted her comfort.

"Images from the television replayed in my mind even more often than on the screen. And photographs in magazines, I would stumble across, then freeze to, searching for something familiar."

"You need to put this to rest, don't you?" Miles asked.

I turned to face her. "Yes. I've been so helpless about — I need to find these killers."

She kissed me, snuggling my head between her ear and shoulder.

"Maybe it wasn't a slip of the tongue, calling Buster and his gang terrorists." I said. "There is a connection. The horse killing is random and yet so planned. The terrorists kill for some insane political reason. Rich performers in horse shows kill, not for money, but for the intangible glory of winning. To replace a loser with a winner. I feel so scared by the coldness of it all."

We lay in each other's arms for a while and I allowed Miles to silently comfort me.

That evening, Miles took a glass dish of lasagna from the freezer chest, then placed it in the microwave on a defrost cycle.

"How'd you like to help with the chores? Norburt should stay in bed. He'll want to get up and help me if he sees me doing them alone. Besides, you have me weak as a kitten."

We loaded the flatbed with hay and Miles showed me how to drive the tractor. While I drove, Miles broke bales and threw them off the back in a long, bright green ribbon. Cows and calves gathered, forming a dark furrow in the hay.

Returning to the house we found it perfumed with the delicious aroma of lasagna. The phone rang. "Hello," Miles' breath came out in a rush. "Oh, sure." She covered her face with her wide hand. "Yeah, you bet. Right. Ten o'clock."

She turned to me, her expression stricken. "I'd completely forgotten. Tomorrow's branding." She shook her head again. "There's a hell of a lot to do. All my relatives, cousins, friends, all with kids, are coming to help. We do it on weekends. Every other week, another ranch. This year I'm last and, look at the house! Will you help?"

Her desperate appeal made me smile. "Of course. What do you need?"

"Could you start cleaning? I've got to set things up to feed in the corrals first thing in the morning. And sort the pairs. Crud! Where did I leave the branding irons?" Miles went through the front door, mumbling to herself.

Later, while I vacuumed, dusted and mopped floors, Miles took a roast beef from the deep freeze and a ham from the basement cold locker. Both roasts would go into the oven tomorrow. She poured three pounds of dried beans into a colander, picked them over, washed, then set them aside to soak. "My friends will bring the rest of the food."

She stood, looking tired, staring at the shining appliances, clean counters and linoleum floor. "You sure have done a nice job in here. Thanks."

24

In the morning, Miles slipped out of bed while the sky was pitch dark. I got up with her to start the beans cooking, get the roasts ready to put into the oven, and help her sort the cow-calf pairs from the rest of the herd and drive them into a large corral. Murna worked hard that morning. When Miles and I came back into the house, the automatic coffee maker had done its job.

"That'll hit the spot." Her eyes smiled over the rim as she sidled up to me. She brushed her face against my hair, then kissed my earlobe.

"That extra dog, Murna, might work out after all and not be just a pet for Norburt. We did a piece of work already today."

Miles set her coffee cup down and slid her hand under the warmth of my shirt. "I almost prayed for rain when I woke up this morning and saw you on the pillow next to me."

I pushed her hand away with a laugh, then firmly did up the buttons. "Oh? What's rain have to do with it?"

Franci McMahon

"Can't brand. Hot irons don't work on wet hide. The steam burns the little critters, and it's rough enough on them anyway. Besides, just think about it. Kneeling in mud, handling wet rope. We cancel when it's like that. While it's a job that has to be done, I find I'm reluctant to miss any bed time with you."

I heard the sadness underneath the playfulness. I sat in Miles' lap, in the sling of her batwing chaps.

"The crew won't start arriving until about ten-thirty. It looks like we are ready, wife." Miles stood easily, lifting me along with her, then set my feet to the floor. She looked pretty pleased with herself.

I returned her smile but inwardly felt a flash of concern that Miles was getting in too deep. The smile lingered on my lips with a twist of irony. It was myself who had me worried. It felt both scary and deeply wonderful to be called wife. And so incorrect.

Miles said, "I took Norburt some hot cereal. He's not getting any better. He's pissed as hell he'll miss branding."

Trucks pulling horse trailers started arriving early.

Tess Reilly, Miles' cousin, a no-nonsense, friendly, plain woman, came in the door with a covered dish and two children around eight and nine years old. Both wore chaps and boots and these weren't Roy and Dale outfits; these kids grew up roping and riding beside their parents.

Miles introduced me as Jane, and I realized our pretense of a different identity had passed its usefulness.

On the porch, I listened to the clatter of horses backing off trailers, shouted greetings among the ranchers, a few aloof growls from the working dogs.

Miles was questioned about Skipper. She cut the story to the bare bone. "In the animal hospital in Butte. Be home on Monday."

At first I felt a little shy, but Miles' friends soon made me comfortable. The relaxed banter, excited children and covered dishes arriving in the kitchen gave a festive air to the day.

I asked Tess, "Do the women work with the cattle, too?"

"You bet! Why sit back and let the guys have all the fun?" Tess laughed, her head tossed back. "Branding is one of the highlights of the social season. Come on. Let's go out and get some action."

Horses stood tied to the hitching rail, sides of trailers, and anything else solid enough to hold them. As we led our horses out to the corrals, Tess filled me in on some local history.

"Used to be the gals worked all day on the food to have it ready for the men when branding was done. They served the guys at a sit-down meal. One year, one of the ranch women — I think it was Mary Carter, of the Forked Diamond — set the tables up for a buffet at her ranch, got on her horse and shook out her rope. She roped with the best. That changed things fast." Tess casually adjusted her own rope bag as she smiled at me. "Want to try? Buck's a good roping horse. I've seen Miles do some nice work off him. He'll take care of you."

I considered this for only an instant. "I guess I won't." Childhood fantasies of being a famous trick roper returned to mind. I smiled as I watched the children riding into the mass of calves, loops swinging above their heads. They probably have the same dreams, I thought.

I'd often wondered how feminism had fared in the West. I suspected it had been met with Brahma bull resistance, but watching Tess take up her piece of ground with authority, I suspected it wasn't an easily told story.

Standing beside Buck on the fringe of the action, I watched for a while. Cows, separated from the calves in an adjacent corral, bellowed without letup in an effort to locate their babies. In the branding corral, calves huddled in a teeming black and red mass, bawling for their mothers. Human voices yelled over the din. Dogs watched silently from the sidelines with no work to do, restless, wanting to be in the thick of it.

The roar of the propane forge, mounted in the back of a pickup, smothered all but the strongest sound. The handles of the ranch branding irons poked out of the forge. The truck was parked just inside the main corral gate. One of the teenagers kept an eye on the propane tanks, guarding the hot branding irons and shooing the smaller kids away.

I watched each calf get roped by the hind feet, dragged away from the herd, bleating pitifully, then get branded, have a piece notched out of one ear, be given an injection, and released. The bull calves had already had rubber bands placed around their testicles at birth, for a slow, mostly pain-free, castration. Testicle Festivals or feasts of mountain oysters, breaded and deep-fried, or simply tossed into the branding fire to cook, were a rarity these days, Miles had told me.

It looked like a football huddle with everyone crouched over a terrified calf. Each person had a different job. At least the procedure was over quickly. When the dazed calf was released to stagger to its feet, the younger children chased it into a separate corral.

The adults stood back to let the children get good roping practice before the calves became too wary. The children loved the time to rope real calves with an admiring and doting audience of parents and peers.

I tied Buck to one of the corral posts and walked over to the branding fire. "Hi. I'm Jane. Anything I can do to help?"

"Sure," answered the fourteen-year-old boy. "Can you give shots?"

At my nod, he ambled over to the table holding the biologicals, stumbling on the way, all legs and angles, ungainly in a graceful sort of way. Someday, I thought, this boy will grow into six feet of coordinated cowboy.

"My name's Ted." He filled a contraption resembling a grease gun with a short needle on one end. He set the large bottle on the table. "Give each calf five cc's in the right arm pit."

"Subcutaneous?" I asked.

"Yeah, just lift up a flap of skin and put it right underneath."

Before long I was part of the action. Into the armpit went my needle as the calves were held down like wrestlers on a mat. Stinking smoke of burning hair blew around me. When the air became too repulsive to breathe, I tucked my nose against my arm. Someone offered to let me do the ear-notching instead of shots, but I refused, imagining the crunch through the cartilage, hundreds of times worse than the gruesome memory of getting my own ears pierced.

Eventually my stomach did a slow turn and I searched for the nearest truck to puke behind. Miles turned up at my side. "Come on, you need a break."

"It's barbaric. Do they have to be branded and ear-notched? Why brand them when you put those plastic ear tags in their ears at birth, anyway?"

Miles raised her notebook. "We record the cow's number and her calf's soon as the tag goes in, that's true, but those tags can get ripped out the first week the calves are up in the timber. Besides, it's the easiest thing in the world for a rustler to cut them out and put in their own. We notch the ears so you can recognize your own stock at a distance. Often, at roundup time, all you can see is a pair of vigilant ears poking up from the brush, and you're looking for a notch in the bottom of the right ear. Those cows can get pretty spooky on summer range."

Miles smiled at me. "Believe it or not, the ranchers are looking for a better way, too. Most of them recognize it's a horrible experience for the calves, even if they only see it in terms of growth rates and losses. But tomorrow these calves will act like nothing ever happened."

Miles watched one of the other women toss a rope, landing it neatly around the hind feet of a calf. "The branding is the hardest part. They'll be sore. I wouldn't be surprised if soon we have a tiny micro chip embedded under the skin that you can scan by running them through a chute."

"They already have that for horses — oh, but you know that."

Both of us fell silent, transported to the seal brown horse at the auction, and the awful sound of legs striking each other as the horse rolled over. Out of the corner of my eye I saw Miles shake the memory away.

"Why don't you try roping for a change? Don't forget to wear gloves, and try it from the ground at first. Start out on one of the young calves. If you manage to catch one it won't drag you very far," Miles said with a snort. She handed me a lariat, then left me standing in the busy corral.

At first, watching Miles thread her way into the hectic action, I thought, no way. But then, why not? Nobody will notice if I miss. Besides, if the kids can do it, I'm sure I can too.

I thought the children cute and funny as the calves scooted out from under the thrown lariats with the ease of a Houdini. The laughter was different when I was out there and had slapped the backs of three calves with my noose and fallen once, slipping on a very wet calf pie. My performance was complete when I roped one of the largest calves around the neck and was then pulled half way across the corral until I realized I could simply let go of the rope.

Leaving the corral, it was hard to see through the dust and grit caught in my eyelashes. Dirt ground between my teeth. Into my head popped the determination that if, IF, mind you, I moved out here, next year I would be the slickest roper they had ever seen.

Tess and one of the cousins smiled encouragingly at me, and with good humor scraped at a calf pie remnant on my sleeve, gently trying to cheer me. I smiled at myself, feeling silly. They were treating me the same way they did the children, to buck up my sagging confidence.

"Thanks. I can see I've some practicing to do."

Just then the overlaying roar of the propane forge died, as though a jet plane had landed. We drifted over to see why it had stopped. Miles stood beside a man fumbling through his pockets.

"The tank's out," Miles said, switching to a fresh one. The guy pulled a match book from a pocket and handed it to Miles.

"Hey, we're waiting on the iron," someone yelled.

"Coming." Miles lit the forge, then asked, "Anybody have a ball point? Mine's dry." Miles shook the pen and tossed it in the trash can.

Someone handed Miles a retractable ball point pen. Instead of thanking him and sauntering away, she asked, "Where did you come across this, Doug?"

She passed it to me without looking my way. In my hand lay a ball point pen from T. J. Buckley's restaurant. The pen had been a fund-raiser for the Brattleboro AIDs Project.

Other than a long shot, too long to be believable, the only way this pen could have gotten out here was to be carried by the horse thieves, Frank or Buster. Or maybe Doug, himself? I looked at him more closely. But there was something wrong here. I guessed none of these guys would dine at T. J's. Buster and Frank were more likely the Al's Steak House type. I knew nothing of Logan. Could someone have picked this up on a visit east?

"Damn, I don't know where I got it. Is it important?"

"I can't tell you why it's important right now," Miles said, "but it is."

"Well, let's see." Under the pressure he turned to stare at Bull Mountain. "I can't remember."

"Try to think where you went over the last couple of weeks," I said.

Doug labored, trying to retrace his life. "Then on this last Tuesday, I had to go back to Montana Ranch Supply again. Damn part for the rake was wrong. Had to get a new one ordered, picked up a box of horse shoes while I was there, and that evening Tess and Pete dropped by."

"I didn't know you shod your own horses, Doug," Miles interrupted.

"I don't. They was for Jack Logan. I dropped them off on the way home. He had a friend from back east visiting. Gave me some good advice on shoeing a horse I have. Stupid thing's always cutting his legs up with his own feet."

We let Doug run on until his memory was spent.

❦

The corral began to empty out, branded calves and their mamas sent to recover from the experience to a large pasture with a long trail of alfalfa hay down its center. I decided to check on the feasting preparations, and placed on the back burner the information just learned. At the house, I found the tables already set up under the cottonwoods on the lawn. Sawbucks held boards covered with paper tablecloths.

The roasts and casseroles had filled the house with delicious aromas, and pies and salads covered the kitchen table. Washtubs filled with ice and pop had been set up on the lawn. A big coffee pot sat to one side. Bottles of Walker's Deluxe whiskey, surrounded by herds of small shot glasses, were arranged discreetly.

The feasting and partying carried into the evening. The children ran in groups like young antelope, making up games as they went along, and teaching the younger children old games learned from siblings and friends.

I listened to tales of other brandings, told in a society with a long past of story telling. Accounts of horses going berserk and bucking through barbed wire fences, everyone concerned for the horse, but the rider's injuries brushed off with a casual wave of the hand. One woman told of riding out with her brother to round up and bring close to the home ranch a band of young horses during a harsh winter. They'd found them grazing among a herd of nearly four hundred elk, driven down from the high country. Stories of Grizzly bears met on the trail. Of packing into the "Bob" — the Bob Marshall Wilderness area. I smiled to myself to realize only three subjects were worth the art of conversation; horses, cows and hunting, in that order.

At dusk, the first mosquitoes drove everyone back to their trucks and homes, back to routine lives.

25

When the phone rang we were sitting in the softest chairs in the living room, hot tea in our hands and silly contented smiles on our faces. It had been quite a day.

Miles reached for the black daffodil. "It's for you."

"Jane Scott?" a strange male voice asked.

"Yes?" I responded with a rising question.

"This is the FBI, Special Agent Smith speaking. We have reason to believe Bernard Wilde is involved in your kidnapping. He seems to have left Vermont. Do you have any information that could lead us to that individual?"

Stifling amusement at Buster's butching up his name, I answered, "He's in this with a rancher up here. His name is Jack Logan. You need to talk with the Sheriff of Jefferson County." I gave him the phone number.

"I have that number," the agent's cold voice responded. "What were you doing at Mr. Logan's farm, anyway?"

"Ranch," I corrected.

"Why do you think Mr. Logan is involved?" Agent Smith asked.

"I recognized a couple of the stolen horses in his corral."

"Oh? Were they branded or something?" The city-bred agent hadn't a clue as to how anyone would recognize a horse.

"A couple of them were. Buster Wilde was there, too. He chased after us."

"We'll send an agent. And, Miss Scott, it would be better if you let us do the investigating."

"Fine. I'd appreciate it if you would. My life is in danger."

"We found what we think is the horse truck."

"Van," I corrected unthinkingly. "Where?"

He hesitated, as if sifting through regulations for the go-ahead to tell me. "Outside Helena. Clancy," he added. "In an equipment barn. We haven't been able to trace the lessee yet. A corporation."

Then he popped the question, "Look, we'd like you to identify the van on Monday. Say, meet us in Clancy in front of the Post Office in the morning at ten?"

"Why not now?" I countered.

"It'll be dark soon and the inside of that shed will be as black as a Commie's heart."

Oh God, was this guy real? I stifled a laugh.

He continued, "Tomorrow is Sunday and I don't work on Sunday. Family day. This is a resolved kidnapping, so it can wait. Ten o'clock Monday."

"Make it nine. I have another appointment." I needed to take Norburt to the doctor. "You'd better coordinate your investigation with the County sheriff," I advised.

It didn't take a psychiatrist to discover he resented altering his time schedule, and any suggestions I might have.

For a moment I thought of calling Vic but it would be eleven o'clock on the east coast. Instead, I dialed the sheriff's office in Boulder. Deputy Bullock was on duty; Lance had gone home. I asked if they had been told the van had been found. "No, the Feds haven't said a word to us."

"It's in an equipment barn in Clancy. Any way to find out if Logan rented it acting as a member of a company?"

"Will do."

26

On Monday, in the post office parking lot I saw three vehicles, one of them nondescript, and one truck. I'd just decided upon the blue sedan as the most likely government issue when the truck door opened and a cowboy swung his long legs to the ground. Clean cut. Tall and good-looking. Not weathered as Miles was. As a chameleon, he was near perfect; however, one flaw told me immediately that this was the Fed.

He sauntered obliquely in our direction. I smiled blandly, waved and called out. "Hi, Agent Smith." He tripped then checked his surroundings over each shoulder. New at this, I thought. He walked to the driver-side window, casting a nervous glance at Norburt.

"How did you know it was me?" he asked.

I smiled. "Your jeans have a pressed crease down the front."

"So? My wife irons all my clothes."

"Ranch wives don't have time to iron blue jeans. If you're going to pose as a rancher you need to get it right."

"What's your name, bud?" Uninterested in my opinion, he questioned Norburt, who looked at his hands and shrank into himself. Murna, sitting on the back seat, fixed the Fed with a hard stare and lifted her lips.

"He's a friend." I wasn't going to let him grill Norburt. "Lead the way, will you? We have an eleven o'clock appointment in town."

The agent returned to his truck, wobbling slightly on his high-heeled cowboy boots. I followed him west out of the small town, where ponderosa pine grew sparsely over grassy hills. The road narrowed to a sandy strip with jack fencing running along the right side. We turned under a huge arched gateway. Hewn trees the size of telephone poles were set on either side of the ranch lane with a cross bar carrying a sign identifying the Running W. The road led down through dense pines to open up overlooking a ranch. The largest building was an equipment shed.

Pulling up my emergency brake, I turned to Norburt and said, "I have to go with this man. It won't be long. Wait here, all right?"

"I'll just sit here," he answered through his chest congestion.

Joining the agent, who showed a search warrant and his I.D. to the woman who exited the ranch house, I felt a surge of tense excitement. I'd believed, even hoped, I would never see the van again. Now I wanted this to be it. To resolve another piece to this mystery and free myself up to deal with the difficult issues ahead in my own life.

The ranch woman swept her thin hair from her forehead. "We rent this shed out. He'll be mad about this."

The agent obtained the renter's name and description. I listened, but whoever had rented the storage space was unfamiliar to me. He acted for a corporation; Big Sky Transport or something. The woman, her day suddenly taking a different shape, went back into the house for the spare key to the shed's padlock. Booming metal doors opened on the half-lit gray van. Here it was, the gray whale, sinister in its sea bottom filtered light. Fear dragged my feet through the dry dirt floor as I approached my former prison.

We entered the van through the cab door. This was my first look at the brain of the whale. Candy wrappers and discarded pop cans littered the space between the seats. Cigarette butts jammed the ash tray. A hula girl, suction cupped to the dash, wiggled as we moved through the cramped area. I pulled the connecting door open: here it was tidy. Someone had swept it out, including the manure, and even hosed off the urine. The horse blanket shackles were gone. But they had missed the little scrap of red material I had retrieved with my teeth from the sharp metal edge. It was close to the wall, partly covered with straw, hard to see in the dim light.

I felt as if something had just run up my neck, fleeing the scene. "This — " My voice was so rough I couldn't finish. Clearing my throat, I tried again. Pointing to the red rag, I said, "This tore off the horse blanket I was . . . " What were the words to show what that terrible prison was like? Wearing? Bound in. Trussed up. Demeaned in. Confined. Abducted. Seized. Trapped. Bagged. Kidnapped.

" — tied up in," I finished.

He pulled a camera from the prop saddle bags, took pictures of the red scrap *in situ*, then plucked it up to place it in an evidence bag.

I found myself staring at the bucket I had struggled to reach, so dry with thirst. I went back into the front of the rig.

"Don't touch anything," he said.

Staring out through the windshield, I saw the ranch woman pacing just outside the door to the shed and I wondered if she was involved. She looked pretty worried. Maybe renting this place made the difference for them financially. It might be hard to find someone else to lease this space.

While Special Agent Smith snooped around in back I imagined myself a driver on a long trip, examining the dash

FRANCI McMAHON

and around the sun visors, anyplace someone might absentmindedly tuck something. A picture of one's sweetheart, or dog, children. A phone number was written on the paint, scratched in light pencil. It seemed familiar. A Brattleboro, Vermont number. Eight-oh-two, five-five-five-two-five-four-four. Not Velma's number. That would be six-oh-three for New Hampshire. I groaned as I struggled to remember. This number was one I'd dialed, I was sure of it. When? I was bad with numbers, had to look them up every time. I jotted down the number on a small pad I carried in my jeans jacket.

When I returned, I'd call the number and see who answered. If there was no answer I knew Vic would know right off the bat, or could find out. I called out, "Hey, Smith. There's something here you might want to see."

❧

The wait at the doctor's office was long and the magazines boring: Wildlife magazines about how and where to kill animals, and dieting in a spotless house. Finally, Norburt was seen and given a prescription and some expectorant samples. We stopped first at the drugstore. The druggist took forever.

An increasing sense of urgency came over me. It was like watching puffy white clouds become yellowish grey storm clouds, the air crackling with electricity. On the way over the long pass going home, I held my foot to the floor, the car struggling to maintain sixty miles an hour.

Miles' truck was parked in front of the house. My shoulders relaxed with relief, and I realized my fingers were numb from gripping the steering wheel too tight.

"I wonder how Skippy is," Norburt said as he got out of the car, standing to one side for Murna to jump to the ground. He looked up at the house, expecting Miles to greet him.

"I'm sure Skip is getting better or the vet wouldn't have let her come home," I said. "Now we need to get *you* feeling better. I'm sure Miles will be out to see you in a minute."

We walked to the bunkhouse. While he got himself ready for bed, I set up a bedside table with the new comic books we had bought in town, cough lozenges and a glass of water.

When Norburt, dressed in his blue flannel pajamas, had crawled shyly between the sheets, I tucked him in. "We'll come a little later to check on you."

"Where's Murna?" Norburt asked.

"Here by the bed."

As I neared the front door of the house, Skipper's urgent barking alarmed me. I found the dog shut in my bedroom. Skip wagged her tail joyously at seeing me and tensely trotted in place; then she ran straight to the front door.

The note on the table seemed innocent at first. It said, *I'm off on a little pleasure ride. Meet me at the old cabin for a picnic. I've left Honey saddled. Becky.*

I read it over, knowing something was seriously wrong. My gaze went to the window. I saw Buck tied to the railing, one hind foot cocked, patiently napping. She called Buck, Honey and would never have signed a note to me with Becky.

Also I knew she never went for pleasure rides.

I looked at Skip, anxiously waiting for me to get a move on. Skip knew. Miles couldn't have made it any clearer; she was in trouble. The one who had taken Miles had laid a trap for me.

I got through to Lance at the Sheriff's office. I told him what I'd found when I got home, then read the note over the phone to him.

Worry came through the trained calm of his voice. "I know where that is. My dad used to go up there with Becky's dad."

"I do too. She took me there a few days ago."

He was silent a moment. "We'll need to get horses together. Damn, the four-horse gooseneck's in the shop — have to find other horse trailers. Don't go by yourself. Look,

FRANCI McMAHON

it could take us a while. As much as a couple hours. Wait for us."

"Two hours? How can I do that when some nut has Miles? No way. Where's Logan and Frank?" I asked. "I'll bet it's Buster who's kidnapped her."

"Can't be Buster. We picked him up an hour ago. He's telling an odd story."

"Don't believe a word of it. Hurry up 'cause I'm not waiting."

My glance went to the drawer beneath the telephone. Slowly, I opened it and lifted the phone book as Lance's insistent voice came over the wire. Then, very quietly, I hung up the receiver.

I stared at the silver Colt pistol. It must have been in the family for generations. I raised my hand to pick up the gun, then dropped it to my side again.

Oh, yeah, gunfight in the O. K. Corral, here we come. I slammed the drawer shut.

I thought, where are the saddlebags? I'd need binoculars, rope. What else?

I dashed out the door toward Buck. Miles had put the saddle bags on when she saddled him. Buck woke up white-eyed as I neared him, alert for danger. Trying to behave in a less threatening manner, I slowed, then examined both sides of the bags. Empty.

I'd have to tell Norburt something. Some reason Miles wasn't here. Making the best show of calm I could, I went to the bunkhouse. I made up something about Miles doing some job on her horse and that I would join her.

"Lance and some of his friends are coming for a visit. Let them know you're here. Keep Murna inside with you, okay?"

"Sis will be mad."

"It will be okay, today!" It was the best I could do.

Tearing back into the house, slamming the door, I tried to imagine the situation I'd be riding into. The edge of my mind licked on the steel of the gun. I pushed the thought away. Her words came back to me, "If someone were trying to kill me . . . " Taking a deep breath, filling every corner of my lungs, I slowly let it out.

I walked toward the door. My hand, almost involuntarily, opened the small drawer and removed the gun.

I didn't notice that I hadn't pulled the front door all the way closed. It was the chance Skip had been waiting for.

27

I wiped damp palms along the tops of my thighs, and gathered the reins. Buck trotted slowly over uneven ground.

How long would it take to get there at this pace? Would I be in time? I would give anything to know whether or not Miles had been hurt. My ears roared from the blood of fear pumping through my veins. Miles would die; I would lose her. I was the one who had brought danger and injury to this family. I groaned and Buck's ears flicked back to listen. He dug his hooves into the trail, responding to my legs.

The sky was a cloudless blue. Everything, from a single blade of grass to the soft sweep of the mountain peaks, held a shadow side as well as an illuminated brilliance.

An image of Buster appeared, arms like anvils, holding Miles. No, that wasn't right! Lance told me Buster had been arrested. It had to be Jack Logan and Frank who had taken Miles. Or, with any luck, just one of them. I didn't think Frank would kill, but I had no idea about Jack. He had quite a lot at stake, protecting his political status as commissioner and his standing in the community. He might be ruthless.

The fear slid from my mind into the deepest part of my belly. I doubled over the saddle horn and closed my eyes, tight.

What am I, some kind of lethal gene that attaches to those I love? Had I, in some hidden dark part of me, believed my love would kill?

If we could just get through this, I'd go back to Vermont and Miles could go on living her life. I'd like to think of her with her feet on the ottoman in front of the gas fire. No, better, in the stirrups.

Buck's ears pricked. Faintly, I heard a horse neigh and brought Buck to a halt. I watched his ears for clues. They swiveled like radar, then locked onto the gulch beyond the old mine drift. A low, almost soundless whicker came from the gelding. I could see Tiger through the trees. He wasn't in the little corral but tied in front of the cabin. The horse was way too clearly bait for me to dismount, tie up Buck and saunter through the door. Hair raised erect on the back of my neck.

Picking my way through the thick aspens, I circled to the rear of the cabin. Angling deeper into the woods, I dismounted and tied Buck to a tree. Reaching into the saddlebags, I removed the binoculars. My hand bumped the rigid metal of the revolver and I recoiled.

I pressed my forehead against Buck's warm neck while he squeaked the saddle with a deep breath. Avoiding the basic decision — to take the gun or leave it behind — I untied the saddle strings and slung the bags over my shoulder.

It was very quiet. The raven too, was silent. The clearing in front of the cabin was a pool of flickering light. I crept closer until I had an unrestricted view of the window above the bed.

Just in front of my boot tips I saw a bright scrap of litter, crackly and fresh. A Hall's Menthol Eucalyptus drops wrapper. I knew someone had sat here looking into the window.

When we were in there? Of course. My stomach churned.

I balled up the paper and pitched it away from me in disgust.

Pulling the binoculars out of the bag, I focused on the cabin window. A slow examination showed no movement. But I couldn't expect to see any. They would be watching through the front window in the belief that I would ride up to the front door, unsuspecting.

Or would they? It was all a bit too obvious with Tiger parked out front. Instead of rushing into a trap I needed to work this out. After all, I did have two hours to wait for Lance and his boys. But when I imagined Miles being tortured or violated I wasn't so sure I could.

What, if I were a spider, would I do to catch a fly? I'd get a clear line of fire, for one thing. To shoot me.

It was hard to focus on an intellectual problem with the fear of a bullet ripping through me so vividly on my mind.

It all depended on if one or two people had abducted Miles. My guess was that Frank would not be involved in this. He would cut and run. That left Jack.

From where I sat I could not see the open mine shaft, but I remembered that from the front door of the cabin it was a clear view of the Lady Smith mine. The distance was no more than a hundred feet. An easy shot with a rifle.

Adding it up, I knew they were not in the cabin. They waited in the mine.

I rocked back to sit on the dirt, scanning the area between me and the mine. Glimpses through the intervening trees showed the orange pile of waste dirt and rock that fanned out from the mouth of the old mine shaft. The dark hole, framed with aged orange fir beams, was not visible. I worked my way a little closer. Raising the binoculars again, I could see nothing but a wooden box near the entrance.

I glanced at my watch to find only an hour had passed. Lance and the posse wouldn't get here for, at least, another two hours. I couldn't afford to wait. If Miles was being hurt while I just sat here waiting I'd never forgive myself.

Then I remembered the horse I'd heard neigh up the gulch. I'd heard a soft hello-nicker from Tiger to his old friend but this other horse was worried. The ringing neigh had come from the kidnapper's horse.

I smiled with an idea. Horses are always freeing themselves. Some untie themselves and others simply set back and break their halters. I'd turn any horses loose so they'd run past the entrance to the mine. A horse was a getaway car. Whoever was there would have to come out to catch them. Either from the mine or cabin.

I backed up, watching the mine. An elk trail led roughly in the direction I wanted. Behind a large cluster of interwoven boulders waited a familiar horse tied to an exposed root. Night actually nickered softly to me. I gave her little scratches in greeting, wondering at my attachment to this feisty mare.

There was no other horse nearby. Must be only one man to deal with, I thought with some relief. I hoped it was Frank, my take on him being that when it came down to it he would shy at murder.

"I'm so glad you're safe," I whispered as I softly pulled her ears. "Now I'm going to turn you loose and I want you to kick ass. Be a mare with attitude."

I led her down near the drift opening, pulled the halter off, leaving the bridle in place, then shooed her into a gallop. Night tore past the mine, happy to run after days without freedom. Snorting and blasting out great farts, she ran kicking through the clearing. Large clumps of sod flew up behind her feet. Tiger reared backward, his reins broke, allowing him to join Night's frolic.

A man in the drift opening scrambled to his feet, shouting. His voice filled the vessel of the mine shaft, rolling over and over the walls.

I was ready with the gun pointed at the dark hole. But I wasn't prepared for the angry man who burst into view.

"Dr. Burns!"

Had Dr. Burns already rescued Miles? Maybe Frank or Jack Logan were out in the woods? I spun around, wildly pointing the gun behind me. No one exploded out of the trees.

Through the fog of crazy denial I heard his angry shouts. His whole attention was on the two horses bucking as they ran. He turned, face red with anger, spittle spraying as he shouted.

I was shocked at the sight of my affable, friendly, yarn-telling vet from New England, now utterly transformed.

"Damn you, Jane. You've screwed everything up." He took a step toward me.

"Hold it right there," I said, the pistol in my hand adding authority to my words. I had seen the writing on the wooden box behind him. DYNAMITE.

It didn't take a genius to add it up: Burns meant to leave us both in the mine, set the charge and ride off. Hadn't Miles said these old shafts collapsed all the time? He must have believed it would be judged an accident. I had to find out if Miles was back in there, and if she was all right. I added another hand to hold the gun steady.

He glanced toward the rifle resting on his jacket in the drift opening. His face emptied of anger as if there were a drain in his Adam's apple, and a mask of heartiness took its place. With two fingers he reached into his pocket, unwrapped the object he withdrew and popped it into his mouth, dropping the wrapper on the ground. A Eucalyptus drops wrapper.

"Now, Jane. You won't shoot me, will you?" he asked with his broad smile. The inside corners of his eyebrows compressed horizontal forehead wrinkles into a tight band. The cough drop pushed out one side of his cheek. He was aiming for the cutely quizzical. He fell far short of his goal.

I needed something other than the gun to stop him. Something I could live with. I reached deep to my Quaker principle of relating to his inner light. "It was very hard for me when we found that chestnut mare dead. You didn't kill her, did you? I can't imagine you harming horses, or people. It's not too late to walk away from this bunch of horse thieves. Testify."

He began strolling across the mine waste pile toward me. He appeared to grow in size as he approached.

"You won't shoot me, Jane. You're a Quaker." He was close enough for me to see his big triangular teeth in his open-faced smile.

He used his horse-soothing voice as he came slowly forward, "Nonviolence is based on the inner light in everyone and no one should damage that. Or own it. The basis for antislavery, too. Isn't that it?"

I knew he was attempting to lull my defenses. "Where is she?" I demanded.

He stretched a hand out to me. "I'll bet you haven't even released the safety."

Damn, he was right. My mind flashed on all those stupidly portrayed heroines in high heels with their guns on safety. Trying to keep my focus on him I fumbled my fingertips over the gun's surface trying to find a button. Then I saw Miles, hands tied but standing at the drift entrance.

He lunged for me. I jumped to the side, the gun exploding a shot into the dirt at my feet. Burns tripped on the mine car tracks, sliding over the edge of the orange dune of drift diggings. His slick city shoes couldn't get a grip on the fine mine waste. He tore at the slope with his hands, his knees rammed into the dirt to stop his backward slide.

I dashed to the mine opening where Miles stood outlined by murky darkness. She held her wrists out, and I struggled to untie the knots.

Burns was making some headway up the steep, slithery surface of the mine refuse. The rope was too tight to quickly loosen. I made a quick decision and threw the gun deep into the drift, kicking Burns' rifle to join it.

FRANCI McMAHON

Miles' eyes over the gag were eloquent.

Burns scrambled up the slope and over the top. I had to do something to stop Burns. My searching gaze collided with the wooden box. I stepped to it, picked it up and running toward Burns, threw it at him.

The heavy box hit him in the middle of his chest, knocking him down and the wind from his lungs.

Then I saw a flash of movement. A blue-flecked aspect of the Furies now stood guard over Burns. Skip exposed her teeth showing a compacted line of snarled dog lip, black nose pointed at his throat. Skipper's growl was low and serious. This time Dr. Burns was down to stay.

Miles pushed a hip forward in mute command. I felt a knife through the denim of her jeans pocket. The knife made the job easy. I tried to undo the hard knot of the bandana, and ended up cutting the cloth away.

Miles licked her lips and ran her tongue around the inside of her mouth. She shook her head. "Too damn close. Lance coming?"

"Yes," I croaked.

Keeping an eye on Burns, Miles shook her arms and fingers, trying to get the full range of feeling and movement back. "Thought I was going to cash in my chips this time. I kept thinking, shoot him, shoot the bastard. I'm thankful Skip isn't a pacifist."

I threw my arms around Miles, relief making my knees spongy. "I was so scared he had already hurt you."

"Well, he didn't. But he still could. We can't rely on Skip to keep him harmless. I'll recycle this rope."

"I've got some more in the saddle bags. I left them up there." I looked uphill.

"Hold up a minute. I'll get a gun first." Miles picked up Burns' dropped flashlight, and went back into the drift. Soon she emerged holding a gun, and squatted near Burns.

"You shot my dog, mister. You better believe I'm no Quaker."

I ran back to the place I'd found Night, returning with the saddlebags slung over my shoulder.

Dr. Burns didn't give me any trouble as I bound him hands and feet. I sat back on the ground. "How did you follow us here the other day?" I had some questions and wanted his answers.

"Jack knew where this cabin was and figured you had the mare hidden up here. I've been staying here ever since I took the mare."

"I'm surprised she let you ride her," I said, skeptically.

"Oh hell, this is a trained horse worth a ton of money. She was in the Olympic trials. The brute will get in a bite when she gets a chance, that's all."

"Dr. Burns, would you tell me how you got involved in this? How could you kill anything? You're a healer."

He looked directly at me. His soft brown eyes seemed so kind. "I didn't kill that mare, Jane. It was Chuck Smith, Velma's husband. So crude. A hammer," he said in disgust.

A subterranean aspect of my affable vet began to emerge. And it was cold in there. I remembered the way he had offhandedly alluded to his aged mare as going "down the road." In other words, to the knackers. I listened with disgust as he continued.

"I had to go up there late that night just to cut the brand off. Sloppy of them not to have taken care of that."

A detailed picture of the chestnut mare seized by death in the spring sunshine came to me. She would look different now. Dogs, birds . . . things would have eaten her. The memory became overlaid with the seal-brown horse in the sale ring.

"You killed that horse in Butte. You would have killed us both. What drove you to do that?"

Kneeling beside me, Miles moved her arm around me.

He avoided my eyes. "Figured I could lick it. I could've, too, if I'd been able to pay off the bookies. I owed them five hundred and eighty thousand, and I'd already handed that much over to them. My ex-wife had to have a goddamned condominium, though."

So here was the story. Motive: greed and addiction.

"The first time was for a friend of mine. A valuable horse of his had a stroke. Well, I knew the horse wouldn't live long, you see, and the insurance was due to run out on him the following week. I just helped nature along. My friend collected sixty five thousand . . . offered me ten."

"It went beyond that, didn't it? Your little mercy killings?" Miles said.

He gave her a fixed stare, then directed his gaze at me. "I reconnected with an old friend. She had this idea worked out, but she needed a veterinarian. She had clients whose horses weren't working out to be top notch. The horses were heavily insured. Easy for me to make death look like an accident, or illness."

I said, "You mean you killed the horses, then certified the death as natural or justifiable destruction?"

"Yes, Jane. Leila is so smart." He seemed unaware he had spoken his accomplice's name.

Guiltlessly, nearly bragging, he told me of four electrocutions he had participated in. "Looked exactly like colic."

"How did you do that?" I asked, the reporter aspect of my personality taking over.

Obviously he was proud of his cleverness. "First all the manure was cleaned from the stall. We ran the horse around until its coat was sweaty, then put it back in the stall. A guy who worked for Leila, the Sandman, made a simple device — an electric cord with a plug on one end, wire split and two alligator clips attached on the other. One clip would go to an ear, and the other to the anus. Plug it in. Quick. And no one would question my findings. Death from twisted intestine and pain due to colic."

With heaviness I realized that their greed and extensive connections in the horse world had given them the motive and opportunity to kill. Killing had now extended to anyone blocking their way.

"There's a lot of money to be made here." He glanced over at Miles. "We could use another ranch, since Logan will probably get picked up."

"Not interested," Miles said.

"I tried to get out of it at the beginning," Burns said. "The Sandman told me he'd kill me if I talked to anyone. When I got word the next hit was a yearling colt named Streetwise, I balked. There was nothing wrong with him. Nothing. The Sandman broke the colt's leg with a crowbar, then shook it at me. When he threatened me, I believed it."

I stood up, confused and sickened. Exposing this ring wouldn't stop the abuses. There was too much money at stake for the show world to be honest. Suddenly I knew I'd never participate in showing again. I turned and walked away.

Skipper flicked an ear toward the clearing just before the Jefferson County Sheriff's Department galloped into it, guns drawn. In the lead rode Lance in his olive green uniform, brown boots and light tan cowboy hat, looking handsome and dashing. He stopped his horse with a slight rear, dismounted handing his reins to a deputy. Approaching he said, "We heard a shot. Anyone hurt?"

Miles shook her head.

"This the guy who nabbed you?"

"Yup," Miles answered. "He meant to blow us up in the drift. He's all yours."

Lance knelt beside Burns, fixing a pair of plastic handcuffs to the veterinarian's wrists. "This must be Doctor Burns."

"Right. How did you know?" I asked, amazed.

"Bernard Wilde told me everything."

"So, he confessed."

"You're right, and wrong. In fact, Bernard worked for an insurance company specializing in horses. As a blacksmith he was situated perfectly to do investigative work. Buster got Velma to hire him on for a couple of local trips. The time you were kidnapped, he worked it somehow that the regular van driver was out of commission when the shipment was ready to travel. He kept a record of every day's activities."

"The little book! I saw him writing in it at Logan's barn."

"When we arrested Logan, picked him up right before you called, he tried to lay it all on Buster Wilde. Frank's on the dodge, but we'll find him."

A deputy trotted up leading Tiger and Buck. "Couldn't catch that black horse. Laid her ears flat at me. She's hangin' out back in the pines."

Miles mounted Tiger. At her nod, I took Skip in my arms. She yelped once as I lifted her up to Miles. Skipper put her long nose into the cleft of Miles' chin and shoulder.

We rode back to the ranch at a slow walk. Night frisked alongside, occasionally galloping ahead, then trotting back, like a dog on a walk.

At the ranch, Miles carried Skipper into the house to bed her down again. This time the dog was content to rest.

I found Annie Bullock in the bunkhouse reading to Norburt. The blond deputy sat on the bed next to him. She jumped to her feet, asking, "Miles. Is she all right?"

"Yes. She'll be here soon. She's taking care of Skipper." We smiled at each other, Annie and I, not needing to fill in the blanks. I rested my hand on Norburt's arm for a moment before I sat on the edge of the bed.

"Glad you kept him company," I said nodding toward Norburt.

Norburt watched for his sister. He flashed a quick smile, just the outside corners of his mouth, and his gaze returned to the door.

Miles came in carrying a package. "This a party?" she asked Norburt, her easy saunter carrying her across the floor.

Happiness mixed with relief created the broadest smile I'd ever seen on him. Norburt sat up a little straighter. I pushed another pillow behind him.

"Did you bring me a present?"

Miles placed the brown paper-wrapped package on his lap. We watched him unwrap it. Uncovering a yellow earthenware dog bowl, he pointed to letters printed on it. "What does this say?"

"Murna." She watched her brother's face light up.

"Murna, come see your new dish. Murna." He looked at Miles, "Can I keep this in here? Does this mean she lives here with me?"

His sister smiled. "Yes."

Franci McMahon

28

The drive to the Helena airport was a silent affair until I reached for the radio dial. Tuning in a station, I stopped at 99.9. I reached over for Miles' hand.

"The Fox!" she said, pleased.

"I think I'll miss it in the east."

"Honey, country is everywhere."

The seat had been confirmed, ticket scribbled on and the gate pointed out. Now the waiting lay ahead.

Miles looked out the window toward the runway, her face stony. The scar running across her cheek shone, like a windshield in the rain. She watched the sleek, snub-nosed airplane wheel and come in close to the airport buildings. A stairway, drawn by a small tractor, was brought to its side, where a curved door swung open. The roar of the plane changed to a high whine, dropped to silence.

"Flight 368 from Seattle to Billings arriving at gate two."

We walked to a more private part of the second story waiting room, sitting side by side in plastic and metal pedestal chairs attached to the floor at an impersonal distance. Miles placed a brown paper bag on the floor beside her.

I took her hand. "You know, I'll miss Norburt. He's a sweet man." I studied the broken fingernail on Miles' thumb. "I can't live with you, Miles. As much as I would like to."

She squeezed my hand hard. "I know you've got a life back there. You were like a bird that's hit the glass of a window, then stays in your hand for a while. Long enough to see the beauty of its feathers. A Tanager."

Miles looked down in her lap, self-conscious at her poetry. She handed me a brown-wrapped parcel.

I opened it. A brand new lariat lay coiled there.

She said, "You can practice while you're gone." Abruptly, she stood. I rose also and we held each other through our eyes.

Miles did nothing to wipe away her tears. She set her city Stetson a little deeper than usual at the brim. "Send me a letter once in a while."

She kissed me on the lips, held my body full-length for a moment, then took the stairs for the lobby.

"Flight 368 now boarding at gate two for Billings."

I watched Miles pass through the revolving door then take long strides, without one glance back, across the parking area to the car. From the car, Skip watched, her ears a sharp silhouette.

I picked up my new canvas luggage.

Minutes later, the brake was released on the twelve seater plane. With a slight jerk the plane rolled forward, taxiing toward the end of the runway. My heart gave a leap when I saw the car standing on the roadside, Miles next to it, her elbow rested on the roof of the car, a hand shielding her eyes from the afternoon sun. She watched the plane glide along the runway, and as it lifted off, raised her hat in a wave.

I watched the car and Miles shrink to join the world of the city below. My stomach yawned, a gaping hollow wound. The plane banked in a sickening turn, my window becoming a porthole looking straight down. I gripped the frame of the seat where it was fastened to the plane's body. Mountains encircling Helena moved into view, and the plane leveled off.

As my heart returned to normal rhythm, I looked at the beauty outside my window. Far off to the west a line of high white mountains reflected the afternoon light. Must be the Bitterroots. The sky was a Pasque Flower blue and I was part of it, a lone molecule.

We flew over a lake fed by a wide river flowing north through broad grassland.

Another broad valley flattened out beneath us, cut by a river running wild and unfettered. Tiny dots of cattle were scattered in black and red dapples across the green range. Then a mountain mass reached toward the plane. I winced as we neared the highest star-shaped peak. Hard, white alpine ridges ran out to the Plains. A veil of cloud spun off the crest, alluringly feminine.

Everything went very fast when we landed in Billings. I transferred to a large-bodied, cold-blooded jet. I watched the horizon-to-horizon squares of cultivated land, etched in their different crop colors, sort themselves from the blur. The land appeared shaped to its use. Domesticated. I thought back to the wild rim of snow-edged rock spinning out to the dry range land.

Victoria waited, eyes bright and searching, at the end of the caterpillar tube. I broke into tears when she took me in her arms. She rocked me as people streamed by.

In the quiet dark of the car, surrounded by headlights flowing past on the interstate as we traveled north, I talked about Dr. Burns. I studied the profile of my friend, sometimes lit brightly, sometimes a dark shadow, and said, "I trusted him."

"There's something sick, you know, about a vet who kills horses for money! Yikes." Victoria shook her head. "Leila's disappeared. Logan must've called to warn her before he was picked up. The police think she may have had a whole other identity ready to take on if this thing blew up."

"She'll do it again. They have to find her."

"I think she was the head cheese behind the ring."

"How are Mooney and Dusty?" I asked as a wash of sleepiness swept over me. Once reassured, I slept like a hedgehog the last part of the three-hour drive home, awakening as Vic exited the Putney ramp, drove through the quiet village, and up Kimble Hill out of town.

The trees arched overhead out of the dark and reached from the verge. I felt a surge of claustrophobia. So many trees here. Everything so lush.

The sound of Victoria's car backing out the driveway left me desolate, in spite of my bravado. The house seemed foreign, even with Scout's song of greeting, her wiggling, squirming body trying hard to show me how much I had been missed. I knelt to pet the little dog, trying to regain a sense of familiarity with my lifelong home. Bugsy, purring, wrapped himself around my legs as I walked into the kitchen.

Western time, which my body had adjusted to, told me it was nine-thirty, but the clock on the wall said eleven-thirty. Far from sleepy, I sat in the middle of the kitchen floor on the hard, cold bricks, held my animal friends, and wept.

When I got out of bed, the clock on the side table read five-thirty. Still tired, I knew more sleep was out of the question.

Vic was coming by for breakfast, I remembered. That was hours away. I'd have some coffee, then go for a ride. All the familiar things I'd always done seemed so awkward. Locating utensils in the drawers or the contents of kitchen cabinets, nothing seemed to be in its usual place. Then, as if breaking through amnesia, the commonplace came back: where the can-opener was kept, how the coffee pot worked.

It felt so good to be back on Star Dust — except my body expected him to be Buck. Moonglow had gotten used to not being left alone and called for her son to return in big neighs as we rode out the driveway.

Who would I call for veterinary help, now? I experienced a pang for the loss of the Dr. Burns I remembered.

"So, tell me." Victoria filled her coffee cup, put in sugar and cream, directed her blue eyes at me, both eyebrows arched. "Why was Dr. Burns so stupid as to get sucked into this?"

"He was in debt from betting at the track and he'd already mortgaged his farm, sold all the horses he could. You were right, Vic, or at least all the gossip was correct. I'm sorry I was so harsh with you."

Vic waved the apology away. "What made him think he could get away with stealing horses?"

"Leila had gotten away with it for five years. She sought out Burns, became his lover, and when she discovered how desperate his financial picture was, knew she had an accomplice. She had to have a compliant veterinarian."

"Still hard for you to accept that Dr. Burns acted on his own greed?" Victoria said with a quizzical smile.

"Well, I guess it's difficult to let go of the way I thought he was. What he wanted me to believe he was like." I frowned, then continued with my story.

"As a money-making plan, it worked well. Logan was the missing link; a place, far from them and any obvious connections, where the horses could be fenced or held until the hue and cry of the theft had died down. Leila had been married to Jack, knew his wild side and that his ranch was about to go on the auction block. Burns or Leila would identify the horses to be stolen, Velma and Chuck picked them up and held them until time to ship them to Montana."

I remembered how all the pieces had fallen into place. "Most of the horses shipped for slaughter went locally. It was Leila and her stable man who transported the horses around New England, rotating the slaughterhouses so they wouldn't be too frequent visitors at any one of them. Frank has talked plenty, trying to lessen his sentence."

"What about the owners of Jameel? You know, the and/ or Phillips?"

"Yeah. They've been arrested for insurance fraud. They're key witnesses. They don't seem like criminals to me, just a couple living beyond their means, with their credit cards maxed out."

"Have they found any owners of the batch of horses you traveled with?"

"Most of them. The one Burns killed at the stockyards in Butte was a top of the heap open-jumper from Virginia who was in Vermont for conditioning. That will bring out the big lawyers."

"And that mare you mentioned?"

Embarrassed, I glanced away. "Night? I don't know. We haven't been successful in finding her owners. Burns claimed she was a second-string Olympic horse, but now he seems to have amnesia. I thought she might have one of those tendon implants with a registration number on it, but no luck."

Victoria smiled fondly at me. She said, beyond sweetly, "I thought you referred to her in other conversations as 'the hell bitch'?"

"I grew attached to her."

Victoria laughed, then took a sip of coffee.

Suddenly I sat up straight. "Vic! You need a horse! She would be perfect for you."

"You think so?"

"I can attest to her being sure-footed, the way she tore over those mountain slopes."

"But she doesn't sound all that friendly."

"A few of your homemade oat-apple treats and some special attention and she'll warm right up to you. She doesn't do well in confinement."

I continued with my story, telling her about Buster working as an undercover insurance investigator.

Vic said, "Sure had me fooled. But why act so weird at Velma's? Remember that day we first saw Jameel?"

"Buster knew Velma was involved in shady horse dealings. He'd gone that day to trim her horses, and see if he could tell what she kept hidden in the barn. He was hoping he could get some hard evidence, or get a job as driver on the cross-country trips. He didn't want me to connect him with that place, or for Velma to connect me with him."

"You know, if it hadn't been for your persistence, this wouldn't have been resolved. They would have continued with their money-making scheme. Quite frankly, I was ready, early on, to get out of it."

"I had to stay with it." I stated this as fact.

Victoria looked deeply into my eyes and slowly agreed. "There's a story I want to tell you, Jane. I think it's connected to all this. One of the most powerful images I have of you is when we were seventeen. It was Christmas break and your parents were due back from their trip in time for the holidays. We'd been watching television and learned of a plane crash on the evening news."

She was telling me about the day my parents died. Why was she doing this to me?

"You said, 'That was their plane. I know it.'

"You packed your suitcase. I watched you fold the dress you and I picked out for your Christmas dinner. It was something special for you to not insist on wearing blue jeans. You folded it with great care, repeatedly, but weren't satisfied with how it fit into your suitcase. Abruptly, you wadded it up and threw it in a corner of my bedroom. Then you changed your clothes, taking a great deal of time to choose just the right outfit. I offered to help but you didn't respond, so I curled up in a chair. I felt so scared . . .

"You pulled on your left sock then put on a shoe. Then right sock, right shoe. You sat very still for a few moments, suddenly unlacing and yanking off both shoes and socks. You would try a new combination, both socks first then both shoes. Finally, you stood, although dissatisfied. Do you remember this?"

"No. No memory at all."

"You left behind all the presents you and I had wrapped with such happiness and excitement. I urged you to take them but you ignored me. You took your suitcase to the living room couch, sat it down beside you and waited for word. Mom was beside herself. You stayed there until it came — someone dressed in a blue uniform, at our front door.

"Later, you gave up on neatness and order, as if it had betrayed you. Now, I see you preparing breakfast cleaning up as you go along — as if you've always been so tidy. I see a change."

"Order is no longer my enemy. I guess I don't hate it for letting me down, or feel that I can affect the future."

We sat quietly for a few moments. "I sure have missed you, my friend," she said to me.

We ate without talking much more. Victoria put her fork down and angled her body forward, both elbows on the table. "Now I want the scoop on your rancher affair."

My fingers shredded the paper napkin. "I'm afraid it can't go anywhere."

Victoria reached one hand across the table to still my fingers. "Why? Does she snore? Have a two-sponge system in the kitchen? Only eat three-inch-thick rare steaks and French fries?"

"Vic, it's the distance. I'm settled in my life." With a stab of anguish, I raised my eyes from the napkin. "I thought my home here, all the animals, you . . . would pull me back into place. But it's all shifted, somehow. This is what's strange." I looked around the room — the paintings, photographs, furniture — then looked back to Victoria.

"Jane, I've done a fair amount of thinking while you were gone. I must admit to some ignorance about your life-style. I don't think I ever bothered to realize before that lesbian relationships have the same variety and problems as we straights have. Besides that, please forgive me for being so frank, but I'll tell you what I've observed about your love relationships. You keep them at a distance, or choose women who can't get close. Either because of a barrier in themselves, or a physical one, like geography."

"I agree, but I do think my having money attracts the wrong women. Or else sets up an imbalance right from the beginning."

"Not Miles, though."

I reached both hands to Victoria, who took them. "Everything was different about this. A different culture. I found myself drawn to something elemental, genuine intimacy. I loved the closeness I felt with her. Similar to you." A shadow flitted over my eyes. "Eventually she'd come to resent my wealth, though."

"Jane, I think you're using your wealth as an excuse. I think you've always done that."

I took a deep slow breath. "It would be an utterly terrifying thing, to go out to Montana to live with Miles."

"Does she want you to?"

"She says she does."

"Any reason not to believe her?"

"No." Shoving the chair out of my way, I marched around putting not quite dry dishes in the cupboards.

"What am I doing?" Vic spoke to my back. "I can't believe I'm encouraging my best friend to move out west. Is this woman worth it?"

"Oh, yes!" I turned, answering in an almost breathy voice.

Victoria laughed out loud, then carried her coffee cup to the sink.

"It's so awfully risky," I said. "I was utterly terrified she'd die. That because of me someone would kill her."

"That didn't happen, did it? Let's just talk about the physical side of the problem. You could rent your house, or close it up. Then, if you moved out there and it failed, you could come back. I'd stop by every now and then to check on it."

"Yes, but what about Moonglow? It would be hard on her to be in an entirely new place."

"She would adapt. Or I could keep her." Victoria's voice was neutral. "I've seen the inner loneliness of your relationship with Rhonda. Don't you think you deserve more?"

"I think I'll call together a Clearness Committee. This is, most certainly, a time when I could use some."

"I'm glad you'll ask for help from your Quaker meeting."

I put my head in my hands. "Oh, Vic, what am I going to do?"

∽

The Montana cowgirl's voice was warm and plain over the wire. "Your letter came. I loaded Night on the van yesterday. They expected a stopover in Billings last night, arrival in about five days in Vermont. Now, you wanted her to be shipped to Victoria Marsh, right?"

"That's right."

"I gave the driver your map and directions. I sure do miss you, honey."

Not wanting to, but unable to stop myself, my voice was a little cool. "Yes, well, I'll try to come out for a visit later on in the summer." My stomach flipped and my thighs ached.

A little cool didn't faze Miles. "You better, or I'll come out and get you." A soft laugh came to me, which made my cheek long for the feel of worn and dusty fabric lifting on her chest.

❦

Victoria, her two daughters and I lined up along the rail fence watching Night run and tease Max and Nutmeg in the adjoining pasture.

"She's a gorgeous mover," Victoria said. "Be great on the trails."

"Wouldn't she be super at Dressage?" Jackie commented.

I laughed, "Or three-day Eventing. I know she can jump. Seems like we all think she can do anything."

Holding my hand out, I whistled. The mare came to a sliding halt, turned and trotted back to us. Her warm breath and whiskers brushed my hand. Victoria touched Night's silky shoulder, spreading her fingers wide, then sang her humming song to the mare.

The soft sound pulled the mare around to Victoria. A low whicker rolled out of her body, flickering the rims of her nostrils.

"She likes you, Mom." Jackie smiled broadly. "Can I ride her sometimes?"

"Me, too. Can I?" I asked, as if I too were one of Victoria's daughters. Jackie took my hand.

"Maybe." Victoria drew the word out.

"I think we'll have to take a number, Jackie," I said, very pleased.

"Any news about what's happened to those creeps?" Victoria asked.

"Yes. Burns and Logan have been indicted. And Velma did some flat-out confessing when she heard the others had been picked up. She did her best to unload the responsibility onto Leila. The police located Leila working under a different name at a Thoroughbred breeding farm in Kentucky. That trainer I interviewed for an article has been tied to the Sandman and Dr. Burns. The Sandman — nobody's found him yet or will say who he is. And between Mrs. Phillips's testimony and Frank, who talked — big time — this bunch will be nailed. Indictments are expected to be handed down next week."

Victoria looked with sympathy at me. "I imagine Dr. Burns may never get out of jail."

"And he was worried about his retirement. Guess he doesn't have to any more. Maybe I'll visit him in jail."

∽

A week later, the day was humid; even at eight in the morning there was a heaviness to the air. As I parked in the small area by the plain white meeting house, I tried to pull myself out of all the scattered places to an awareness of being in the moment.

With a special tenderness I greeted the other arrivals. They had missed me, and I them. We were all drawn into the high-ceilinged room with its circle of mismatched chairs as the time neared eight-thirty. Without looking at our watches, the group of ten or twelve found our familiar places, sat, and entered the silence.

Not a soundless silence, but a silence giving space to the mind. Squeaks from a wicker chair, a sigh, whispers from a child; it flowed like water around us, connecting everyone in the room, rising, pushing the seaweed, waving, swirling in the rock-hollowed tidal pools. Crabs skittered across the edge of vision. Licks of foam caught on mussel shells. Birds called to each other, gulls transformed themselves back into warblers outside the window.

FRANCI MCMAHON

When the silence deep inside was calm, there was room for my absent father and Miles. I was amazed to discover that the place within, which I had kept reserved for Spenser, was larger than I had thought. Much larger. In fact, memories of joy and intimacy had become intermingled with the old loss and pain. The place which Miles had reached released them. And she set free my ability to love in spite of my belief that loving was lethal. I knew I wouldn't be able to trust this for a long time, perhaps the rest of my life, but if lucky, I might recognize that my distancing moves consisted of plain old fear.

In the safety of the warm circle of Friends, I let tears creep down my face leaving shiny tracks. A farewell for an old pain, guarded and strong, mixed with a boundless future joy. I opened my eyes, looking up to the beams supporting the roof, which I had helped frame on a workday long ago. Yes, I did know something about building things that last.

I settled back in my chair, then turned my eyes to the window. Outside, white birches leaned toward one another, bending, swaying — intimate and graceful.

About the author

Franci McMahon, a western native, brings her passion for horses into gripping stories, appealing even to those born without the horse gene. She lives and writes on a Montana horse ranch. *Staying The Distance* was her first novel.

Franci McMahon can be reached care of Odd Girls Press or via email at <kestrel@mcn.net>.